D.W. GILLESPIE

THE TOY THIEF

FLAME TREE PRESS
6 Melbray Mews, London, SW6 3NS, UK
flametreepress.com

Distribution and warehouse:
Baker & Taylor Publisher Services (BTPS)
30 Amberwood Parkway, Ashland, OH 44805
btpubservices.com

Thanks to the Flame Tree Press team, including:
Taylor Bentley, Frances Bodiam, Federica Ciaravella, Don D'Auria,
Chris Herbert, Matteo Middlemiss, Josie Mitchell, Mike Spender,
Cat Taylor, Maria Tissot, Nick Wells, Gillian Whitaker.

The cover is created by Flame Tree Studio with
thanks to Nik Keevil and Shutterstock.com.
The font families used are Avenir and Bembo.

Flame Tree Press is an imprint of Flame Tree Publishing Ltd
flametreepublishing.com

A copy of the CIP data for this book is available from the British Library
and the Library of Congress.

HB ISBN: 978-1-78758-048-0
PB ISBN: 978-1-78758-046-6
ebook ISBN: 978-1-78758-049-7
Also available in FLAME TREE AUDIO

Printed in the US at Bookmasters, Ashland, Ohio

D.W. GILLESPIE

THE TOY THIEF

FLAME TREE PRESS
London & New York

To Grant and Lily, Daddy's little monsters.
As long as you two are around, I'll never run out
of things to write about.

CHAPTER ONE

You're probably wondering what it was like being a girl named Jack. Both my parents named me, but not in the usual way. Dad told me, years after the fact, that Mom wanted to call me Jacqueline. A sweet name. A *girl's* name. He agreed, but I always got the sense that my name was something of a loss for him, like his team got kicked out of the NCAA tournament in the first round. It didn't really matter in the long term. He ended up getting his way when I ripped my way out of her. Babies do that sometimes. You don't know me very well, but believe me when I say I didn't kill her on purpose. I was just a…difficult pregnancy, which naturally led to a difficult adolescence and difficult adulthood.

Jack.

Difficult.

Was it the name or the lack of a mom that made me who I am? That's the question of course, the big one, the one I've been trying to answer ever since I was old enough to ask the question. It was just before summer, the long summer with me and Andy, when all that awful shit went down in that dark hole in the ground. Everything changed that summer, and once the dust finally settled, I think that was when the question actually occurred to me.

Why am I me?

People always ask me about my brother too, the usual stuff like what was he like, did you suspect anything, did he ever hurt you? I won't deny that it pisses me off, but I don't really blame them. I can't. Not because it's just human nature doing its thing, the words behind their eyes clawing, twisting out, like something kept in a cage for too long. No, I can't blame them.

Of course he hurt me. I hurt him too.

Brothers and sisters are just like that, the best and the worst of relationships, the entire world rolled into one. I can still remember the way we'd go at each other, the ways that only we could hurt each other, simply because we knew *how* to hurt each other. Insert knife here and twist it like so. Oh, he could hurt, and I could hurt even worse, and we could both make promises with hands on a Bible that we would die hating each other. So why did I go after him after he came up missing? And why did he risk everything for me? To have a sibling, especially a close one, is to have a greatest enemy and a truest friend, but it's always been like that, hasn't it?

When people ask about Andy, I get ruffled around the edges, but I've learned to smooth out and shake my head in good nature. Of course Andy hurt me, but there was more than just that. There was the time Billy Callahan ripped my skirt off. I was only eight at the time, just old enough to have a sense of sex as a vague, far-off thing that grownups did in the dark with their clothes off. I was flirty with Billy in that way all eight-year-old tomboys were flirty. I called him names, kicked dirt on his shoes, told him to eat shit when he pushed me down.

I liked him. He was eleven. I think he liked me too.

Then one day at the creek behind his house, he told me he wanted to see my panties, and I froze up, all of the silly flirting evaporating like a puddle in the middle of summer. I didn't know about sex, not really, but I got the sense that Billy did, and when I told him I didn't want him to see my panties, he grabbed a handful of my hair and started twisting it. I knew, *just knew*, that he was about to pull a clump of it out by the roots, skin and all. He didn't though. He just pulled me close and reached down for my skirt and ripped it clean off. I pulled away, stumbling down into the mud and grass, ass straight up in the air. He got a good enough look that day. One of his friends was laughing at the dirt stains on my underwear, sing-songing, "Jack shit her pa-ants."

I didn't even know Andy was there. He might have been hiding, watching it all unfold, waiting for the right moment. Or maybe he just walked up at the perfect time. I never knew for sure. He had a half-rotten stick as thick as a Coke can, and when he swung it into the side of Billy's head, it exploded in a shower of bark and termites. Billy's friend stopped laughing just long enough for Andy to raise it back up and catch him under the chin in another cascade of wormy wood.

Both looked up, saw Andy, and they knew. Without words between them, the boys crawled away and Andy stomped off toward the little clearing near the creek bed, his favorite hiding spot. He never even glanced back to see if I was okay, but I didn't expect him to. Andy never was much of a talker.

★   ★   ★

A while back we had a little baby shower for a girl at work, a sweet gal as round as she is tall, a plump face like a bullfrog. They dragged her husband in for the whole thing, him feigning a smile as they opened the presents one after another, a pile that grew like mushrooms after a week of rainstorms. I had never done the whole shower thing before that. Never had a reason to. I can still remember strolling into the baby toy store, printing off the registry, and just marveling at all of it. I was pushing 30 then, babyless, likely for good unless something drastic popped up. Whenever I met someone, I always felt like I was breaking bad news to them.

"Yes, thirty."

"That's right, not a *single* baby."

"Who knows why? Could be that I'm completely unfuckable. Maybe my pussy just don't know how to grow one."

People don't like a woman that jokes like that. Believe me, I've learned the hard way. So I'd smile, the fingers on my right hand itching, and somewhere, in some far-off place, God would start laughing.

Anyway, the whole baby industrial complex was new to me, and the sight of the place put my jaw on the floor, for more than one reason. One, because I had no clue that such a place even existed, that there was this hidden economy, an entire ecosystem that could keep this place, this shrine to the newly born, afloat.

And two...

I've seen that many toys before, and the memory nearly put me on the floor. Toys, stacks of them, new and old, stretching as far as the eye could see in that subterranean place, that nightmare. And somewhere, hidden in the back, I could see him, the Toy Thief, tall and gaunt, crawling on the ceiling toward me like a pale spider. I couldn't do it, so I stumbled out of the baby store, back into the sunlight, to lean against the concrete wall and let the moment pass.

One breath in. One breath out.

Soon, the world returned. That dark place was gone. I saw the smoke rising from it. I set the fires myself. It was just a bad dream. Eventually, when I found the nerve, I ventured back into the aisles, staring with wide eyes at the rows of factory-produced rattles, dolls, and battery-powered things that spit out an endless prattle of nursery rhymes. Would these toys ever mean anything? Would Frog Face's child bond with them the way I did with my toy?

My only toy?

I tossed a few rubber duckies into the cart and followed them with a pack of diapers. After paying, I drove home and drank shitty vodka until I was woozy enough to sleep. It took a lot of vodka.

★   ★   ★

My memory is shit nowadays, but I've tried to think about Andy when we were at our youngest, delving deeper into my subconscious, trying to unearth the earliest memory I can. I do this from time to time in the hopes of uncovering something *good*, only to come up time and again with something horribly frustrating.

The mouse, for instance.

I don't know for sure if it's my earliest memory, but I've convinced myself that it must be. I mean, it shines brighter than its siblings, and it's not very hard to see why. Andy had started a little bonfire down by the creek – his hidey-hole we used to call it. The little flat spot was ringed with trees and shrubs and was surprisingly well hidden, even though it was maybe a hundred feet from the nearest house. Pissing distance as Dad used to say. The only thing was, no one could get in there without some serious effort. For a kid, that meant crawling through about fifty feet of drainage pipe or going hands and knees under a thorny wall of brush. Once inside, there was a good ten-yard square of patchy grass, smooth gravel, and slick creek bed. It was a wonderful place to smoke a stray cigarette or peruse a dirty magazine – a *Playboy* if you were lucky, an *Easy Rider* if you weren't.

I can remember seeing the smoke from the back porch, which wasn't really a porch in the literal sense, just red bricks in a stack with a metal pipe jammed in for a handrail. Dad was quite the homemaker. I had borrowed one of Dad's lighters, using it to melt crayons onto the porch, watching the colors swirl and blend like beautiful little starbursts. I think my original plan was to mix the colors together and make one big supercrayon, a brick of color that would leave kaleidoscopic comet tails across a blank piece of paper. Once the thick globs started to drip onto the bricks, the plan went out the window. I just couldn't stop myself. I held the lighter until my thumb nearly blistered because I wanted to watch the crayons all disappear, like that feeling you get as a kid when the bathtub drain makes a tornado. It's so small, but maybe, just maybe, it could suck you down into that lime-crusted darkness.

I looked down at the blob of color, like a pile of Halloween vomit, and when I glanced up, wisps of smoke were rising from the circle of bushes that hid Andy's secret spot. He had his own lighter, several to be honest, and he liked to burn just about anything he could get his hands on. Curious, I trotted down there, across the empty road on bare feet, the bottoms gone black with dirt.

He had a pile of sticks, trash, whatever he could find, all of it stacked in the center, a small pyre fueling a weak flame. A plastic drink bottle caught with a *whoosh* and a thread of black began to rise and vanish overhead. He had a sharpened stick, digging around in there like he always did, only more focused than usual. His back to me, he was fiddling with something, a gleaming piece of metal that shined just on top of the fire.

"What are you up to?" I asked, and he jumped half a foot off the gravel before turning on me with guilty eyes.

"You? Nothing. Just get back to the house," he said. Andy always did like to bark orders, but if he ever knew how much he sounded like Dad, he probably would have knocked it off. I ignored him, same as always, and peered into the fire. There was a tiny little can in there that probably held cat food or maybe dog food for the world's smallest mutt. Something was inside, and Andy was tipping it back and forth like a chef.

"What's in there?" I asked on my tiptoes.

"Nothing! I said get!"

But it was too late. I realized now why he was so mad. Not because he was embarrassed, but because he was scared. There was a mouse inside, a dead one to be sure. I never knew when or how it had died, but even then, I had my suspicions. The dawning realization seemed to instantly wake up the rest of my senses, and all at once, I could smell the fur, hear the crackle of juices dribbling onto the scalding tin.

I never said a word, but I just stood there, mouth open, wondering what sort of satisfaction he was getting out of this strange moment.

"I hate you," he blurted out, kicking at the fire and knocking the better part of it into the creek to fizzle out. He stormed off through the bushes and refused to talk to me for the rest of the night. That was the part I remembered: the stark, cold realization that the people you love might not be who you think they are.

I think I grew up a little that day, but there was something else. Something I had forgotten, or maybe chosen to forget. It came to me one night in my twenties, when I had a dream about a burned man lying in bed next to me. He drew back the sheets and showed me his sides, all charred and peeling, and he asked me to touch him. I did, and the tips of my fingers caused the skin to split and a wall of white fluid pressed out, spilling onto the bed like old milk.

It was an awful dream, but I've never been one to put much stock in dreams, to chop them up and sift through the pieces, trying to see what might be inside. No, it was just a bad dream, but it did trigger something. A memory of that day with the mouse. Andy had stormed away, leaving me alone with the remains of his fire. Despite his kick, the coals still burned red hot, and the tin can was resting on one side just next to them. I remembered picking up a stick and tilting the can onto its bottom. The mouse was still there, the singed fur stuck to the edge of the can. With the tip of the stick, I pressed it against the humped back, which split, spilling a ribbon of white ooze into the empty can.

It was awful, a truly horrific moment, like attending your first funeral once you're old enough to know just what it means.

I kept watching anyway.

★　★　★

Dad wasn't much of a talker either. Most nights, he'd plow in with a handful of sacks from KFC or McDonald's, or maybe even a stack of pizzas, drop them on the table, and say "Get it while it's hot." Then he'd load up, testing the structural integrity of his paper plate, bending it with the weight of his food. Construction work makes a man hungry, to hear him tell it. Then Andy and I would do the same, pouring ourselves plastic cups of too-red Kool-Aid, nuclear fallout in liquid form. Our stovetop gathered dust, and eventually we even started storing linens in the oven. It was clean, so why waste the space? I can't remember ever seeing him cook, but I do remember eating chicken noodle soup whenever I was sick — microwaved, I assume.

In the days before DVRs, we would watch whatever was on, occasionally popping in a VHS copy of *Ghostbusters* or *E.T.* or the handful of horror movies we'd taped. The TV remote was a piece of junk that sucked batteries dry in what felt like a few weeks. Dad would stomp around in the kitchen, sifting through the junk drawer, swearing up and down that he'd just bought a pack of double As.

"To hell with it," he'd inevitably say. "We're just watching a movie tonight."

If it was a TV night and Andy and I couldn't agree, the old man acted as judge and jury, dropping the gavel and declaring that he would pick tonight. That usually meant whatever sitcom was on the networks, and that was just that.

When he got too tired to hold open his eyes, he'd circle the room, kissing my forehead and scruffing Andy's hair before heading off to his room and leaving the rest to us. No bedtimes. No homework checks. Just one big roommate and two little ones. I can't remember him ever tucking me in, but I know he must have at some point. There were years there when I was too young to do anything for myself, and as far as I know, it was all him. I try to picture those wide, granite-cut fingers holding a bottle, and my imagination just fails me.

He did always, and I mean *always*, tell us he loved us before he retreated to his room. And I always believed him. Maybe it was because I was the youngest. Maybe it was because I was a girl, whatever that has to do with it. Regardless of the reason, I believed him when he said it. I think, in some small but essential way, that simple fact accounts for so much of the difference between Andy and me. Everything that's happened, every choice the two of us have made, has been shaded by the fact that I believed it and Andy maybe didn't.

There was always something sad about my father's bedroom, something that made me want to stay out of there as much as I could. It was musty and musky in equal parts, a mixture of undusted clutter and aftershave. It was always dark, the bedsheets over the windows in that room only, a yellowed glow peeking in around the sides like the edges of sun around an eclipse. That accounted for some of the melancholy, but mostly it was the bed. It was huge, bigger than mine and Andy's put together, wide enough to fit four easily. There was a hollow where he lay every night, a perfect mold of his tall, heavy frame. It wasn't in the center like you might imagine, but over to one side, so close to the edge he would have tumbled off if he rolled over in the night. Next to him, tucked messily under the blankets and sheets, was a line of pillows for him to drape an arm over. It wasn't the bed of a bachelor, a man who never shared a bed. No, my father had shared his bed for ten years, and he was still sharing his bed long after his wife was gone, long after I, his sweet daughter, came into the world and took her away.

What a day that must have been. To gain and lose everything in the same, awful moment, your entire life cut into two. Before and after. And your daughter, your sweet little angel, was the knife that sliced your world in half. Whenever I worked up the courage to peek in that room, all I could see was all that I had taken away from him. I was the reason that bed was half empty, and because of that alone, I stayed far away.

Despite all the reasons he had to hate me, my father was a good man. He didn't know what he was doing, and there were certainly times I hated him because of it, but I'm too old for that silly shit now. None of us know what we're doing. All I'm left with now is the question. Yes, he was a good man, but if my mom were still around, could he have been a great one?

*   *   *

I'm stalling, and I'm sure you can tell, but this stuff is important. I have to make you understand who I was, who Andy was, who Dad was, because you won't believe me. You can't. What happened when I was nine was…impossible. A dream. Something you forget a few minutes after waking up, not because your memory is playing games, but because it was too awful to stick around.

No, if you want to understand the most impossible parts, you have to understand us. Stitched up. Not quite broken, but held together by duct tape. A family adrift at sea. If that…thing…hadn't come into our lives, we might have just kept on drifting out onto the horizon. But these things *happened*. I saw the back door slide open, and I saw it slink in, crawling over my bed, touching my face, light as a shadow. For years, I've argued, convinced, bargained, and refused to make peace with the thing that invaded our home, with the toys that vanished that long summer of '91.

The toys.

That's all they are: worthless things, scraps of cloth and hunks of plastic. They don't mean anything. They aren't *worth* anything. Every shred of meaning and value and substance comes only from what you put into them – the innocence and hope that they absorb like sponges.

Just toys.

I never had much use for them, not the way I grew up, but when I was about seven or so, I found a box marked 'Jack-Baby.' It was near the back of the garage, hidden behind old Christmas decorations I'd never seen out, relics as strange as cave drawings. I wondered if my mom had hung them up back before I came along. I sat there trying to picture the house filled with winter decor, maybe with the smell of cookies in the air. I pushed the thought aside and dug into the box, rifling through a few foam blocks and baby rattles before finding a single, green-around-the-edges teddy bear. It didn't make a lick of sense. The box was too big for just a few toys, and I got the distinct feeling that it had been full at one point. Maybe Andy had scrounged around in there, looking for something to burn.

It didn't matter. When I looked at that bear for the first time, I didn't see a toy that meant something, some sort of far-off relic of my early years. Just a bear. Cotton and button eyes, staring straight at me. My hand caught hold of something on the back, and I turned it over to find a little metal clasp. I turned it, winding it up, and a slow, plinking version of 'Twinkle, Twinkle, Little Star' began to play. It wasn't familiar, not exactly, but I couldn't stop staring at it, listening to that song play all the way to the end.

But there was something. A twinge of a feeling. A subtle hint at something bigger. Looking at that bear, listening to that song, I saw that someone at some time had cared enough to buy it for me. Dad still bought me toys, but for as long as I could remember it had been a perfunctory thing, a motion we went through. He'd take me to Walmart on my birthday with fifty bucks in his pocket, and we'd stroll around, doing the math, seeing how far the cash would go. They aren't bad memories, not really, but that bear spoke of something else. A different life. A life of anticipation and surprise. A life with sleepless Christmas Eves, and birthday presents neatly wrapped.

That bear, in more than one way, was my mother.

I drew it out of that musty box, and I clung to it. It moved into my room permanently, going with me wherever I went, and I slept with an arm slung over it, the smell of dust filling my nostrils every night. That's how it was.

Until he came.

That summer changed everything, and I've never told anyone until now. The girl I was, without question, is gone, but those memories, the weight of what happened, will never leave me until I get it out. I mean to tell it. What I saw. What I did. Every last moment. So buckle up.

CHAPTER TWO

Sallie Renner was a rich girl. Or is a rich girl. Or woman, or whatever. She's married off now, and the two of us haven't spoken in probably eight years or so. It's easy now, so many years out, for me to try to trivialize our friendship, to try to make it less than it really was back then. I mean, she was a wealthy girl from the other side of town, the nice side, you might say. I was the daughter of a single father, a construction worker no less, and the pair of us never really had that much in common. It's fair to ask, were we ever really friends at all? But no matter how I try, that narrative doesn't quite hold as much water as I wish it did. It would be easier if it were true. But the reality is, she meant a hell of a lot to me. When I think back on the time we spent together, before the thing with the toys, it burns like a patch of dry brush catching fire in a dark field.

Warm. Inviting. Bright as daylight.

That was Sallie, or at least, that was *Sallie and me*, together, that little electric connection that certain friends have. There were sharp edges, moments that could bleed from blissful laughter into instant, dark reproach if the unspoken rules weren't followed, but in those days, there were no rules.

Out of all my handful of friends, she was the only one who ever slept over alone, not like the small gaggle that roosted on birthdays or over the long, endless summers. No, Sallie and I usually slept over at one of our houses at least once a week. Her home was all wide spaces. Huge rooms, a football-field yard, endless walk-in closets, and yet we were never really alone there.

Her dad and brother more or less let us be, but her mother – a crane-necked shrew named Ruth – never let us out of her sight. It was me, of course. Even when I was nine, I knew it. Compared to the rest of the PTA inner circle, my father was an unknown variable, something possibly wild, likely dangerous, and most importantly, poor. I never felt poor until I started going over to Sallie's house, but her mother had a way of letting me know I was.

"These are steaks," she once said as she stared down the long, straight ruler of her nose. "You'll need a knife."

Despite the room, it was stifling over there, and after a handful of times and countless begging, Sallie somehow convinced Ruth to let her spend the night with me. I can still picture her perched on the edge of the porch as we drove away, the three of us piled into the front of my dad's filthy truck that farted black smoke as we drove away. She was right not to trust us, of course, but one time was all it took. Once Sallie got a taste of freedom at my house, I don't think we ever spent the night at hers again.

It's not like we were getting into trouble, not really anyway. Sure, there were more than a few bad influences around Tristan Circle, that wide loop of road dotted with single-floor homes, some impeccably kept, others practically spilling trash onto the street. There was a row of squat apartments behind us, just across a short span of creek, and that was where most of the trouble started. Sallie saw her first fight behind those apartments: two fifteen-year-olds, shirtless, spitting, rolling in the mud until they tired out and just sort of gave up. She took her first puff of a cigarette back there with me, though neither of us felt compelled to keep it up after that. We both saw our first thirty seconds or so of a porno in one of those apartments, a grainy VHS that showed something so anatomical I couldn't quite wrap my brain around it. We walked back into the daylight shaking our heads and questioning whether it was real or just some kind of kinky special effect.

All this is to say that, yes, I *was* a bad influence on Sallie. I never held a gun to her head, but just being in my presence was enough to rub off on her, as if my upbringing and inherent griminess were somehow absorbed into her skin. Over time, she opened up more about her mom, specifically about her mom and me. It was a pretty simple concept. Ruth didn't want us to be friends anymore.

"Forget her," I told her, and I meant it too. I'd gone my whole life without a mom. So could she.

But soon I started to see a change happening, some kind of backlash against a backlash, you might say. Having me for a friend was, in many ways, a middle finger to her mother, a knife to cut a hole in the blanket that was smothering her to death. This was all well and good for both of us, but after a while, Sallie began to revert. It's hard to explain, but she started to turn...*childish*. I mean, we were kids, I have to stop and remember that, but we were just old enough to not *feel* like kids. We knew what we were doing, we knew who we were, and the last thing we needed was for Ruth to stick her pointy nose into our business and tell us what to do.

The source of the whole thing was my inability to grasp what Sallie's life was like. I guess I couldn't really understand the power of parents the way she did. My dad was more of a nonentity than anything else, a swell guy I truly loved, but not a major player in my day-to-day. I woke myself up, ate a bowl of cereal, caught the bus to and from school, and let myself in with the key we hid under a rock next to the porch. In other words, I was calling the shots.

But Sallie relied on her mom and dad for everything. They took her to movies. They ate dinner at a table. They had family game night once a week. There was power there because, quite simply, there was love there as well. I didn't see that when I was nine. How the hell could I? But I see it now, and in hindsight, that change in her makes more sense now than it ever did before.

She started carrying a doll with her when she came over. Started quietly snuggling with it when we finally went to bed. She didn't lug it around nonstop, but it was always there, in a backpack, waiting for her to sneak it out when I wasn't looking. It was a girl, all felt, in a pink dress with yellow yarn hair. I'd leave the room for a minute and catch her twining the gold locks into fat braids. It wasn't like my bear. That was mine, something secret, a thing I kept hidden from Sallie whenever she came over. We were girls now, not children, and so I hid my toys away.

But this.

This sudden reversal to silly girlishness felt wrong somehow. A betrayal even. A slap across my face.

So I made it very clear that I hated the doll, hated all toys in fact, hated how childish they were. Hated them even as I hid my own away from her. It was a wedge, a sliver of distance between the two of us, a thing carefully slid into place by none other than Ruth herself. It was a very clever thing, a reminder of who it was that truly loved her more than I ever could, and it might have been enough to do the job by itself if given enough time. But something else intervened and did Ruth's work instead.

It was a Saturday in late May. I can't remember the exact date, but I knew that school was almost out for the year, maybe just a couple of weeks left, I think. I remember it so clearly because we were putting on an end-of-the-year show in my living room, a big production like kids do. There was a musical number (Sallie), a deep, well-rehearsed monologue (me), and a dance number performed without consent by my fat, tiger-striped cat named Memphis. Sallie had brought her dad's video camera, a small one for those days that recorded onto small tapes about half the size of cassettes. We meticulously set it up on the end table near the back door, one of the few places open enough to record our masterpiece. The two of us made hand-painted title cards, selected the music, and rehearsed until we were nearly bored of the whole thing.

By the time the actual show time rolled around, it was nearly eleven, and after yawning through the first two acts, we prepared the stage for Memphis, who was sleeping next to the water heater, just as I knew he would be. The stage was a three-sided wall of cardboard lit by a pair of flashlights. The words, *Kitty Kat Dancin'* were crudely scrawled on the back wall. Andy strolled out of his room to get a drink while we were setting it up, and he just shook his head.

"What?" I said defensively, suddenly feeling childish, something I hated.

"You're asking for it," he replied. He didn't joke with me very much, and generally, my brother seemed to want to stay away from me the older we got. Still, if the moment struck, we could have some good times, the sort of deep belly laughs that only siblings could inspire. It had been years since I had seen him really smile at me, and he didn't smile then, not quite, but I could tell he wanted to.

"Asking for what?" I demanded.

"Have you ever *met* Memphis?" he said sarcastically.

"Uh, he's my cat, ya butthole," I replied. Not very clever, but right along my usual operating speed.

Again he shook his head, and I fully expected him to stroll off into his bedroom. With a grin, he poured himself a glass of Coke, pulled up a kitchen chair, and waited for the show to start. He didn't have to wait long.

I'm still not entirely sure what our plan was, but I was certain, once the cameras were rolling, that Sallie and I would be able to make a convincing dancing cat. I scooped Memphis up from his endless nap, and he purred and curled into me, no doubt expecting me to bring him to bed with me like I did most nights. Instead, I carried him to the clear spot near the back door where his stage, his chance at stardom, awaited.

"Action!" I told Sallie, and the show began.

As the director of this particular piece of art, I took the majority of the scratches myself. I felt like it was my duty. In his defense, Memphis was surprisingly slow to anger. It wasn't until the second verse of 'Pour Some Sugar on Me' that he really dug his claws in. The whole thing was a disaster, but the truly amazing part was hearing Andy's laugh. I had forgotten what it sounded like.

"Shut *up!*" I demanded, but it was too late. It was like my brother had sprung a leak, and the laughter was just pouring out uncontrollably. My face was red, and blood was dripping from half a dozen small cuts on my hands. I could have walked away, could have joined in and laughed myself, but instead I walked over and slapped him hard enough to leave a bloody print across one cheek. He was, as I well knew, the mean one of the two of us. I'd seen it, the way he could instantly grow violent and threaten the people around him, so I flinched, waiting for it. He only let his head drop a bit and slunk back to his room. Still fuming, but a little ashamed, I grabbed Sallie by the arm, and we stomped off to the bathroom to tend my wounds.

We also, all unknowingly, left the camera running.

Ruth had promised to pick Sallie up early on Sunday, a promise she kept, and the gentle, almost polite beeps from the driveway sent Sallie scurrying. In seconds, she was gone, and I was left to pick up the remains of our show from the night before. Ironically, I had to kick Memphis off the cardboard stage.

"Get!" I spat. "If you didn't want to dance on it, you don't get to sleep on it."

It wasn't until I had the thing folded up and tucked under one arm that I noticed the camera. It was dead by then, the battery sucked dry overnight. I stashed it away in my room, careful to hide it in a dresser just in case Andy came digging around for it, looking for some way to exact revenge. I still felt bad about the night before, but I wasn't ready to apologize, not yet anyway. I didn't think much more about the camera until that afternoon when the phone rang. My father got to it first, and after a few words of bland, inoffensive chitchat, he handed the phone off to me.

"Sallie?" I asked.

"Her mom," he answered with a cocked eyebrow.

We never talked about Ruth, but I got the sense that he wasn't nuts about her either. I suppose that handing the phone off to a nine-year-old was proof enough of that theory.

"Hello?"

"Jack," a tart voice said, "Sallie brought a camera to your house."

It could have been a question, but the tone made it a simple, blunt statement.

"Yeah…" I said, and my dad tapped a knuckle on my forehead and frowned. I looked up just in time for him to mouth the word *ma'am*.

"Yes, ma'am. We were making movies. She left it over when—"

"It's very expensive."

I didn't really know what to say to that, but she didn't give me a chance to respond.

"I can't come just this minute. I have too much to do. Can I trust you to keep it safe until this evening?"

"Uhh…yes, ma'am."

I wasn't quite sure what she thought I would do in a couple of hours. Maybe sell it for crack.

"Good. I'll come over after work…wait…I'm on the phone…"

I could hear some kind of commotion on the other end of the line, and I instantly recognized the voice. Sallie sounded worked up, and despite Ruth's protests, her daughter kept nipping at her heels.

"Yes. *Yes.* Fine," she said to Sallie. "I'll be over tonight," she directed at me. "Now Sallie wants to talk to you."

There was a fumbling of the phone and a smattering of annoyed whispering.

"Mother!" Sallie said. Then footsteps, plodding away, followed by a slamming door. "Ugh. Jack, you there?"

"Yeah. What was that all about?" I asked as I too fled to my own room on the cordless phone.

"She's just ridiculous. Dad doesn't even care about the camera, but she's in there shitting bricks."

"I noticed."

"Look," she added, a bit nervously, "I also left...my doll." She paused for a second, just long enough to let my eyes finish rolling. "I just got out of there so quick this morning. I'm pretty sure it was over by the back, where Memphis made his big debut."

She was right. I remembered it from the night before, because I had been especially annoyed that she felt the need to drag that stupid thing out when we were so busy. It was sitting on the end table, just next to where the camera had been.

"I remember," I said, sounding annoyed. "I musta missed it this morning when I got the camera. I'll find it."

"Thanks," she said quietly.

After the call, I kept thinking about the way her mom had talked to me, and I muttered something smart-assy to myself when I walked into the living room. I checked the spot where I had seen the doll the night before. Then I checked the floor underneath the table, behind the couch, and under the couch.

Nothing.

I knew, almost at once, that Andy was to blame, but I knew better than to go storming in there without any proof. Then it hit me.

The camera.

I had no clue how long it had been running, but I felt confident that it had lasted long enough to catch him in the act. Even as disinterested as he was, Andy knew how much Sallie loved that toy, and getting back at her would be wonderful payback against me.

Sallie had had enough forethought to bring her dad's power cord in case the battery went dead, so I hooked it up along with the AV cord – one of the white-yellow-red setups. We still had it plugged in up in the cluttered playroom from the night before. I don't know why we called it a playroom. There was a tiny TV, some board games, but little else. It was really just another hiding place for us whenever my dad felt like being conversational and we just wanted to be alone.

Once everything was plugged in, I hit Rewind and ran the whole thing back to the beginning. Then I hit Play and sat back against the orange beanbag chair. There were some sputtering images of our rehearsals: Sallie wearing a black wig that made her look surprisingly like me. Me slowly explaining how the choreography of this scene or that scene would work. Jump to the stage, half askew, the camera being nudged into place and the world turning slowly into focus. I squinted and cocked my head this way and that, trying to find where the stupid doll could be hiding. Just once, for a second, I saw it, leaning against a lamp on the end table, right where I remembered it. Then we adjusted the camera again, and it was gone from the frame.

I fast-forwarded a bit, bored now, but still hopeful that I might catch Andy in the act. It would be a special moment for a little sister to have irrefutable evidence like that. If he hadn't dissected the damn thing, I might even have a chance to get it back. The screen flickered, and there he was, Memphis in all his fat, orange glory. With a cringe, I hit Play and watched it unfold.

That damn cat.

In the scramble that followed, the camera dropped onto the edge of the couch, and the unmistakably sweet sound of Andy's laughter rose up, filling the room once again. Without a moment of hesitation, I turned down the volume to a whisper. I wasn't ready, despite how pissed I was, for Andy to hear it all again. Part of it was fear of retaliation, but much more than that, I hated the fact that I was the one who silenced that amazing peal of laughter. It was true, deep regret that I felt in that moment, knowing that I might not ever hear a sound like that again.

There was the light sound of my slap, and the laughter was gone, followed by the slight sound of stomping feet. And then nothing at all. The image showed the edge of the couch, the bottom of the end table, the cardboard stage on the floor, and, farthest away, the sliding glass of the back door, a sheet of blackness. I had to get closer to the screen to make it out, but there it was: the single cotton foot of the doll, resting at the corner of the screen. Pink. Soft. A physical manifestation of everything sweet inside Sallie.

Ugh.

I waited and watched, not quite ready to fast-forward because I was so certain that the deed would happen at once. After we fled to the bathroom, Andy had nothing but a cold glass of Coke and a red, stinging cheek. I know exactly what I would have done in that moment. I would have found the first thing in reach that belonged to him, and I would have destroyed it. Shredded it. Pissed on it even. Anything to give that pain away to someone else.

I don't blame a nine-year-old for being petty, but it was amazing how poorly I understood my brother in those days. He never hurt me, other than by simply ignoring me, and I don't know why I felt so certain he would this time. Something about that slap had tipped some invisible balance, like a globe spun upside down, and suddenly, I was the one on top.

I'm not sure exactly what Andy did with the rest of that night, but he never did reappear in front of the camera. So I watched, and watched, and watched, and when I finally couldn't stand it, I hit Fast-Forward and let the world spin by, minutes reduced to seconds. Even at double or triple speed, it was terribly boring, and my attention had fluttered to something else in the room when I heard the tape stop. I'd come to the end, and as far as I knew, I had nothing to show for it.

Instead of giving up, I ran the tape back a few seconds and hit Play just to be sure, and there it was. The door still showed black beyond the thin glass, and the cat stage still waited unused. But the doll...

It was gone.

Again, I hit Rewind and stared at the corner of the screen, waiting for the single moment when the foot reappeared, and in a flash, it did. I think I gasped a little when I saw it, and I fumbled for the Play button. There was some movement, a lightly shaded shape that glided around the side of the couch. Memphis, his tail curling up as he explored in the dead of night.

"You," I said bitterly. Of course he was responsible for all this. I rubbed my thumb across my gnarled, bandaged fingers and cursed him under my breath. I was about to stop the tape, wondering briefly where the cat must have dragged the doll off to, when I saw Memphis step further into view onscreen. His head tilted this way and that, and without warning, his back began to arch, fur standing straight up, ears folding neatly back against his head. He was staring at the back door, and after turning the volume up, I could hear his low, vibrating growl echoing in the empty room. Memphis could be temperamental. He was the type of cat that might decide to bite you after letting you pet him for half an hour. He wasn't a bad cat exactly; he just liked to do things on his terms. Even if you were doing him a favor by stroking his back, he always seemed to think *he* was the one doing the favor. But despite his prickly nature, he wasn't the type to growl at strangers or stare out the window, hissing at birds. To be honest, the outdoors didn't really seem to exist for him, and that made the sight on the TV all the more strange.

All at once, the cat darted away with a hiss, gone from the screen for good, and before I could even begin to wonder why,

I saw it. The glass door, as silent as a quiet breeze, began to inch open. I must have screamed when I saw it. Honestly, I don't remember, but I heard Dad calling from the next room.

"You okay, Jack?"

"Fine," perfectly calm. I was very, very good at turning my emotions on and off. Even at nine, I knew it. But as the tape played on, the last thing I felt was calm as I watched the door to our home opening like some kind of black mouth. There was a puff of breeze from outside that caught the thin drapes, then…a shadow.

There's no other way to describe it. From the angle, I could just barely see the top of the door and a blank patch of white wall leading up toward the unseen ceiling. A smooth, dark shape seemed to melt up the wall, like liquid defying gravity. The thin line rolled up and out of sight in less than a second, disappearing out of view onto the ceiling somewhere above. I tried to wrap my brain around the layout of the room, tried to convince myself that all I was seeing was just the play of light from a passing car. Then a pair of thin, black fingers reached into frame from above, and just like that, the doll was gone.

CHAPTER THREE

I never pressured Dad much into talking about Mom, mainly because I knew he wasn't a talker, but also because I knew how much it had to hurt, thinking about her, dwelling on the past. Even so, I learned a lot just from diving through the old pictures he kept in albums tucked away in the ancient, undusted cedar chest in the corner of the playroom. I found the albums the first time when I was about seven or so. There were five of them, mostly small and cheap plastic things that held dozens of moments locked in time, relics from before my mom and dad were married. There were beers in nearly every frame, and more often than not my dad had this sort of cross-eyed look that I couldn't recognize yet as pure, ass-faced drunkenness. But he was always smiling, and so was Mom. You could feel the joy edging off the pages, out of the frames – the sort of joy that is exclusively reserved for young people in love.

Dad's hair was longer, shaggy even, and he wore button-down shirts with his chest showing, the tiny patch of hair just starting to show. He was cute too. Not the sweaty, filthy guy who walked in every night with bags of garbage food. This was a young man, a handsome one, and I could see why my mother would have fallen in love with him. More than anything else, he looked like the kind of guy who carried the party around with him, a fella who always seemed to be humming a tune.

On the other hand, Mom was me, because of course she was. Add a couple years, some boobs, sun-kissed hair, and there I stood. It scared me, because I wondered if I too could be gone so quickly, my own life little more than a blink. Even so the pictures excited me a bit too, because she was so damn gorgeous. Her hair was pure Seventies: feathered and layered in a Farrah Fawcett style that might have been laughable on a plain Jane. On her, it was radiant, and my stomach fluttered a bit thinking that I might look like that one day.

Then there was the gigantic wedding album, all white, meticulously kept, and there they were, a few years on. Dad's hair was shorter then, his face lined with a short cut of a beard. His eyes were straighter. Apparently he had laid off the beer, for the wedding at least, but he was no less happy. This was his day as much as hers. She was a pearl next to him, white and gorgeous, and the pair of them smiled, fed each other cake, kissed and kissed again. After that, there were a handful of honeymoon pictures, vacations in exotic places I had never seen, tan skin, fruity drinks, the whole nine yards.

And then...Andy.

An entire album. Smiling, cooing, laughing. In flipping through a handful of pages, I had seen my brother happier than I ever knew was possible, and I could only stare at them, wondering why he had grown so sour and cold. More than anything, I wondered with some bitterness why I hadn't gotten a brother like that of my own.

Of course, the world looks very different as a grownup. I can't believe it took me so long to notice it, but the pictures ended with Andy. When I realized this fact, I was furious, until I understood that it was my mother who had done all this. She was the one who brought out the camera and forced people to smile. She was the one who printed off the pictures, bought the albums, arranged them just so. It was sad really. It wasn't just one life that ended when I was born. It was three.

I put the albums away in the back of my closet for years, but when I was about seventeen, long after everything had happened, I came across the pictures again and started flipping through them. I noticed things I hadn't seen before. Little things really, but enough to tell a story if you cared to look close.

Like the picture someone snapped at a party where my mother stood chest to chest with a guy twice her size as my father pointed over her shoulder. I don't know who took it, or even what exactly is happening, but it's clear that an altercation is very close to breaking out, and she's the one standing in the middle. Or the pictures of her knee-deep in a garden, sweat slick on her brow, my father behind the camera. I can tell where the spot is in our yard, and for as long as I've been alive, not a single thing has grown there.

There were others too. Andy on one hip, a bag of groceries on the other, her thin arms straining. Her on all fours, laying a rock walkway through the backyard, a path that is still barely visible to this day. I'd probably looked at those pictures dozens of times before the weight of them really hit me.

The moments. This was who my mother was. Tough. Brave. Hardworking. And, quite possibly the most important thing of all, not someone who was easily rattled.

Now that I'm nearly the age she was when Andy was born, there's no question that I look just like her. But it wasn't until I saw that doll disappear that I knew how alike we really were.

★　　★　　★

So many of the moments from my youth are lost in a haze, brief bits of memories that have changed, blended, or been created whole cloth by my mind. In other words, I don't always trust my memory, because most moments aren't memorable enough to move over to the long-term area, like a stamp in steel. With that said, I can *vividly* remember the few minutes after seeing that hand snatch Sallie's toy away. Me sitting there, staring at the blank screen, trying my damnedest not to scream. Dad was milling around in the next room, Andy was hidden away out of sight somewhere, still stewing from the night before. Whatever this secret was, it seemed to be mine and mine alone.

It all started there, but it ended several days later, and in between were chances, opportunities for me to share the burden with someone else, to get help. Who knows what might have happened if I had. But once my heart stopped pounding, I jumped up and quietly shut the playroom door.

I'm not sure how long it took for me to work up the nerve to rewind the footage and watch it again, but it was long enough for me to convince myself that I had been mistaken. The door wasn't open, it was just the jittery beat of the video. The dark shape was just a shadow, Memphis probably. And that hand. It was Andy's of course. It had to be. He had just sneaked back in after the coast had cleared to snatch the doll as a bit of vengeance against me.

And then, after watching it again, all attempts to rationalize what I had seen flew out the window. The door *was* open. The shadow was something solid, something real. And those fingers, those gaunt, bony things, like Halloween decorations, they were painfully real. I stopped the tape and popped it out of the side of the camera before slipping it into my pocket. I knew why I was afraid, because someone had somehow broken into my house last night, but I couldn't say why I was so secretive about it. This entire scenario felt as if it had somehow sprung from me, like the slap across my brother's innocently laughing face had been the catalyst that started…well, whatever was happening here.

As shocking as it was on the second viewing, I was able to catch the rest of the scene before losing it. That's when I noticed the dark shape slipping out once again, quick and silent. Then the door slowly sliding shut. A moment later, the latch slid back into place, locking the door behind it. Once more, I ran the tape back, realizing that I had never noticed the latch the first go-round, but there it was. Seconds before the door began to open, the latch flipped and slid out of place.

Immediately, I went back into the den, where it happened. I needed to see it for myself, to try to process what the hell was going on. I walked in silently, careful not to touch anything, struck by the odd feeling that whatever had let itself in and out of the house had somehow infected the place. I snatched up one of the flashlights we had used for our show the night before and peered at the walls, searching for...what exactly? A trail of slime? Bits of hair? Fingerprints?

I found nothing at all, so I turned to the door, flipping the latch and sliding it open with my shirttail, still unable to touch it. I checked the handle, the walls, the concrete-and-brick porch, the eaves hanging over my head. In each case, I found nothing more interesting than bird shit and old chewed-up bubblegum I had spit out. I glanced through the murky glass and saw Memphis peering at me.

"You saw it, didn't you?" I asked when I walked back in.

He purred and nudged my leg, but he didn't have any more answers than I did. I watched the video three more times before I finally worked up the nerve to tap on Andy's bedroom door. It was a little after noon, and depending on the day, he might not even be up yet, but the familiar sound of his Nintendo told me he was wide awake. I tapped. Waited. Tapped again. Knocked. Banged my fist.

"What?" he snapped as the door flew open.

The room behind him was a dark pool, somewhere forbidden, the realm of the reclusive teenager. I peeked over his shoulder and he narrowed the door to a crack.

"I said, 'What do you want?'"

"Nothing," I spit back. "What's up your ass?"

Already off to a rough start, even though it was intended to be an apology. I've never been much for saying I'm sorry though, and Andy knew it.

"Leave me alone," he said before slamming the door in my face.

"Andy…jeez. I'm sorry," I said to the closed door. "I lost my temper. You know how I am about stuff."

I waited, but the sound of his game being unpaused was the only response I got. The door was locked, but I knew how to pick it. He didn't *know* that I knew, and I'd been saving that particular surprise for a very special occasion. I couldn't imagine there being a bigger reason than this.

"What are you playing?" I asked as I sat down on the bed.

"Get the hell out of my room," he demanded.

"Wait. Please, just listen. I'm sorry I acted like a butthole last night, but there's something I need to show you. Something I *have* to show you."

In the time it took to convince him and run back the tape yet again, I was starting to feel silly. Now that I had an audience, I'd see that it really wasn't as terrifying as I thought it was. It simply couldn't be. Then the tape started, and I felt my heart pounding in my ears, felt my lungs refusing to fill up, a reminder of the asthma attacks I'd had when I was five.

"So, what am I looking at?" he asked.

"Watch," I whispered, wanting to turn away.

The latch. The door. The shape. The dark hand.

When I finally glanced back up into Andy's face, it took a minute to register what I was really seeing. Some sort of embarrassed, stoic fear hidden there. Maybe outright terror. So why did he also look so mad?

"Well?" I said finally, still staring at him. "It wasn't you, was it?"

"Me?" he barked. "You slap me in front of your dumbass

friend, then you stage this bullshit, and you have the nerve to ask if it was me?"

"But I didn't...I mean, I wasn't even..."

He wanted to hit me. I could tell that much by the way his fists were white around the edges. He didn't hit me though. Instead, without a word, he dropped to one knee next to the camera, popped open the case, drew out the tape, and threw it as hard as he could against the wall. It exploded in a fan of plastic bits, leaving a hole in the drywall the size of a nickel. I was frozen, my eyes and mouth gaping as the evidence shattered in front of me. Andy's abrupt turn into violence was so sudden, so unexpected, I could barely speak, my words falling out in a strained whine.

"Why would you—"

"Get the fuck out of my room!" he screamed.

The rest was a blur. Dad was there, stomping his foot, demanding answers about the wall and the screams. I lied. I told him half a dozen stories about how Andy was picking on us the night before, about how he broke Sallie's tape just to be mean, and how all I wanted to do was spend time in his room. In between screams, Dad listened, fussed, told Andy he should know better, that he was the bigger brother, that it was his responsibility to be the grownup. I watched it all, stewing and self-righteous, but not really triumphant. The wedge between me and my brother was only growing wider by the day, and for the first time in a long time, I felt like I actually needed him. To this day, I don't know why my natural inclination was to turn on him at the first sign of trouble.

As for Andy, all the fight was gone. He stared at the floor just in front of his feet, blinking every once in a while. When Dad finally gave him a chance to speak, he only shrugged his shoulders.

"Come on," Dad said, putting a hand on my shoulders.

"When he's like this, you just have to leave him alone."

I glanced back, just once, and I saw that Andy wasn't staring at the floor anymore. He was staring at the wall where the tape had exploded, studying what he had done.

CHAPTER FOUR

I went on a date a few months ago. I finally understood why they use the term "blind" date. You have to be visually challenged to agree to go on one. Calling him fat would be kind.

Now, before you start thinking I'm even more of a bitch than you already do, you have to understand the situation here. I'm no catch; I realize that. My issues, stacked one on top of the other, would cast a shadow on the Eiffel Tower. But it doesn't change the fact that I'm still quite pretty. That's not bragging — it just is what it is. I've heard it my entire life, from the age of three on. On multiple occasions, I've had people tell me I could be a model. Granted, those people were idiots, but it doesn't mean their opinions were completely invalid.

My hair is black, but my eyes have always been a vibrant, cold blue. I'm too short to be a model, but not so short that it's noticeable. I've tried hard to stay slim, even though I have enough of my dad in me to completely blow up if I ever stop trying. In other words, I'm used to getting looks from just about every man I meet. It's distracting enough that I tend to keep my eyes on the ground, just to avoid the awkwardness. They see me coming and like what they see, and the reactions are as varied as the men are. Polite smiles. Curt nods. Aw-shucks glances at their shoes. Outright creepiness in the form of making my clothes vanish with their imaginations. The message, regardless, is clear: "Hello. I'm a man. May I?"

That changes when they get close, when they really see me, really see the parts I don't want them to. All of a sudden, that nervous energy shifts, and the balance of power tilts in their favor. It sounds awful to say, but there are, quite simply, tiers that exist between the sexes, instantly recognizable categories that we all fall into like colored marbles into jars. I hate it, but I, more than most, can't deny it. If my life had progressed differently, had I just ignored the thing that crept into my house, I feel certain that I would be in the high end of the tiers. Certainly not the top, but miles away from the bottom.

This thought occurred to me when I met my date. His name was, I dunno, Bob maybe. He certainly looked like a Bob. Thin hair, parted to minimize the damage. Beard that acted as camouflage, hiding a weak chin. Striped polo, tucked into khakis. Vanilla pudding made sentient.

We talked. We ate. He laughed. He was, simply, over the moon. Somehow, by some insane alignment of the planets, he found himself on a date with someone he shouldn't have been on a date with. The type of girl who had no doubt shunned him for the better part of his life. The type of girl who moved in flocks in high school, running him down, making him feel small, making every ounce of fat on his body feel like a ten-pound weight. And yet there I was, sitting right in front of him, smiling, nodding along, trying to make the best of the whole thing. Regardless of how the rest of the night might go, the simple act of eating a meal with me was a victory, and he basked in it.

When it was all said and done, he drove me back to my car, which was parked in front of a grocery store – a neutral meet-up suggested by a coworker whose ass I would ream on the following Monday. As he drove, I actually fretted over how to end this whole thing, not because I liked Bob, but because I was so damn lonely. I'd made an effort to hide everything throughout the meal, keeping the worst parts of me hidden as best I could. I'd grown remarkably good at it over the years.

I considered, *really* considered, going home with him, if for no other reason than to lie beside another human being in bed. Then, as we made small talk, he saw it. It was my fault. I'd been careful throughout our meal. I was always so careful, but sometimes, you just mess up. You slip. Though his gaze was still focused on the road, the shock in his eyes was bright, sharp, and totally familiar. He realized, in a single instant, what I'd known since the date began. The world flipped, and the balance was thrown upside down. As he pulled into the lot and parked beside my car, he looked at me, not as an object of desire, but just an object. In a single moment, the power shifted completely to him. I was no longer his desire, just his pity, someone he could throw it to just to make me feel better.

"So," he said, grinning, "let's go back to my place."

I stepped out of the car, pausing just long enough to turn back and say, "I'd rather drown in shit."

★   ★   ★

I spent a few minutes attempting to piece the tape back together, but it was all for nothing. With a sick feeling in my stomach, I dropped the shattered bits into the trash can just as the doorbell rang. It was Ruth of course, there for the camera, foot tapping, eyes narrowed on me. I handed it over, hoping against hope that she wouldn't notice the tape missing.

"Sallie said something about her doll." It wasn't quite a question, but it made me breathe a sigh of relief.

"I...uhhhh...I'm not sure where it is, Miss Renner."

"Mrs. Renner."

She stared at me. I stared at my feet. Neither of us spoke for an awkwardly long time. Finally, she sighed, as sharp a sound as a tire springing a leak.

"You know, she really loves that toy. It means a lot to her."

She studied me, waiting for my reaction. "I can't imagine it means anything to you."

I shrugged and she turned on the heel of her pristine white sneaker and she was gone.

The next day at school, Sallie wasn't happy with me, but I told her the truth. Part of the truth at least. I didn't think it would do any good to tell her about the...thing that took her doll, even if I desperately wanted someone else to know. I promised to keep looking for it, and that was just about all I knew to do.

I was more concerned about the Toy Thief anyway, which was how I had begun referring to the creature in my head. Whatever it was, I was equal parts horrified and mesmerized by it. So, despite my fear, I decided it would be best to try to catch it in the act once more, to regain some bit of evidence to replace what Andy had destroyed. It was, in hindsight, nine-year-old logic. There wasn't much else I could do, but this felt like some kind of momentous secret, one that had come to me alone to explore and understand. I wasn't going to let the opportunity pass.

I planned a stakeout for the next night. *Planned* might not be the right word. I might have been watching too much *A-Team* at the time, but this particular little adventure turned immediately into an opportunity to get equipped with whatever sort of gear I could find. As you can probably tell, I'd always been a bit of a tomboy, and any chance I got to play adventurer, I took it. There wasn't much to speak of in the way of legitimately helpful equipment, but I began to dig into my closet all the same, clawing my way through old boxes of junk in search of anything that might help, again with nine-year-old logic applied.

I had a pocketknife, a cheap brass and wood job with a lock on the back. It was too dull to cut butter, but I still wasn't sure exactly what I was up against, and a weapon is a weapon. I found a handful of bottle rockets, probably too old to actually fire, along with half a dozen roman candles. Powerful firearms, equivalent only to rocket launchers in the mind of a child. There was a roll of thickly threaded string, probably from a kite, that I figured I might be able to set a trap with. Batteries of all sizes, perfect for cracking open to gather the acid within. The deeper I dug, the longer the list grew, but the greatest treasures were relegated to the garage.

Cans of spray paint and old, half-working lighters, aka flamethrowers.

Garden trowels, perfect for digging spike pits in the yard.

A rusty box cutter.

And last, but certainly not least, a sledgehammer so heavy I could barely lift it.

It was a veritable arsenal of tricks, traps, and weapons, and by the time I had compiled my notes neatly in my unicorn Trapper Keeper, I was beginning to feel very good about my chances against whatever it was out there.

But despite all my offensive capabilities, there was really only one legitimately useful piece of equipment that I found. Tucked in the back of my closet, lost and all but forgotten, was a Polaroid camera with three pictures still left. Dad had gotten it for me two years earlier during my sudden, temporary fascination with photography. Those were different days back then, long before everything went digital, and instead of wasting a fortune on a real camera with real film, Dad settled for the cheapest Polaroid he could find.

I'm not sure how I had forgotten about the thing, especially with all the evidence plastered around the house. I had a bulletin board in my room that was wallpapered with pictures of Memphis staring at the camera, my dad smiling with a beer in his hand, and even a few of Andy, his hand held in front of the lens, clearly uninterested in having his picture taken now or ever.

Mostly, though, there were pictures of me and Sallie. A few of the stills were of other friends, the peripheral sort who drifted in and out, background players in the play that was my life, but only Sallie stood out. Little did I know how even that would change in a few short weeks, but then, everything would change, wouldn't it? My spotty typing at work is proof of that.

The first night after seeing the Toy Thief, I attacked my goal hard. I was well intentioned in my planning, but my results left a bit to be desired. If everything hadn't gotten so bad later, or maybe because it *did* get so bad, I couldn't have helped but laugh at my attempts. I started by tying a thread to the sliding back door in long, looping knots and attaching the other end to the living room lamp. In between, I attached three empty soda cans to the string by the pull tabs. They hung limply in the center, dangling like cow udders. It was a pathetic attempt at an alarm system, but it would make at least some noise if anything touched it. Andy, who had only just begun to acknowledge my existence again, sat back and sneered.

"What is that supposed to be?"

It was Monday night, a little after nine. Just about the time that everything in the house wound down, the heartbeat at its slowest. We'd eaten leftover pizza from the night before, and Dad was in his recliner in the other room, probably dozed off. I had waited until the sun started dropping to begin enacting my plan, and by then, Andy was usually in his room, playing a game or watching TV. I hadn't expected to even see him out here, and I let out a little yelp when he spoke from behind me.

"Nothing," I barked.

He stared at the glass door, at the exact spot where the camera had caught everything unfolding.

"You making another bullshit movie?"

"It's not bull," I answered, not quite sure my father wasn't in earshot. Andy had long given up any pretense that he didn't cuss like a sailor. We both did of course, but I was still my daddy's little girl. I thought I could keep that up for a few more years, use it, take advantage of it.

"Sure," he said, turning away without another word. I considered following after him, my instinct urging me to get in his face, to be relentless, to refuse to let up until he saw that I was right. That's what I always did. But tonight, though, tonight was different. I let him walk away without another word and went back to my work.

During my digging, I'd come across another old toy of mine, a plastic pony frozen mid-gallop, with a honey-colored coat and a white mane blown back in the breeze. Quite striking really. For the life of me, I couldn't remember where it came from. Some well-meaning relative who had no clue that I never had and never would give a shit about horses. It did, however, serve well as my bait.

I placed it on the end table just next to the sliding door, in exactly the same spot Sallie's doll had been. Then, on the opposite side of the room, I set up shop on the dust-covered sofa. It was old-brick red, covered with afghans as ancient as Methuselah's balls. No one ever sat there, mainly because it was so damn uncomfortable, but when my father strolled through half an hour later, he barely even noticed.

"Have a good night, honey," he said with a quiet peck on the top of my head. "Don't stay up too late. School tomorrow."

In many ways, the scent of beer mingled with aftershave had become "Daddy's smell" during those years. He wasn't a drunk, not in the traditional sense, but he was a drinker. More nights than not, he would "have a few," as he liked to call it. In the years between then and now, I've thought a lot about my dad's drinking. I've had my own brushes with addiction, things that I won't go into here, but I've always come out on the winning side, able to sweep the little gremlins into a closet and slam the door shut. My tendencies, I've learned, are much more extreme, just like pretty much everything else about me. I get mad quicker, I laugh harder, and if a fight breaks out, I hit harder. Dad and Andy were both a smoother, quieter variety, and even though I never had a chance to ask him, I think my dad's drinking was less about self-destruction and more about a mellow, smooth numbness. After losing my mom, I think I can understand that.

When the coast was finally clear, I finalized my supplies for the evening. First, I pulled the cushions off the couch, frowning at the mess of old gum, loose change, and bits of ancient food underneath before sneaking down the hallway to pull a sheet from the linen closet. I carefully laid the sheet down, plopped a pillow onto one end, and began to set out the rest of my gear. I decided, with some regret, that the fireworks would be a bad idea. No matter how ferocious a weapon they might prove to be, setting the house on fire could turn a win into a loss very quickly. I unfolded the pocketknife and slid it under the edge of the sofa, just in reach if I needed it. I tucked the heavy metal flashlight I'd found in my dad's toolbox into the folds of the sheet, and I slung the strap of the Polaroid around my neck. Then I slid down into the sheet, nestling as deep as I could manage before pulling the cushions up on top of me.

It was, admittedly, very bad camouflage, but from a distance of fifteen feet or so, I might be nearly invisible if you weren't looking for me. Through a narrow slit of cushions, I could see the back door, a gaping, empty blackness. With a few fidgety adjustments, I pulled the camera up closer to my face and peered through the eyehole. It wasn't a great angle, but it would work.

And the waiting game began.

I listened to the music of my house. Every house has its own tune, a unique series of sounds that takes years for you to fully realize is even there. Ours was no different. The icemaker on the fridge would hum, pop, and dump a fresh load with a crunch. The water heater, long on its last leg, would hiss every so often. When the central air came on, one of the loose vents would rattle just loud enough to hear. Still I waited.

Soon, the industrial saw of Dad's snoring began to drift in, and a few minutes later, the constant clattering hum of the mingling games and music from Andy's room ceased. The house itself seemed to calm down, breathing with the wind outside, and the cracks and pops of the cooling frame grew silent. Never in my life up to that point had I felt more surreally and irrationally afraid. I was, after all, at the scene of the crime, a place where the unreal and mundane collided, a place where anything might happen. I huddled deeper into the musty folds of the couch to hide myself as I shuddered. There wasn't anything to see, and even less to do, but my mind, like the minds of most children, abhorred the vacuum. The empty space filled with a thousand images, all overlaid too fast for me to even discount them as foolish, like a deck of cards being shuffled by an expert dealer.

Eyes at the door.

Footsteps on the porch.

The unmistakable sound of dripping blood.

A hand, black and skeletal, reaching down from the ceiling to pluck me up, to whisk me away to the place where toys go.

It was too much, all of it more than a nine-year-old psyche could handle. I lay there for what felt like hours, but somewhere in the haze of irrational panic, my body decided I'd had enough. So I slept.

I awoke to a nightmare. The room, previously lit by the hanging fixture in the kitchen, had gone as black as crow feathers. My bones seemed to lock at the joints, and my heartbeat pounded in my ears like native drums. I couldn't hear or see a thing, and I gripped the cushion in front of me as if it would somehow shield me from whatever unseen horrors lurked out in the world. In a few long-drawn-out minutes, my eyes began to slowly adjust to the blackness, a fact that only heightened the fear. Every stray shadow felt as if it were glaring at me, every breeze against the windows felt like a breath against the sliding glass door, every swaying branch became a hand grasping at the handle.

Time means nothing in moments like that. It becomes an abstract thought, something impossible to understand, like imagining what comfort feels like when you've dropped a soup can on your toe. If you'd asked me then how long that span of darkness lasted, I would no doubt have told you I had been on that couch for months, maybe even years. But soon, the yawning black mouth of the glass door grew pink in the back, then gray, then blue as daylight spilled in.

I never knew who it was that turned off the light. Likely Dad or Andy stumbled into the kitchen for a drink of water in the middle of the night. Either way, the hunter had come up empty-handed.

★   ★   ★

The next week passed without much worth mentioning. For a few more nights, I kept my vigil, certain the thing would return, only to turn up sore and sleep-deprived for school the next morning. Sallie was more or less despondent about her doll for the first few days, and more than once I nearly broke down and told her the truth. Once, in the bathroom stall, I practiced what I would tell her, whispering into my hand so no one else would hear me. The sound of my voice explaining what had happened, while a line of little girls pissed next to me, convinced me it wasn't the best idea. All I had was the feeling, that bone-deep terror of watching the thing slink up the wall like a liquid shadow. I don't quite know if I have the words now, as a grownup, to truly relay that dread, but I'm certain I didn't have them when I was a child. If it weren't for Andy smashing the tape, I'd at least have had someone to share the burden with, and the thought made me bristle whenever I saw him stroll into a room.

"What's your problem?" he would ask from time to time, whenever he caught me glowering at him.

"Your face," I'd reply with characteristic self-satisfaction.

By Thursday, I gave up. I simply didn't have much choice in the matter. My body just wouldn't let me continue like that for another night. I resolved, even after retreating to my own bed for the first time in four nights, that my hunt was far from over. Even so, I'm not sure I've ever felt quite as snuggly as I did sinking into my own bed that night. I was out before the sun set all the way.

I felt better on Friday, but by the time afternoon rolled around, bringing with it an uncontrollable series of yawns, there was no doubt left in the matter. My late-night stakeouts were over for the foreseeable future, maybe even for good. The realization brought on a wave of disappointment, even despair, as I wrestled with the idea that I might never know exactly what the thing that slunk into our house had been. If there was some higher purpose, some hidden design to stealing a girl's toy, I would likely never know. The memory of the tape would continue to turn hazy around the edges, blurring into something so unbelievable that eventually, my weak, human mind would stop trying to reconcile it. The image would change, transforming into something easily digested and understood, and all would be right in the world once more.

I took a long path home after the bus dropped me off, curling through the woods just outside of our neighborhood. Sometimes I would cut through the wide field at the edge of the subdivision, mainly because it was the closest route to Dee's Food Town, a little market that Andy and I would stop at whenever we had gathered enough change to buy a Ring Pop or some candy cigarettes. I always settled on a Yoo-Hoo, and by the time we hit the curb out front, it would be gone. Inevitably, I'd end up having to squat in the shrubs lining the field to keep from pissing myself.

The field itself wasn't much to see. The real tourist stop for all the kids in the area was a claustrophobic tangle of woods known rather ominously as the Trails. I've never seen a place quite like the Trails before or since, with the low-hanging trees that snaked over each other like something out of a twisted dream. There were scratchy paths within, made originally by deer and raccoons before being filed down by hundreds of sneakered kids over the years, and the trails seemed to run right over each other, doubling back, leading into dead ends and creeks, steep drops and gullies. In other words, the place was chaos made whole, and any kids in walking distance couldn't stay away. It was a fine place to play hide-and-seek or capture the flag, and the low, gnarled trunks almost guaranteed that grownups would stay as far away as possible.

There was something magic about that place, about the realization that a small slice of the planet belonged to people too young to drive a car. But there was something dark there too, the promises of more complicated things that waited for all of us, the truth sneaking in. The used condoms. The syringes. The empty whiskey bottles, broken and jagged. Neighborhood kids, especially the older ones, talked about Devil worshippers holding court there at night, warning any in earshot to stay clear of that place when the sun went down. There was evidence too, proof that they weren't just trying to strike fear into the next generation of kids who called Tristan Circle home. There was the pentagram spray-painted on the far side of the giant water tank on the hill past the woods. There was a dead possum, all but unrecognizable without its skin, that turned up in the alley behind Dee's. And the cross, carved jagged and upside down on the back of a dead husk of a maple tree.

Everyone knew these things, and some of us had even seen them, but that didn't do much to kill the magic of the Trails. It might have drawn us even closer. Even so, I refused to ever set foot in that place at night. But in the hazy hours between school and nightfall, I just wandered. I was tired, more so than I could ever remember being, but more than that, I was just plain bummed. There was something fascinating and big about the intruder, a secret that was mine, a mystery waiting to be cracked. Now it was clear that I would never know anything more than I already did. After watching the tape, I had kept my own special toy – the green bear from Mom – with me at every available minute to keep it from being stolen as well. I set it outside the shower, tucking it into my loose pajama pants whenever Dad walked in with dinner. I even packed it into my book bag, deep down underneath everything else. I wanted it, needed it even, but I didn't want a soul to know that I had it.

At the edge of the Trails, I dug into my backpack and plucked the bear out. I don't know that I had ever been in that particular thicket of dark roots by myself, and I wanted the bear with me, as if cotton and wool could somehow protect me from whatever horrors might lurk within. I plunged in, following the closest thing to a main path that there was. It was two feet wide, the packed dirt smooth and rolling, but knotted with knurls of roots that ran underfoot like great, thick veins. The path veered right, under a broad trunk that grew vertical to the ground, and I had to duck underneath it. The bear dangling in my hand dragged on the ground and jostled against the trail as I walked, but he never complained, and I was glad for the company.

As I wandered, I thought about the strange thing in the house. I thought about Andy, seeming to hate me more by the day. I thought of Dad, and for some strange reason, I kept picturing the version of him from the snapshots I found, clearly drunk but absurdly happy. I wondered if that man might ever be found again, coaxed out, and resuscitated. And then, as if my past had swung a hammer straight at my head, I thought of Mom, and I was overwhelmed by the unquestionable truth at the core of my family. If I had never been born, all of them would be better off. My mother had been, from everything I could gather, the beating heart at the center of our little family, and I was the stake that was driven through the middle of it.

By the time I made it home, I was all but spent. I curled into my bed early again after the three of us ate Chinese takeout, camped around the TV, our faces bathed in blue light and teriyaki sauce. Dad had stopped by the video store and rented a horror movie, I think it was one of the Jasons. I could never keep track of them, but he and Andy loved that kind of stuff. This was one of the few scenarios that I didn't bitch about until I got my way. Don't doubt for a second that if I'd tried hard enough, we would have been watching whatever I wanted, week in and week out. But there was something about those nights, the three of us, watching gruesome movies about teen campers being sliced and diced that was so…normal. It might sound stupid, especially if you lived a stable home life, but for us, it was special. This was our family dinner table, our weekend bowling trips, our overnight excursions into the mountains. It was the only time that all three of us found some sort of homogeneity, where the odd, bitter mixture of three people coalesced into something altogether different and individual. The giant, gaping hole left by my mother's death was still there, but invisible. Unseen. Beyond our reach.

We were whole.

Dad would laugh whenever a particularly brutal kill happened, and more than once, I heard Andy chuckle as well, the sound still so rare as to be special. I could tell things were starting to cool off between us, so after getting up to dump my plate in the kitchen, I intentionally sat down on the couch closer than I had been before. He shifted, a bit uncomfortably, but he never made me move, and by the time the last act of the movie rolled around, I was leaning my head on his shoulder and snoring. He could have easily pushed my head off, told me to go to bed if I was so damn tired. But he didn't.

I finally did wake up when the movie was over. Dad was stretching and yawning loud enough to wake the dead, but Andy just sat there quietly, waiting for me to rouse myself. I'm not sure how long he would have waited, but part of me believes he just might have sat there all night.

CHAPTER FIVE

I think, had things gone differently for all of us, that I might have been able to make it as an actress. I never set foot onstage. Even though the idea interested me, my dislike of theater kids was far too overwhelming for me to take a run at it. I'm basing all this on my inherent ability to manipulate people. It happened almost daily with my dad, but then again, he was terribly easy. I was also able to do it with my teachers, friends, coworkers, whoever was around. It wasn't because I'm some great beauty, beguiling everyone with my good looks. I look good enough, but I've got a strike against me. Two strikes, in fact. There go my itchy fingers again.

It's certainly not because I'm the nicest person in the world. I am, to be perfectly honest, the only person I know who has ever waited outside of a movie theater to threaten a group of teenagers who wouldn't shut up during the movie. That was pretty stupid in hindsight, but the sheer sight of me, all one hundred and fifteen pounds, using language that made rowdy high school kids blush was enough to get the job done. I've spit on double-parked cars before keying them, and I once told a rude waiter that I hoped he got AIDS. So no, it's not my rosy personality.

It might sound horribly pretentious to say it, but the simple fact is that I'm smarter than pretty much everyone. Let me edit that at least a little bit. I'm not smarter than *everyone*. Just everyone around me. I have a feeling, had I been born in some big city or gone to a respected Ivy League school, I might be totally average, maybe slightly above. And I'll admit, there are plenty of people who know more shit than I do. I work with a guy in his forties who watches *Jeopardy* every single day. He can quote Shakespeare and count pi up to, like, twenty-five digits. He's smarter than me. But if I get behind and need some help, I can easily get him to do it. If push came to shove, I could probably collect a paycheck for six months just by using the various people I work with.

In a way, it seems weird to say things like this about myself, but I can't really deny it. Everyone who ever comes close to being themselves, really living in their own skins, they have the same kind of moment. It's that single slice of time when they say, "*This is who I am. I do this better than just about everybody.*" It's like Michael Jordan being humble about playing basketball. After a while, it just sounds silly.

I mention all this to tell you about one of my best skills. From a remarkably young age, maybe even five or six, I could fake being asleep. I know, it doesn't sound like the most impressive skill in the world, but it's harder than it looks. You have to let go of certain parts of your body, let your muscles loosen and relax in ways that just don't happen while you're awake. Your mouth droops open, your eyes are slitted just a tiny bit, while your pupils aren't focused on anything at all. The kicker though, the one that really sells it, is your breathing. Deep and guttural, with hints of a slight snore on the end of it. All of it, combined together, is just another form of control. No one seems more helpless than when they're asleep. People drop their guard, because, as far as they know, you're not really there. But when I'm laying back, slobbering on my chin, I'm really the one calling the shots.

⋆　　⋆　　⋆

Somehow, after the horror movie and the absolutely draining afternoon in the Trails, I had the wherewithal to hang the Polaroid from the edge of my headboard. I figured, even if the hunt was more or less over, I would want it close at hand if I heard anything scurrying about in the night. That would turn out to be a rather serendipitous move on my part.

I slumped into the bed, wrapped up in the loose sheets once or twice, and began to drift. The room was awash in the same cold, blue glaze it always had, lit by the small freshwater aquarium on the desk in the corner. The fish were dead and gone by then, the last one having gone belly up six months or so back, but I kept it on just because I'd gotten so used to it.

Once or twice, Memphis pawed against the bedroom door. I knew how stubborn he could be, how much he liked to curl up at my feet in the night, but I was too tired to care this time. He gave up and slunk off to some other area of the house, probably next to the water heater. The house grew still, my eyelids turned to lead, and I wandered softly into sleep.

Hours vanished. Then there was a sudden, sharp hiss somewhere down the hall, followed by the surprisingly heavy clump of fat paws tumbling across the floor. I jolted awake, mind racing. Memphis running sprints in the dead of night was nothing new, but the hiss? That was completely out of character.

I considered getting out of bed and just letting him in once and for all. I was still too tired to care what the silly cat was up to, but my bladder was beginning to tighten from all the 7 Up I'd downed during the movie. I didn't necessarily need to pee yet, but I knew I would soon enough, so I just waited, trying to muster up the energy to actually stand up and go. I had nearly given up when I heard it.

The latch on my door as it clicked open.

Instantly, I narrowed my eyes down to slits, certain that Andy was either letting the cat in or maybe sneaking in for a more devious plan, some long-brewing revenge. Either way, I went immediately into fake sleep mode, and all the key signs were engaged at once. My breathing changed, my body went limp, and a light, subtle snore rose from my lips. The room went blurry, but I could see well enough with the aquarium light.

I waited.

I can't say how long I held that position, but it felt like several minutes. There was a small slice of blackness running up the wall: the narrow crack of the barely open door and the empty, lightless hall behind. What the hell was Andy doing? Spying on me? Taping me? Some sort of sick, slow-burn vengeance that I hadn't even considered? I couldn't begin to guess, but the tape of the Toy Thief felt so far away that it didn't even cross my mind for a second. That is, not until the door crept open further. That was when I saw the eyes.

A pair of gleaming, reflective orbs hovered two feet above the carpeted floor, as shiny as shot glasses. They bobbed like glowing phantoms, turning slowly to each side, scanning the room for – what, exactly? Danger? Me? It was the measured movement of a thing that was beyond careful, beyond apprehensive, beyond patient.

I was dreaming. I had to be. If it was Andy, he would have to be kneeling, crawling on all fours, prowling into my room like a dog. None of it made sense, and so I knew it was all just a dream. I could feel my heartbeat racing, and I wanted to stand up, to end this thing, to force my frozen limbs to move. But I didn't. I couldn't. So I watched.

It leaned forward, and I saw something else glinting in the blue light – a jagged crown of metal across the forehead, a strange, decorative circle of bronze. It didn't make sense, but dreams never do. I thought about Memphis and felt a sudden pang of fear – not for myself, but for him – and the terror ran through me like fire. As much of a pain in my ass as he could be, I loved Memphis dearly. I couldn't imagine a cat as stubborn as him hiding in a dark corner of the house as this thing slunk past. As I stared at the creature through the slits of my eyelids, my imagination began to run wild with visions of Memphis lying in the den, skull crushed, throat sliced, maybe even skinless, his fur lying across the back of the couch like a blood-slick banana peel.

No. Not that. Nothing like that was going to happen. Nothing like that *could* happen.

Just a dream.

It stepped into the light. It was a slow, measured step, but I knew what I would see before it appeared. A thin, black hand reached into the pool of blue-tinged light and rested there, so gentle that it didn't make a single sound. I'd seen that hand before, and now I knew. I didn't want to know, I begged to God not to know, but it was too late. It was the same hand that had plucked away the doll, all bones and sinew wrapped in black skin, and so I knew.

It was no dream at all.

The hand was followed by another, reaching forward in the shape of a man walking on all fours – not like a dog, but a spider. Now, even through my half-closed eyes, I could see it all. The eyes didn't just look glassy, they were glass. They were glass lenses, round, perfect circles set in what could only be a ghoulish mask.

It looked like it might have been carved out of wood. The face of the mask was flat-nosed, with a pair of nostril holes that pointed straight at me. The overall shape was human-like, but twisted horribly, changed just enough to seem *wrong*. Most unsettling of all was the mouth, lips curled and pulled back like some sort of snarling animal to show the rows of narrow, yellowed teeth. They were crooked, the ends of them refusing to line up, each one askew and angular and awful. My bladder threatened to burst as I took in that horrid, dead-eyed face, and the only comfort to be found was in the realization that it wasn't real. It was only a mask.

Then the lips moved.

In all the days from there to here, I still can't even begin to guess how I held myself still in that moment. The strange, flat nose twitched, the nostrils flared as it sniffed quietly, and I saw that crude mockery of a human mouth open and close, tasting the very air.

Real.

That word echoed, firing from one dark corner of my brain to the next. An impossible thought, an unreal fact that was undeniable as it stood there, hunched on all fours on the floor of my bedroom, mere feet away from me.

Real.

I felt my eyes creaking open as my resolve threatened to shatter. I needed to see more, to know that it was real, to stand witness to something unnatural and impossible as it padded in, one step closer. I saw the whole body in that moment: long, wire-thin, clad in dark clothes that covered all except the ghastly face. The sight of it was enough to snap me back, and I focused once more on narrowing my eyes and keeping up the ruse for as long as my body would allow. It was, as near as I could tell, my only defense.

A hand reached forward, then the foot behind it, then another hand, all of them completely, utterly silent. My mind struggled to reconcile the lack of sound, and the more it moved, the more I believed that the entire thing was nothing more than a waking nightmare, an idea that was all but confirmed when the left hand came to rest on a plastic grocery bag filled with books I had checked out from school. I knew what I was seeing – that ghost thin hand touching the plastic – and I knew what I should hear – that characteristic crinkle of cheap synthetic material. Instead, I heard nothing at all.

So I let my eyes drift closed for a moment, certain in the thought that when I opened them once more, the thing would be gone. My lids lifted to reveal it across the room, kneeling next to the aquarium, again seeming to move in a soundless vacuum. It was studying the tank, reaching here and there with darting hands, its curious head tilting like a cat's. There was a faint *click* that seemed to echo in the silence of the room, and the aquarium light was gone.

Real.

Really real.

In that darkness, I felt on the verge of crying, of letting my resolve shatter and break into a thousand pieces, of giving up and letting it take me. I knew, of course, that I was the reason it was there. I had to be. All that time, I'd felt like some kind of clever little hunter, but the reality was quite plain. I was a child, helpless, a mouse cowering between the paws of a cat.

A toy.

I couldn't hear it, but I could sense it, so close that it could breathe on my cheek. I thought of the video, of the photographic evidence I had captured, and I realized I had signed my own life away, all unwitting. It knew. Somehow, this creature of the shadows had let itself be caught on tape, and it had returned to the scene of the crime to clean up the evidence. Sallie's doll would never be seen again, and neither would I when all was said and done.

Then I heard it: a quiet little clicking noise like a bug chattering. I focused on it, trying to understand what exactly it was I was hearing. A light appeared in the center of the room, a tiny pinprick that sliced through the gloom. It was too small to show everything, much duller than the aquarium had been, but I could make out the creature's face, hovering in midair, disconnected from everything else by the harsh blackness of the room.

The light was floating just above the glassy eyes, and I realized what I was seeing. The strange crown atop the creature's head had a hook resting there, and a tiny, bronze-colored lamp dangled from it. It looked like a miniature lantern, and when the thing turned its head, the lamp swung on the loose swivel just above the center of the eyes. I heard it, just barely, as the hinge creaked a bit, a sound like a rocking chair. The Toy Thief heard it too, and with a deft hand, it slipped its fingers into some unseen pocket and reached up with a thin cylinder that I can only assume held some sort of oil. It tapped the hinge. Then, as if to test out its work, the creature shook its head. The lamp rocked back and forth without a sound, and I could almost see a grin on the edges of that horrid mouth.

As odd as the light made the creature look, I think I understood. I thought of the anglerfish I had seen in a textbook from school, one of the many odd and amazing creatures that lived in the punishing depths of the deep sea. They too carried their lights with them, luring unsuspecting fish into their cavernous mouths.

Something about the light seemed to soothe the creature, and I watched it move freely around the room for the first time. It would stop here and there to sniff at the carpet, the door handle, the edge of the bed. It was careful to stay clear of me, and I was doubly careful to keep up my calm, steady breathing. It was, for me at least, an exhausting affair, and more than once, after growing impatient, I almost let myself drift off completely. It might sound insane, but the more I had a chance to really observe the thing, the less fearful it seemed. Once, when there was a popping sound, it turned toward the hallway and froze for a good five minutes before resuming its search. It was, without question, deathly afraid of being seen, and yet it was still here. There must have been some reason for it.

The creature sniffed its way over to my desk, a mere two feet away from where I slept, and it tried one of the drawers that I kept locked. There wasn't any real reason to lock it, but something about having a hidden key made me feel grown up, as if I were finally old enough to have secrets to myself. For the first time, it sat upright, and I had to stifle another yelp when I saw how big it really was. It perched on its feet, resting like a baseball catcher, and in this position, the thing was nearly five feet tall. The long legs, ending in knobby, sharp knees, came up next to its shoulders as it turned its head this way and that, staring into the lock. It looked, for that brief moment, like the world's biggest tree frog.

It straightened its back, and I thought it was stretching for a moment, but I soon saw what it was up to. Its shirt, an old, shabby-looking thing stitched with ancient material and ebony buttons, was lined with dozens of tiny pockets, two rows of them, stretching from neck to belt line. With a single finger, it reached up to the lantern and turned the light to one side. I realized it wasn't a crown at all, but some gear-toothed mechanism that could be adjusted as needed. The gears of the headpiece clicked softly, and the lamp came to rest on the left side of its head, giving the Thief a better view of its work. Then it dipped into one of the pockets, fished out a handful of tiny tools, and slid them soundlessly into the lock.

Words can't express how quickly the creature worked, how deft its fingertips were, but before I could realize exactly what it was doing, the drawer unlocked and slid open, and its contents were perused before it was shut and locked once more. The lock picking took less than two seconds, and the entire search through the drawers maybe ten. Then the tools were back in place, and its face was turned straight toward me. It had searched the room, sniffing around every corner of the place, and it all led here.

Me.

It lowered its strange, flat nose to the edge of the bed and began to lightly sniff. Every attempt to stay even, to keep up the ruse, began to unravel, and I felt my fingers twisting into tiny knots. I couldn't fight this thing, this monster, not with its long, gangly arms, its massive, jagged teeth. But I was prepared to try. There was a moment when the head dipped so low, so very close to my face, that I was certain the gruesome mouth would open and tear out my throat.

Then it stepped over me, placing a hand so lightly on the bed that I couldn't even feel it. The face went past mine, ignoring me completely before setting on something a foot behind my head. I held my breath as another hand crept past, alighting on the headboard, both feet following, sprawling its body above mine like a spider creeping down from above.

For the life of me, I couldn't guess what it was doing, but I was still convinced it was just sinking into place, making sure it was exactly where it wanted to be before striking, finishing me without mercy.

Then I heard the sniffing. The face was low, so close that I could practically taste the smells that drifted off of it. Oil. Grease. Musty places, like the way Memphis smelled after chasing mice through the basement all day. Regardless of how close it was to me, of how powerless I felt, I realized in that moment that it barely even noticed me. The sniffs were getting louder now, deeper, like a little girl in a patch of flowers. It was enough to make a man pass out if he kept it up, and with some sense of horror, the truth hit me.

I had been so tired when I came in from school so many long hours ago, but I still had gone through the usual motions when getting ready for bed. I'd peeled my socks off, because I couldn't stand to get hot in the middle of the night. I'd flipped on the aquarium, because I was so used to the extra light.

Most importantly of all, I'd gotten my bear, the old, green, moth-eaten gift from my mother, and placed it in bed next to me. And there it was, perched delicately, practically sleeping on its own pillow next to mine. As I rolled and tossed, as I always did, I'd drape an arm over it. That was all I needed to make it through the night, to know that there were good things in this world. That someone, at some point in time, loved me.

I don't know if, up until that point, I had ever really internalized what that bear meant to me. Something about the way it had been tossed into the garage, swept away, a relic of a life that no longer existed. I never asked Dad why he put it away, but the look on his face when he realized I had found it had given me some ideas. He didn't look mad, or even upset in any noticeable way. He just looked sad, the same way you might look if you came across a picture of someone you loved a long time ago. It was a pitiful face, and when I saw it, I made an effort then and there to hide the bear from him. To bring it in and out inside my backpack, to keep it up in my room instead of lying around where he might come across it.

I might not have really known just how dear my toy was, but I did know that it wasn't something I wanted to give up, at least not without a fight. And the longer I waited, the more clear it became that the creature was here, not for me, but for my toy, just as it had come for Sallie's pink doll.

The events of the day came back, and I remembered the trails, the fields, the woods, dragging the bear along, waving it around like meat in front of a starving dog. I could imagine that the Trails would be a nice place for this thing to hide. The way it sniffed, the way it hunted, it reminded me of a bloodhound. For reasons I could only guess at, my bear was a delicacy, something worth risking coming back here for, worth risking being seen, being caught, and I, stupid little Jack, had practically led it right into my bed.

Without thinking, I let a sigh escape from my lips. It was a single, deep breath, the sound of someone dangerously close to being roused from a deep sleep. I could hear the sniffing stop, and within the span of a second, the room was shrouded in darkness.

Silence.

Blackness.

These became the world. I never felt the bed shift, never heard a wild scramble as the Toy Thief scurried away, and in that blackness, I no longer questioned whether or not it would end my life in the next few moments. I *knew* it would, and in that span of frozen horror, my will finally broke. With a shaking, silent motion, I reached up for the Polaroid, found the button, turned it toward the bed, and pressed it. The room flashed, and in that brief, horribly clear moment, I saw it – not on the bed, but above me, half on the ceiling and half on the wall, waiting as patiently as a black widow. The glassy eyes leered down at me as the mouth opened in a wordless scream.

An instant later, the world was dark. I heard nothing, not a single movement or hiss, and I felt nothing except the most subtle of breezes as something swept past me. A few seconds later, I heard Memphis growl on the other side of the house, followed by his thumping, racing footsteps down the hall and into my still-open door. I screamed when I felt him jump up onto the bed, but it didn't matter. The Toy Thief was gone.

Too terrified to take a single step from the bed, I dropped the camera to the floor, grabbed Memphis, and pulled him up next to me, clutching the terrified cat against my chest. He didn't fight me like he often did when I tried to snuggle him, but he was still bristling, his back still curled. Every so often, he would growl a bit, and I would sink deeper into the covers. But within half an hour, the growls died away, replaced by contented purrs. At some point across that vast gulf of night, both of us slept, reasonably certain that our home was ours once more.

CHAPTER SIX

It was almost absurd how scared I was the first time Andy got suspended from school. We weren't exactly the Brady Bunch, but we never really got into much trouble growing up, either. I think I was maybe six when he first got suspended. It was only for a day, but to me, it was a monumental moment – one of my earliest memories, to be honest. It meant that the boy who I looked up to, idolized even, wasn't quite who I thought he was.

I knew, even by that age, what trouble looked like. There were kids, handfuls of them in our school, who never knew what it was like not to be in trouble. I remember this one girl, Angie Breyers, who nowadays would probably be diagnosed with half a dozen things, each with their own medication. In second grade, after an especially wild day, the teacher actually pulled out a roll of masking tape and taped her to her chair.

"If you get up, you *will* get a paddling from Mr. Kinney."

My God, had there ever been such a threat? Our principal was a bear of a man with a gray beard and fingers as thick as Polish sausages. Word had it that he had an electric paddle that he could plug into the wall, which would shock you every time he hit you, multiplying the pain by an absolutely immeasurable amount. In those days, none of us ever doubted such irrefutable facts, so when I saw Angie start to pick away at her belt of tape with a pencil, I tried to stop her.

"Psst. Psst!"

I can still remember her face when she turned and looked at me, a face like a dog that has just been hit by a car. She seemed dazed,

24/7. Her brain in an eternal stupor. She wasn't stupid. I'd seen too much of her to think that. It was just that her mind, her senses, her very makeup weren't fit for the world she was born into. Could there have been a place for her where she could have been okay? If her parents had done a better job, would it have mattered? If she had known someone loved her, would it have made any difference at all?

"What?" she said with that stony, confused look in her eyes.

"Don't," I said. I was pleading, nearly on the verge of tears. I didn't want her to get hurt. In those days, I never wanted anyone to get hurt.

"Mind your business," she said, her eyebrows arching down like wasps. With one more flick of her wrist, she tore the tape away and slowly began to wad it into a tight little ball, which she promptly stuck on top of her desk. I half expected her to throw it at the teacher, but she never did, and the longer I watched, the more I realized there was no greater plan in that moment, no grand scheme. She just didn't want to sit still. Maybe even couldn't sit still. Within a few minutes, she had edged out of her seat and was picking at a scab on her knee with the end of a ruler.

The teacher finally did catch on, and Angie did indeed get escorted all the way down to Mr. Kinney's office. I never knew what happened down that terrifying stretch of hallway, but I swore then and there never to end up in his office myself.

I'm not sure if Andy had any similar moments, but his eventual fall from the good graces of his teachers filled me with some kind of existential dread, a well of fear I hadn't even known existed. The idea, the very thought, that my brother could be one of *them*, cast in with the likes of Angie Breyers, left me utterly despondent.

I found out, years later, the extent of that first indiscretion that got him banished from school. It was in the bathroom, a decidedly frightening place in grade school. I remember overhearing some of the older girls talk about the boys' room, me listening in as they demonized it, turning it into something terrifying.

"The stalls don't even have doors."

"How are you supposed to poop?" I asked, eyes dropping.

"You don't. Not unless you don't have any choice at all."

I still shudder at the thought. It sounded less like a school and more like an institution, a prison, the kind of place you might get shivved if you weren't careful. I was thankful in that moment that I was born a girl.

His first infractions were, in hindsight, all small-potato type stuff. His first time was for nothing more frightening than writing the word 'Fuck' on the wall of one of the stalls with a Sharpie. A teacher happened to stroll in and that was that. Enjoy your day off, son. Now, that was how it got started, but it wasn't until a few years later that Andy really took a step into the other side of the law.

That particular story, as told by my dad after banishing Andy to his room for the night, went something like this. One of the older kids – some boy named Patrick – had been picking on him. General, hazy details were all that really existed, but it had something to do with Andy's teeth. This was the year before Dad's insurance added orthodontic work, and my brother's mouth was a mess by then. There was a gap in the front, which was bad, and one of his bottom teeth had turned sideways, which was worse. To hear my father tell it, which was no doubt the same way the principal told it, Andy had attacked the boy when his back was turned. They had to take him to the hospital.

There was, of course, more to the story. One of the girls in my class the following year – Mary or Marie, I forget – but her older brother had been there, and he saw the whole thing.

"Oh," she said, choking a bit when she realized who I was. "You're Andy's sister."

"Yeah?"

"I remember him," she replied. "I mean, my brother told me about him."

According to her brother, the bullying had gone on for the better part of the year. The boy in question, Patrick something, had started calling Andy 'Snag,' short for Snaggletooth. Andy had tried his best to avoid it, even going so far as walking out of his way to use a different bathroom. It didn't matter. There was blood in the water, and the game of picking my brother apart, piece by piece, was just too delicious to give up. I've known the type my whole life, people like this Patrick, people so small inside, so pitifully devoid of anything at all approaching a sense of humor, a personality, a soul, that the only way they can connect with their fellow humans is to destroy someone different from them. They can sense people like Andy – quiet, naturally soft souls – and they hone in on them, tracking them, hunting them, and eventually eating them alive unless they push too far. Usually, they don't get their comeuppance, but in this case, Patrick did.

Andy did attack him from behind, but the details were much more wonderful, gruesome, and poetic. After a particularly cruel round of bullying in the boys' bathroom, Andy decided he'd had enough of being called Snag. He quietly left the bathroom, stopping in the hall to draw out the heaviest book in his backpack. Social studies, I imagine. Then, with a patience that only my brother could have, he waited for Patrick to emerge, to stroll down the hall, to dip his head to the water fountain for a drink. That's when Andy swung the book like a sledgehammer into the back of his head.

I don't tend to believe people who give stories about really stressful moments. I say this, quite simply, because I've been in enough awful moments to know that no one really remembers the details, not when the mad scramble of panic sets in. That said, when Mary/Marie told me that her brother swears up and down on a stack of Bibles that he heard Patrick's teeth shatter, I believe it to be a true story. The metal guard of the water fountain sliced through his lips and broke four of his teeth. Andy never yelled, never screamed, never promised future retaliation over the prone body of his torturer. Instead, he tucked the book under his arm and went to his next class as the crowd grew and Patrick's wails echoed through the halls.

That one, the worst of his offenses, got him suspended for a full week. I wish I could say it was his last, but that moment began a slow, spiraling landslide. In time, it even started to change me. Once I had seen that the world didn't exactly end when you got in trouble, I started loosening up a bit myself.

As for Patrick, I hear that his classmates started calling him Snag, short for Snaggletooth.

★　　★　　★

Memphis woke me up the next day, the same way he always did back in those days. He'd start by scooting up next to me, about six inches away from my face. Then he'd start purring. Depending on how late I'd pushed it with Cokes and movies the night before, this first salvo wouldn't do much of anything, forcing him to move on to phase two. His next step usually consisted of gently tapping on my chin with his soft feet. Occasionally, just out of sheer annoyance, this would get the job done.

But the night before had been brutal and mostly sleepless. Even with my fitful dreams, I still wasn't ready to get up, especially now that the light was pouring through the windows and my bed seemed safe and real once more. So Memphis moved to his final solution. With a careful, quiet step, he crawled onto my chest and began slowly inching his way up to my face. I think he was solely responsible for my recurring dreams of being crushed to death in a dozen different ways, be it by car, train, or elevator. In slow, incremental steps, the fat cat inched closer until he was covering my face and my mouth was full of fur.

"Get off me!"

He mewed loudly, jumped to the edge of the bed, and watched me. I remember lying there – half under the covers, letting my eyes adjust to the dawn before casting them up at the ceiling. Had my room ever looked so alien, so not my own? I turned to the side, saw the picture from the night before lying on the edge of the bed, and hesitated to reach for it. What if I saw it, the eyes gleaming, the mouth hissing? In a weird way, I was glad for the past week of childish denial. Andy had truly done me a favor when he smashed that tape. I could have just gone back to pretending that it never happened at all.

But that picture.

If there was so much as a thread of evidence in that frame, I'd never sleep soundly again. With a shaking hand, I snatched it up and raised it to my eyes.

Nothing.

Just my room. Dark around the edges. The flash turning everything a washed-out white. I took a deep breath, letting it out slowly as my heart stopped threatening to crack my ribs. Then Memphis mewed.

"You saw it, didn't you?"

He mewed again.

"I wish you could talk. Then maybe I'd know if I was crazy or not."

The light on the aquarium was out, but I could have been sleepwalking.

"No," I said aloud. "Just...no."

I reached back for my bear, who was still sitting on the pillow. Then I ventured into the kitchen to silence the hungry cat prowling after me.

I didn't see Andy leave that morning, but I do distinctly remember when he finally returned. There was a knock on the door, and Dad had to button his pants before answering it.

"The hell is that?" he said as I met him in the hallway, watching from a distance. I couldn't hear everything they said, but I saw enough to know within seconds just what was going on. Blue suit, black belt weighted down with a gun, cuffs, and all other sorts of toys. Nodding heads. My father bringing a hand to his brow in frustration. And all at once, I knew. Without hearing a single word, I knew.

I darted down the hall, into my room, and straight for the window, which faced the road. There it was, a patrol car parked on the curb. It was hard to tell in the warm, early morning sun, but I could see there was someone in the back, someone who looked, even through the glare, to be young. The cop escorted my dad down the yard before opening the door to let my brother out.

Andy.

Arrested.

Jesus.

All the shine had been rubbed away from my brother years before, but this. This was entering the big time. Thirteen years old and already being picked up by the cops. Even at nine, I knew where this was headed.

There was an exchange between the three of them, not heated or angry, just resigned. My dad's posture, firm but tired, exasperated, and embarrassed. The cop, good-natured, understanding, and clearly certain that this wouldn't be the last time. And then Andy, sallow, sullen, and absolutely uncaring. Dad shook the cop's hand and motioned for Andy to do the same, which he did with as little effort as possible. Then, with a giant hand across Andy's bony shoulder, Dad guided him back inside. I met them there, my eyes as big as teacups, watching every moment, but not daring to say a word. Dad gently closed the door behind Andy and locked it. He never locked it.

"Anything you want to say?" he asked, turning back to Andy.

My brother shrugged.

"Go to your room. Get all the cords for your games, your stereo, your cable box. Bring them to me."

"Fine."

"We'll be talking about this later. Now..." He paused, probably thinking about exactly what he wanted to say. "You don't want me to talk about it now. Think about what you want to say. I expect some kind of explanation."

Andy didn't have much to say about that. As I watched from around the corner, he gathered up the cords in question and laid them in the hallway like a coil of poisonous snakes. I waited until Andy's door was tightly closed before I dared to walk out and survey the scene.

I know I'm a pill. I mean, I always have been. I'll bet my mom was too, even if my father was never able to truly admit it. But it's moments like that one that show a part of me I'm not entirely proud to admit exists. Me, hiding, watching from afar, tiptoeing around the situation like a scared little mouse. I guess what I'm trying to say is this: I talk a good game, and I can even walk a pretty good one. I want people to think I'm tough, and I'll show them if they make me.

But Andy.

Andy was cut from something altogether different. He was part stone, something cold and hard and nearly impossible to break. I could see it in his eyes then. To me, the cops were figures of almost mythic proportion, the very sight of which made me weak in the knees. To Andy, they weren't shit. They couldn't hurt him, not really, and so he shrugged them off. As clear as I can tell, that attitude came from my dad – a man who had the benefit of two parents, each of them picking up the slack for the other. As an adult, that coldness had melted into something mellow, a healthy dose of 'fuck it' that made him likable, fun to be around. But for Andy, raised by a single, somewhat bumbling father, it coalesced, hardened. I'm not saying that my dad was necessarily to blame for Andy's fall from grace, but he played a part to be sure. So did I. He didn't kill our mother after all. That was all me.

Anyway, when the coast was clear, I sneaked into the living room, where Dad had already flopped back into his chair. He had a beer in hand – early for a Saturday, but I think even back then that I understood it. The talk with Andy, whenever it happened, was going to be rough, and he needed to prepare. I sat down on the couch without a word and kicked my feet. Nothing to see. Bored girl, watching baseball with her dad. I sighed. When that wasn't enough, I sighed louder.

"You okay?" he said finally, looking over at me.

"Ye-ah. I guess," I said in a worried tone.

"Go ahead," he said, taking a sip.

"What?"

"Just get it over with. I know you saw everything. What do you want to know?"

I considered playing coy a bit longer, but there wasn't much point. Dad knew me too well to pretend.

"I saw the cop," I said, leaning forward. "What happened?"

This time he sighed, a sound as tired as any I'd ever heard. Another big swig of beer was followed by, "Your brother..." He trailed off. "Andy's...he's just kinda lost. Has been for a while now."

I nodded empathetically. "What did he do?"

"Got busted stealing cigarettes." He looked down at his beer. "Down at Dean's. The clerk snatched him up by the arm and dragged him into the fucking back room."

He glanced at me and shook his head. "Don't cuss," he added, like he was performing a public service announcement.

"Never do," I replied. "So then what?"

"What do you think? Clerk called the cops, and Andy got to take a little ride. Jesus, he didn't used to be like this."

I sensed something at the edges of the conversation, something Dad would have liked to say but didn't dare. I could only imagine exactly what that might be, but I had a strong suspicion it had to do with Mom. We were always stuck, Dad and me, when it came to her. All I ever wanted was more: more details, more pictures, more of her clothes, her makeup. How had she talked? What had she laughed at? How many friends did she have? For him, it was the opposite. Every mention made him squirm, but I don't think it was because he missed her. I'm sure he did, but he squirmed and avoided the subject to save me the heartache of being the one who took her away.

So I let the moment die and drifted back to my room sometime later to stare at the ceiling and ponder every crazy thing that had happened in the past week. After an hour or so I heard Andy's door open as Dad slipped inside. Even through the walls, I could hear Dad's voice – firm, deep, booming – as he laid down the law as gently as he could. For the life of me, I can't ever remember him yelling, but things got heated all the same. I'm not sure what Andy said to get it going. Whatever it was, Dad wasn't having it. About a quarter of an hour later, Dad stopped, half in and half out of Andy's door, and for the first time, I could hear him clearly.

"I expect better from you, Andy," he said. "I expect better because you can do better. I've seen better."

There was no answer, and I heard him take a step away, pulling the door closed as he did so. Then Dad opened the door once more.

"I love you."

No answer.

I sat in my room for the next hour or so, headphones in, sketching out pictures of the Toy Thief on a notepad. None of it was easy. Being a dad, especially alone. Being a son. Being a daughter. I thought of Sallie, of their perfect home, perfect family. Perfect teeth even. Her mother, miserable, determined to make them all just like her.

None of it was easy.

I thought of how hard it must have been for Dad to swallow however mad he was, to open that door even after he had closed it, all to let his son, his first and last son, know that he loved him. And what did he get for his trouble?

Silence.

Bitterness.

Casual hatred.

The longer I thought about the whole damn thing, the more I began to boil. None of us deserved what we had, that was true, but the simple fact was, Andy didn't deserve our dad either, didn't deserve a man who never hesitated to tell his family that he loved them. I don't think I fully grasped the feelings I was processing back then, but I picked up on the basics. In the years since, I've seen families crumble, broken chains of broken people, linked together one after the other. At any moment, any of them could have changed the trajectory of their families forever, if only they'd known they were loved. It was everything, and we were lucky to have it. So when Andy finally worked up the nerve to exit his room, I met him in the kitchen, fuming.

"So," I said, instantly accusatory.

"What?" he replied as he grabbed a bag of chips from the pantry.

"I saw all...*that.*"

"It's not any of your business," he retorted, scowling as he skulked back to his room.

"It is when the cops come knocking," I said, following him right into his room, even being so bold as to kick the door that he attempted to slam in my face. "What's the matter with you?" I demanded.

"It's none of your fucking business," he repeated, balling his hands into fists. He hadn't ever hit me before, but I took a reflexive step back all the same.

"What is it?" I asked, genuinely curious. "What do you have to be so pissy about?"

"Don't go there," he replied.

"Go where? What is it you hate so much?"

"You," he replied flatly. He might as well have hit me. In that moment, he saw the confused hurt on my face, but he didn't let up. "You changed everything. You ruined everything. Life was so different before you, because she was here."

I'd never heard him mention my mother before, and the last thing I expected was for this moment to be the one where he decided to.

"You don't mean that…"

"Yes, I do. Don't try to tell me what I mean. You fucked up everything. All you've ever done is fuck things up."

My jaw was on the floor and embarrassing little tears were blooming on the sides of my eyes. I wished he had hit me, and he could read it all over me.

"Now get out of my room."

Without another word, I did as I was told.

★　★　★

I've always wondered about having kids of my own. I mean, it's hard to know for sure just exactly how kids will affect you. Will the best part of yourself come out, that little seed inside you blooming, changing you forever? Or will you take one look and run? I don't think I'd be a runner, but I worry I could be something even worse. I'd be the type to stay, no matter how bad things got. No, that's not quite right. No matter how bad I *made* things.

I already told you that I was broken. It's true. My family was broken, so what were the chances that I would be any different? It's Andy that kills me, though. I would go see him at least once a month. More when I could bear it. Sometimes less. It was hard to get to know him as a grownup, especially through a layer of wired glass. It was especially tough in the beginning, the first few times I finally worked up the nerve to show my face there.

Everyone I knew – coworkers, my therapist, the girl who cuts my hair – they all told me how brave I was, like I was risking my life just by sitting across from him.

It kills me, because I always thought that Andy was one of the bloomers, that a kid would change everything for him. That shell, that wall of scar tissue built up around him, it was always hiding something. The shrinks, the cops, just about every person I met, they all thought they knew what was hiding there. After all, things played out the way they did for a reason. Andy showed exactly who he was – at least if you ask them.

Those people were fucking idiots.

I always figured that if anything ever cracked that shell, you'd find a flower growing inside. Dad, stuck with the two of us, used to try to explain how people worked. I think he was trying to smooth the edges between Andy and me, trying to give us something to work with for the inevitable moment when we were the only ones left. I'm sure he imagined the scenario: brother and sister, each hating the other as strongly as was humanly possible. I can't speak from experience, but I can't imagine a worse feeling of failure than having two kids that hate each other.

The way Dad explained it, we were all born with gifts. You could call them strengths, talents, areas of expertise, or whatever, but the important thing in life was identifying them, honing them, using them to get ahead. I think Dad, had he noticed his own gifts, might have been able to be an artist. Andy, if left to his own devices, could have been a writer himself. I've seen some of his work, and I'm stunned at how complete it is, stories as varied and lovely as any I can find on a bookshelf. For me, I could have been an athlete with a little more guidance. Every shred of physical prowess that seemed to skip Andy was drawn directly into me, but it wasn't just the physical side. I was aggressive, more standoffish, unable to give an inch. Pitiful traits for a mother perhaps, but quite helpful on a field.

The idea of gifts wasn't anything revolutionary, but it has stuck with me to this day. Most important of all was finding out what gifts you weren't born with. These were the things you had to get out there and earn, to find, to take for yourself. My aggression left me cold, so I had to learn how to care about other people. That's why I never wanted to bring a kid into this world. Not for my sake, but for theirs.

★   ★   ★

Later that afternoon, I caught Andy walking out of the bathroom with his shirt off. He was pale, always so pale, but slimly built, wiry, and almost strong-looking despite his aversion to all things physical. He glared. I glared back. Then, as we passed in the hall, I caught a glimpse of a patch of red on his back.

"What's that?" I asked without a moment of hesitation, not because I was a caring, doting sister, but because I never respected his boundaries.

"What's that?" he asked, pointing at my face.

"Seriously, turn around for a second."

He turned toward me and pressed his back against the closed door. "Leave me alone," he spat.

For a moment, I thought of him and Dad going back and forth behind the closed door. Then I thought about how mad Dad was, a quiet, brewing sort of anger, remarkably like Andy's. I'd never known my father to lay a hand on either of us, but the red, swollen patch of skin looked remarkably like a handprint.

"Who did that?" I asked, straining to get a look.

"Did what?" he demanded. "Just leave me alone. I don't want to talk to you."

He spun around, flinging open the door, and I saw it, clear as day. It was a hand, but longer, thinner, inhumanly narrow. The skin was pink, slightly swollen, and speckled with dots of red where the skin had broken. I gasped and began to push into the room. Andy slammed the door in my face and locked it. I started down the hall for my wire to pick the lock, and I heard the recliner being pressed against the door. It was no good – not now at least.

I spent the rest of the day in my room, thinking, plotting, sketching in my notepad. The pictures of the Toy Thief were growing grimmer, more outlandish as the day waned, and long, ghoulish fingers tipped in yellowed claws began to run up and down the sides of the page. More than anything else, I was afraid. Andy could be a pain in the ass, but I didn't want anything bad to happen to him. I went back and forth, considering the possibilities. Would Dad have ever hit him? And even if he did, would he have been able to make such a gruesome mark?

No.

As the sun faded through the blinds, I became more and more certain. That thing, whatever it was, had visited Andy just the same as it had visited me. It wanted my bear, but there was something else at play here. Never more in my life had the thought of nightfall brought such dread in me, but I knew, without a shadow of a doubt, that if anyone was going to protect my family, it had to be me. It was an absurd thought – again, nine-year-old logic – but I truly believed it through and through. Being a kid was like that a lot for me, and probably for you too. Some things just *were*, and questioning them didn't get you anywhere.

I overheard Dad calling in pizza, and I caught him in the kitchen when he hung up the phone.

"Heading out in a minute for dinner. Need anything else?"

I tilted my head a bit, rocking back on my heels as I watched him hovering over me.

"Mmmm…nope."

I wanted to say something else, to warn him about the almost certainly dangerous thing hunting our family. Instead, I just reached up and gave him a hug. My arms barely fit around him, with a foot and a half between my fingertips.

"What was that all about?" he asked as I stepped back.

"Nothing. Just wanted to."

He kissed my forehead and smiled. "Well, whenever the mood strikes you, feel free. Love you, baby girl."

I heard him a few moments later at Andy's door, the two of them discussing the terms of his punishment. Apparently, the music was back on the table. The games and TV would have to wait a while longer. Even after sneaking up on them, I couldn't always hear what either of them was saying, but neither raised his voice. Whatever fight the two of them had in them had burned itself out.

Dad stepped back into the hall and stopped short. "I'll run by the video store," he added. "Anything you want to see?"

There was a long pause. Then Andy replied, "Something scary."

"Again?" Dad said, good-natured like.

"Why not?" Andy said. "Something gory, too."

"You're gonna give your sister nightmares."

"She can handle it. I'd get a nightmare before she would."

I realized in that moment that I was smiling, and I felt a little bit like my mom must have felt. Just a pair of boys.

My boys.

When Dad was gone and Andy was safely back in his room with the boombox roaring, I went to work, spending the rest of the next hour or so working out my plan. I went from room to room, checking doors, windows, any possible way that thing might make it into the house. I couldn't set any traps, not until Dad and Andy were safely in bed, but I at least wanted to have a plan before I got too tired to do anything constructive.

Based on everything I had seen up to that point, the Toy Thief was remarkably skittish. The fact that no one knew about this thing was proof of that, and the reaction after I took the picture only confirmed it. It could have – probably easily, based on how it looked – killed me in my bed. Instead, it ran, getting out of the house in the span of a few seconds. It was fast, silent, and good with locks, all qualities that I assumed allowed it to come and go as it pleased. Even so, darkness was its greatest weapon, and I had no doubt that those lens-covered eyes were designed for nocturnal vision.

So, with these facts in mind, a plan began to emerge. I couldn't fight it, or at least I didn't think that was a very good idea. It reminded me of reading about animals in science class, the ones that didn't really look for fights or hunt for food, but could become wonderfully dangerous when cornered. If I tried to force it into some kind of trap, it would only turn out badly for me.

With fighting out of the question, I had to find a way to use what I knew about it against it. Again, the skittishness, the fear of light. I looked at the sliding glass door, and I thought of the tin cans. A decent idea, just poorly implemented. I needed something heavy, something that would be loud. And just like that, I knew.

Dad had bought me a secondhand drum set a few years ago, and it included a freestanding cymbal that would make your toes curl if anyone tipped it over. It was perfect. I dug it out of my closet and tested it, leaning it against the wall behind the drapes. It was completely hidden. A few pieces of thread here and there, and boom, my own personal alarm system. If anyone so much as nudged open the sliding glass door, the cymbal would topple, waking everyone in the house.

There were, to be sure, more plans, but most of them were too nonsensical to give much mention to. I had my pocketknife tucked into the back pocket of my jeans, along with plans for half a dozen other traps when the time came. Then Dad was back, movie and pizza in tow. We ate, watched, pretended that the events of the day had never happened. It was, more or less, like any other weekend night, with one exception.

"Don't stay up late," Dad insisted as he headed back to bed with a stretch. "Got some things I want you to help with around here tomorrow, Andy. Do a good job, and you'll be playing games this time tomorrow night."

Andy nodded, rising to his feet, not nearly as sullen as his usual self, and the two of them retreated to the solitude of their rooms. I knew their habits, their schedules, pretty much every move they would make. Dad would be back out, at least once, maybe more, for a big swig of water from the kitchen tap. Given the stressful day he'd had, a beer wouldn't be out of the question either. Andy, always more of a snacker than an eater, would be out in the next hour or so for one last bite before finally going to bed.

I checked the clock over the TV. Just about five after ten. I had plenty of time. By eleven, maybe 11:30 at the latest, I'd set my traps and head to bed myself, Memphis tucked under one arm. I thought of Andy, the handprint on his back, and I considered trying to sneak the cat into his room after he was asleep, an extra layer of security just for him. It was a lousy idea though. The cat didn't really like him, and if I did somehow coax Memphis in, he would just wait by the door, mewling, until Andy let him out. No, Memphis was better with me anyway, another personal alarm system. Plan firmly set, I leaned back onto the arm of the couch, surfing channels with sweaty palms, waiting for the right time.

There were countless holes in my plan, but the most gaping was my underestimation of how tired I was. The previous night had drained me in ways I didn't quite grasp, and despite the fear gnawing at my stomach, my body decided I'd had enough. I awoke to a darkened room, the house all but silent, and immediately, I knew it was much later than I had planned. All my traps were still waiting to be set, so I wasted no time, leaping off the couch, ignoring the clock when it told me what I already knew. It was nearly 1:30 now, and not even Andy would be awake at this hour. I focused on the sliding door first, dashing across the room and setting the cymbal up just like I had practiced. Then I turned into the kitchen and saw it, resting in the center of the room under the weak glow of the light that hung over the stove. The most horrifying thing I had ever seen.

It was Sallie's doll.

It sat on the kitchen table, upright and smiling, as if it had never left. As if the entire episode were all just an awful dream. I walked to it, dazed, lost to the world, and I reached out, placing the tips of my fingers on the cloth skin. I needed to touch it. I needed to know it was really there. It tipped over on one side and stopped, caught by something I couldn't quite make out. I edged my hand to one side and felt the thin, nearly invisible wire that held it in place, a wire that ran through the kitchen, down the hall, into Andy's room.

It was in that instant, when I heard the door creak open, that I knew it wasn't a thread, not really. It was a web. A spider's silk. A trap, just like the one I had tried to set a week ago. Only this one was crafted by hands that knew what they were doing – thin, quick, astoundingly clever hands. When the Toy Thief emerged into the hall, slipping out of Andy's room, it moved slowly, carefully, the anglerfish light on its head bobbing left and right as it crawled toward me.

I understood, at least on some level. We both knew the other existed, and so there was no need to play silly games. No more hiding, no more creeping, no more running. It walked onto the linoleum floor, each footfall absolute silence. For the second time in a week, I felt certain that I would wet my pants. It turned its head this way and that, and I noticed for the first time how big its ears were, how well they must be able to hear. The pitch-black hands looked soft and delicate to the touch, but I had seen what they could do, what they were doing. The thought of Andy alone in that room with this creature made me sick in ways I can't really explain, but more than anything else, it made a part of me bubble with a fury I had never known.

"What do you want with him?" I asked quietly as it passed into the kitchen, mere feet away.

I wasn't sure if the thing could even speak, if it even understood a word I was saying, but almost instantly, I had an answer. The crooked, hideous mouth curled up in a smile, the only answer I needed. That playful grin was like a knife into the part of me that had fight left in it, the bold, brash, loud-talking part. I felt myself withering, growing smaller and smaller as the awful thing drew itself up onto its feet.

"I…I won't let you hurt him," I said in a voice as weak as a breeze. "I…I…"

On two feet, it was taller than my father, towering over me, its head seeming to touch the ceiling. Then, with a slow, careful motion, it reached up with both hands and flipped back the lenses that covered its eyes. I don't remember if I was crying before I saw the eyes, but I distinctly remember the warmth of tears when I did see them. They were pink, shiny buttons, round and featureless, without irises or pupils to speak of. I couldn't remember exactly when I had seen those eyes before, but I instantly knew where.

The pet store at the mall.

Andy, Dad, me.

Cute things. Puppies. Kittens. Fish. Even birds.

And piled into a single cage, a dozen of them, curled together with rope-like tails.

Rats.

Some brown. Some dark. But a few bone white, with pink, dead eyes.

My perception changed in that moment, transformed, and I no longer saw the Toy Thief as an it, but as a *he*. He was a bent, broken excuse for a person, but there was something human within him all the same. He was close now, close enough for me to touch, and the smile grew wider. I could finally see those awful teeth for what they were: jagged, uneven, tough enough to chew through walls. Rat's teeth. The posture, the curving back, the white skin, the quickness. There was no more doubt in the matter. He was, quite simply, a rat-man.

Somehow, I found the courage to draw out the pocketknife, to unfold the weak blade, to hold it in front of my face. The smile became something worse. The laugh was a quiet, wheezing sound, the sound of a creature that no longer knows how to speak if it ever truly did. I expected him to reach down, to wrap those bony fingers around my neck, and to choke the life from me. Instead, he reached behind his back and pulled out my bear.

My God, the sight of it. The only relic of my mother, clutched in that awful, bony hand. I would love to tell you that the sight of my bear made me break into a righteous fury, that I dove on the creature and attacked for all I was worth, that I knew, even at nine, exactly what to do. But I can't tell you that. The sight of the bear, clutched in skeleton hands, made me wither, and I fell to my knees with tears welling in my eyes.

"No…" I begged. The idea of losing the last shred of my mother had broken me, shattered my feeble attempts at toughness. I had no plan. No idea. No hope. And so all I could do was beg.

"Please," I whispered, careful not to wake Andy or Dad. If I did, it would be over. The creature would be gone, and my bear would be gone with it. "Don't take it."

The smile grew ever wider, and I became convinced that my life was about to end, right there, on that very patch of linoleum. It might have too, if not for the deep growl that rose from the hallway. It was Memphis of course, my fat, surly savior. He wasn't attacking – even he knew better than that – but he was standing his ground, ears laid back, fur bristling. I wondered why he would do such a thing when running was the easiest option. If a burglar had broken in, I could just about guarantee that lazy bastard would have found a quiet corner to sleep. Then it struck me. What could possibly hate a rat more than a cat?

The smell of the thing alone must have been enough to drive Memphis into a frenzy, and as I watched him, I realized my instinct was right. He wasn't doing anything as silly as defending me. Every ounce of his being was in conflict as he stared at the gigantic rat thing before him, his mind and his instincts at odds, his senses telling him to attack while whatever common sense he had told him to flee. He kept doing this little half dance, stepping forward and back, as if the carpet under his paws were on fire and he couldn't bear to step on it for more than a few seconds.

And there we were, the three of us locked in place, frozen in time, until the Toy Thief reached down with a lightning-quick hand and swatted the cat away. There was a growl, a spitting hiss, and like a flipped switch, the spell over me was broken. I ignored the knife in my hand, and I dove for the bear, hoping to wrench it free. I snagged one of the legs, but he was quicker than I had any hope of being. He snatched it clear and pushed me back with a leathery hand on my face, flipping me onto the linoleum. His horrid, loathsome mouth filled my vision from end to end, and the only thing that existed in the entire world was teeth. All I could do was close my eyes.

"What the hell are you doing to that cat?"

Andy's voice. Sleepy. Confused.

Then a sharp gasp of air as he saw it.

The Toy Thief glanced back at him for half a second. Then, in a frenzied blur, he was up the wall, on the ceiling, scrambling toward the door. And like a bad dream, he was gone, and the bear was gone with him. The sliding glass door still sat open, the dark breeze outside blowing in, catching the curtains in playful wisps as Andy stared with awestruck eyes.

CHAPTER SEVEN

The worst dream I ever had.

Does everyone else have one? A moment that just sticks out, the few seconds of images flashing by, like a movie you watched too long ago to really remember, but too awful to really forget. I've never asked anyone else about their dreams, mainly because I just don't share my own experiences with them. The memories are too awful, too close to real life to just take your shoes off and play around in.

It was that first night, after coming face to face with the Toy Thief. Somehow, I slept, once the night had nearly bled into dawn and the sun had banished that awful darkness. I was in my bed. That was the scariest part. It might sound funny if you've never had a dream like that, but every other nightmare is just...*off*. "Surreal" might be a better word, that feeling of your room being just different enough to make the whole thing seem silly when you think of it hours later. I mean, they're plenty scary, but this dream went beyond that. It was *my* room. *My* bed. *My* aquarium glowing in the corner.

I became suddenly aware that there was something in the room with me. Without a thought, without even seeing a thing, I knew it was there, and I knew it wanted to hurt me. Where, who, or even what it was, I couldn't begin to guess, but that sense of bitter hatred toward me seemed to radiate off it. I wanted to move, to scream, to get up and run as fast as I could, but my body was frozen in ice, my joints locked into place. For hours I lay there, that feeling of utter dread permeating the walls, the floors, my skin and bones.

The sun began to glow through the blinds, and I felt my heart finally loosening because I knew. Nightmares, no matter how deep and terrifying, always fade when the sun hits. But the sun didn't end it. It spilled through, the light creeping across the room, brightening the corner enough to see it, to finally lay eyes on it: the shape of something not quite a man, something bent and gangly, carved out of darkness itself, so black that it seemed to swallow the light that pressed against it.

The light won't save you…

The Toy Thief was a child compared to this voice – less than a child, a game maybe, or…a toy. I wondered how I had even been afraid of the Toy Thief now that this true darkness had emerged for me, and I realized I had never actually been afraid before this moment. Every moment of my life had just been a dream, and now, for the first awful time, I was awake, horribly, endlessly awake. That silhouette solidified, growing solid around the edges, the dark taking physical form as it stepped closer to my bed.

I'm coming…

Tears ran down my cheeks, and my heart promised to stop if the nightmare didn't. If I'd had the ability to end my own life in that moment, I would have, I truly would have, just to stop it from coming a step closer.

I'm coming for him, and when we're gone, you'll never see him again…

A hand carved from pure ebony reached for me, and behind it, in that featureless face, bloody pits of red opened up.

Eyes.

They saw everything.

They saw me.

No death for your brother…he'll never get that kind of peace.

★　★　★

Andy shook me into consciousness at about ten. I could have slept until at least three if left alone. The late nights were catching up with me. I felt sore all over, and I honestly didn't remember when

I had finally fallen into sleep. I thought of the dream, of the shape of a man, of the eyes made of blood, and a pain shot up through the back of my neck.

"What?" Andy said as he stopped at my door.

"I'm just…sore."

"Did that thing hurt you?"

For a moment, I wasn't quite sure what he meant. The lingering nightmare was still metallic in my mouth, and I wondered how he knew about something that had just happened inside my mind.

"Thing?"

"The thing in the kitchen. Jeez, are you all right?"

Everything came into focus as the events of the past week, of last night, spilled all around me.

"Yes. Just a bad dream."

"Good. Garage," he said without another word.

I followed him out, shaking the sleep out of my eyes as we went. With everything that had happened, I wasn't sure what he was up to, but I also wasn't about to question him. When we were safely out, far away from Dad, he said, "Now show me."

It took a second to figure out what he was asking.

"Showww youuuu…"

"The toys."

The fog lifted, and I remembered everything we had talked about the night before. After slamming the sliding glass door and locking it, I had dragged him into my room and closed the door behind us. Then I'd told him everything. The video he'd smashed. Sallie's doll. The late-night encounter. And most important of all, the handprint on his own back. There were tears in his eyes when he drew up his shirt and stared into the mirror at the gruesome mark, which had already started to fade a bit.

"How," he said, his voice quivering, "how did I not feel it?"

I didn't have an answer for him.

"Why me? What does it want with me?"

Again, I had nothing with which to soothe him. I thought of the bear, my last piece of my mother, gone for good, and tears began to fill my own eyes.

"My bear," I whimpered.

"What? Your bear? The hell does that matter?"

I thought of what he had said earlier that very day, about me, about her.

"You should know exactly what it matters. It matters because it came from her."

"What do you know?" he asked, the fury clouding his face. "You didn't love her. You didn't even know her."

"Don't you think I know that? You at least had something. You have memories and pictures and…and kisses and hugs. You know what she smelled like. You know what her laugh sounded like. All I had is that damn bear. And now it's gone."

Tears were pouring down my cheeks by then, but I refused to wipe them away. It would have made me look weak. He shook his head, the storm clouds lifting.

"I'm sorry."

It was just about the last thing I ever expected him to say, but it was a welcome surprise. I didn't push it, didn't pry, didn't demand that he say more. I just took the simple apology for what it was.

"What's going on?" he asked.

We talked through the night, talked until the two of us couldn't stand it anymore. And then, when I crawled into my own alien bed, Andy sat down on the edge, his face sincere. "I didn't know. About that…thing. About everything."

"I know you didn't," I said, pulling the covers over my shoulder. "How could you?"

"No," he said suddenly. "There's no excuse. Not for me. Not for the way I am…sometimes."

I sat up, staring at him, preparing to tell him that everything was fine, that everything *would* be fine, but he was already up by then, halfway out the door. I expected to hear the familiar drone of his music rocking him to sleep, but I never did, and it wasn't until he was shaking me awake a few hours later that I knew anything at all.

"Why are we out here?" I asked, motioning to the garage.

"The toys. Last night, you talked about finding your bear in a box. Where was it?"

I waved a hand at the wall of junk, the old boxes, the mismatched furniture, the bags of clothes too small for us to wear.

"I dunno. Here somewhere."

"Think," he demanded as he began poking around himself. "How long ago was it?"

"A year or two. I don't really know. Why does it matter?"

"The box. You said the box was almost empty. That it had *your* name on it."

He waited for me to get it, and when I clearly didn't, he sighed.

"Why put just a couple of toys into a box and put it out in the garage?"

"Who knows?" I shrugged. "You know how Dad is—"

"No," he said, cutting me off. "Dad's not like that, even if you think he is. That's something an idiot would do. Dad's not like you. *I'm* not like you. But neither of us is stupid."

I readjusted my tone and said, "I didn't say he was stupid, or that you were stupid. He's just a little flighty."

"The reason," he said, ignoring my logic, "that the box was almost empty is because, at one point in time, it was almost full."

I tried to do the mental gymnastics to catch up with him, but it was still too early. "I guess," was all I could eke out.

"This thing…it's been coming here for who knows how long. Taking what it wants. Leaving little pieces for later. Saving them for…who knows?"

"There wasn't just one thing in there," I replied, finally getting it. "There were a few."

"But it was mostly empty, right?"

I nodded, and we dove in. It only took a couple of minutes to dig the box out, and as soon as he lifted my box from the pile, I already knew. It was too light, as if the box were filled with nothing more than air. Then he tore the top off, and we saw it, filled with nothing more than dust and dead spiders.

"You never came out here?" I asked.

"No. You?"

I just shook my head.

"What about mine?" he asked.

It was a good question, one that we spent the next two hours trying to answer. It wasn't until we dropped down the ladder to the attic that we finally found what we were looking for. Cardboard box after cardboard box, dozens of them in a neat stack near the back of the stifling attic. They looked, from a distance, as if they had never been touched. The words scrawled on them, in fat, black marker, told a story that made a part of my heart wither.

ANDY/BABY

ANDY/TODDLER

ANDY/2 YR

On and on it went. I had a box. I had a bear.

He had a toy store.

I'd always had a sense of the difference between his early life and mine. The pictures had shown me that. They told one story. This stack of boxes told another one entirely. I felt a few pangs of anger as I gazed at them, fury directed at my father for more or less abandoning me. But that fire burned out in seconds, only to be replaced by a deeper feeling that I had never known before.

When I glanced over at Andy, I saw the look on his face, and I knew he was reliving it. He reached for the first box he came across, ANDY/SUPERHEROES, and he ripped it open. All the usual suspects were in there, but he dug through them, dozens of tiny plastic figures in search of something special. The one that stood out. The one that meant something.

It was the only one not there.

He slammed the box down and shook his head. "I had a Superman," he said in a pained voice I had never heard from him before. "I took it everywhere. It was…shit. I loved that thing."

He grabbed another box, and once again he came up short. Again and again he searched, digging through the pile, finding nothing more than junk he could not care less about. As I watched him, silently taking in the pain and desperation on his face, that alien feeling grew deeper. I thought once more of Mom, of how I acted whenever her name was brought up. Every time, I struck back, throwing the issue back at anyone who dared question me.

I was the one who was hurt.

I was the one who never got to know her.

I was the one who really lost.

But now, as his desperation grew into a frenzy, I couldn't feel anything other than pure, empty guilt. I *had* killed his mother, and for that, I should feel guilty. The truth at the bottom of it all was that Andy had been hurt a thousand times more than I ever could be.

"Stop," I said, putting a hand on his shoulder.

"No," he whined. "The ones I cared about. The toys she gave me. They're all gone."

The still-bitter part of me wanted to ask him why, if he loved them so much, he had let them rot up here, but I think I already knew the answer to that. Dad, as lost and confused without my mother as Andy was, did what he had to do to survive. That meant that life as they knew it, these two, drifting bachelors, had to begin again. Every nook and cranny of the house before I was born had been packed with reminders, and now those reminders were here, stuffed into boxes and labeled in black ink.

I wanted to tell him it would all be okay, but that felt wrong somehow. There was no easy answer here, and giving him a simple solution would probably just make him mad at me. Instead, I took a different tactic.

"We don't know what this thing is or why it's doing this. So," I said, kneeling down eye to eye with him, "the question is, what are we going to do about it?"

★　★　★

"Okay."

Most of the day was already, inexplicably gone. The two of us had gone round and round about what we knew, what we thought we knew, and what we were still completely clueless about. We were holed up in his room, long enough for me to get accustomed to the stuffy, slightly stinky smell of older brother. I sat on the edge of the bed while he lay flat on his back, staring up at the ceiling. He was shredding an empty bag of chips, ripping the metallic paper into ever-smaller pieces as I sketched away on my notepad.

"Okay. Okay."

His eyes were darting side to side, his mind clearly racing. The desperation of hours before, when he realized some of his earliest possessions were missing, had faded into something more like dazed panic. The weight of this strange, inexplicable situation was only now hitting him fully, and he didn't really know what to do. It was easy for me to recognize that feeling because I had been there myself just a week before. In the years since, I also think that being a few years younger helped immensely in this situation. I might have been stepping into something resembling adulthood, but I still had one foot firmly planted in the world of children. Part of me – probably a larger part than I would have admitted – believed completely that monsters were real. The fact that they might steal toys was just a detail at that point.

"What do you think we should do?" I asked when I couldn't stand to hear the paper rip one more time.

"Okay," he said, staring up at the ceiling, apparently not hearing a word I said. I leaned over and snatched the bag from his hand and tossed it on the floor.

"Snap out of it," I demanded.

"What do you want from me?" he said, leaning up on one elbow. "I mean…what the hell are we supposed to do?"

He was scratching at his lower back without even thinking about it, and when he realized what he was doing, he recoiled in disgust.

"What *can* we do?"

There weren't many options. We both knew it.

"One thing or the other," I replied.

"What is that supposed to mean?"

"Offense or defense."

Andy hated football, but it was something that Dad and I watched whenever the mood struck us on lazy Sunday afternoons. Even so, my brother still got the point.

"Defense didn't work so good last time," he replied.

I sneered at him, but I couldn't argue that he was wrong. My planning, such as it was, had been undone by nothing more out of the ordinary than a nap.

"So? The two of us together might do a better job." My voice was pitifully unconvincing, and it trailed off at the end. Andy picked up on this instantly, and he could have used it to attack, to break me down, to force me to see things his way. It's exactly what I would have done. Instead, he seemed to carefully consider the idea, and even if he was just humoring me, I felt better.

"Maybe we could. If we came up with some kind of plan to keep it out. Changing the locks or something."

"That won't do it," I told him. "I saw him pick the lock on my desk. It took him all of two seconds. He's got all these little tools…I bet that's what he does, just going from house to house, taking things while people are sleeping. You can't hear him. He moves so fast you can barely see him. I mean, this thing could have been walking on our faces while we slept and we wouldn't know it."

He shuddered and scratched at his back.

"Then we tell Dad."

Again, the years between us from kid to teen began to shine.

"No," I said bluntly.

"Why not? I mean, he could help us. Give us an idea of what to do."

"You really think he would believe us?" I asked.

"No," he replied as he cast his eyes down on the floor. "I barely believe it and I saw the thing."

I was corralling him now, leading him down the only path I knew to take. I was already there; I just needed him to get on board, and the only way he ever would was if he got there himself.

"So what's left?" he asked.

"I think you know."

"Offense," he replied softly.

"Offense."

There was a sudden change in him. I saw it in his eyes as he raised them to meet my own. They were gray eyes, like my mother's. They could be, in his younger days, wonderfully sweet, but there was also an icy coldness to them, a frozen glare that spoke of the ability to go much farther than I would ever dream of. My gaze was fire that burned on the surface, hot but not nearly as dangerous as it looked. His was an ember, hidden inside, boiling, hot enough to melt the world.

"Then we kill it," he said plainly. "No traps. No tricks. Just dead."

I think I must have shuddered when he said it, but I didn't disagree, not when he had me locked in those frozen eyes.

"But first," he added, "we have to find it."

★   ★   ★

As I thumb through this, I realize I've probably been a little too hard on Dad. I'm not the most mature person in the world, even knocking on the door of thirty, and I feel like I've only just started to really look at myself in an honest way. Writing all this down, even if no one ever reads it, is part of that. Dad might not have been the perfect guy to be stuck with two kids by himself, but he did the best he could, and he did teach us a lot of things I wouldn't have picked up otherwise.

Some families went skiing.

Some families played sports.

We went camping.

First off, I don't want to make it sound any grander than it really is. We didn't own a camper. We didn't know anyone who had a cabin. What we did own was a tent, just big enough for the three of us. Dad had to lie in the middle, because the sides were too narrow for him to squeeze up against without bringing the roof down on us.

No matter what time of year we went, the first part of the first day was usually the same. Andy and I would stroll around, gathering whatever sticks we could find, working our way up from small to large, with plenty of dry kindling like Dad had shown us. Meanwhile, back at our campsite, Dad would spend an hour, sometimes two, cussing and kicking at the dirt as he fought to get the tent assembled and up in one piece. Before night started drifting down on us, we would gather around the pit and take turns trying to start the fire. Dad smoked in those days, but he never let us use his lighter. He had a long rectangle of steel, and he'd pick up chunks of flint from military supply stores. It wasn't that he was some kind of survivalist. Hell, we had a cooler full of Yoo-Hoos sitting three feet away. It was just that he wanted to teach us something.

Sometimes, we'd bring rods and reels and take them down to the lake. Whatever we caught, we'd lop its head off then and there and take turns slitting open the belly and sliding a finger through the hole. I can still remember the slightly gaggy feeling I got whenever I glanced down at the string of entrails, but I did it all the same. Andy didn't seem to mind at all, and it was clear that he was simply better at this outdoors stuff than me. More in tune, you might say. Regardless of whether it was bluegill, catfish, even the occasional bass, we would take it back to the fire and roast it on a spit. Usually, there wasn't enough for more than a few bites, but everyone got to taste it whether they really wanted to or not. A bite or two of half-burned fish, followed by a premade bologna sandwich. Something like heaven.

Sometimes we stayed out there for one night, sometimes for two. We never bathed, because where would you bathe? We pissed and shit in the woods and brushed our teeth with water from Igloo coolers. When it rained, we wore ponchos and didn't mind when our feet began peeling in our tennis shoes. We ate out of coolers or bits of whatever we found, skinned, cleaned. It wasn't surviving, not exactly, but it was closer than most of my friends ever got. We grew to understand that being dirty, being grungy, was part of being human.

Usually we went to the public state park, but from time to time a friend with land would let us camp out there. In those cases, we'd shoot the handful of guns that Dad owned. Sometimes we'd set up aluminum cans and pick them off with .22s, easing into the tiny kick, the sharp report, our eyes learning not to close as soon as we touched the triggers. Once in a while, Dad would buy a box of clay pigeons and we'd move up to shotguns. A twelve-gauge was a fast teacher. Keep the butt tight to your shoulder, or wear the bruise for a week. Hold it just so, careful to glance down the barrel, or get a black eye. I never did get comfy with a shotgun like Andy did, but I might have, given enough time.

I shot a squirrel when I was eight. I wasn't crazy about the feel of it, knowing that, in an instant, it was dead because of me. I didn't have one of those movie moments where I leaned over it, crying my eyes out. I just stared at the little hole under its eye, wondering how bad it hurt. It flailed for about half a minute, and that was that. Dad made me help skin it, clean it. He had a grill grate that he sat over the fire, propped up on a few rocks. Over and over, he kept turning each half of the squirrel, basting it with packets of barbecue sauce from McDonald's. It was, without question, the best thing we ever ate out there.

In those days, Andy liked to stalk through the woods, gun in hand, and search for tracks, trails, signs of where a buck had bedded down the night before. He never actually shot a deer, but he did get really good at tracking them. We were, in a sense, learning about what the world might have been like before the power went on, and for both of us, it was a powerful lesson. Andy especially. As much as he lived for video games, he really seemed to find himself out there, to tap into some dormant, forgotten part of his humanity.

★　★　★

"I went through there," I said.

Andy stood next to me, an old, rusted machete in his hand. He had found it behind our shed, buried under a stack of cordwood. I can still remember him swearing up and down that the red marks weren't rust, but blood. Otherwise, why would anyone hide it? It was a pitiful weapon, likely to split in half the moment you hit anything with it, but it made him feel better just the same. I had dragged him out to the Trails, promising to retrace my steps with him, and even though it was the middle of the day, I felt the need to bring my pocketknife.

"And you had the bear with you?" he asked nervously.

"*Yes*," I said in frustration. "I already told you."

He ignored my tone and kept looking at the wild tangle of trees and ferns. It was dark overhead, the looming clouds threatening to soak us at any minute. The darkness gave the entire place an even more ominous look, as if the creature wouldn't think twice about leaping from the shadowy thicket to rip us to shreds.

"You think…it's in there?"

I shrugged, not wanting to answer either way. "Dunno. I don't think so."

It was true. I wasn't just trying to convince myself. The way he responded to light, sound, people. He was skittish, the type of creature that would hide in a cellar, a mausoleum, maybe even a burrowed hole in the ground. Something dark, cool, and musty.

"You sure about that?" he asked, still staring at the horizon.

"I'm not sure about anything. I just know it hates people. There ain't many here, but there are some."

He nodded, clearly agreeing with me.

"I think we're good. But I also think you're right. It smelled your bear. It had to pass through here."

He swung the machete nervously and said, "All right. Just wait here," and he marched in.

"No," I said, grabbing his shoulder. "We have to at least have some kind of plan or something."

He brushed me off. "This is how we make a plan. We have to check things out first. See if we can track it. See if we can learn anything about it."

"I know that," I said, having to step in front of him to keep him from entering the Trails. "But we need…I don't know…a method or whatever."

He reached into his backpack and retrieved a giant grocery bag, which he shook just in front of my face. "See this?" he asked. "This is my plan."

I peered in, squinting at the multicolored contents before frowning in confusion. "Jelly beans?"

He smiled.

"Yep. Dad's Easter presents. Haven't eaten them for probably three or four years. I kept throwing them in one of the drawers in my room. I've told Dad a couple times that I hate them, but he just forgets, I guess. Either that," he snorted, "or they're just the cheapest thing he can find."

The frown on my face didn't lighten in the slightest. "What the hell does that have to do with anything?"

"Well, he has to save money somehow, and I guess—"

"No," I blurted out. "Not how expensive they are. I mean, the jelly beans. How the heck are jelly beans going to help?"

"Oh," he said. "They're markers. See…"

He took a few steps toward the Trails and dropped one. Then a few more steps, and another jelly bean, then another. Finally, I figured out what he was up to.

"It's such a maze in there," he said. "There has to be some way to mark where I've been. And these are pretty damn easy to see. Whenever I start down a trail, a few jelly beans here and there will let me know it's good to go."

"Sooo…we're like Hansel and Gretel."

"If that helps you," he replied sarcastically. "And who's we? I told you to stay out here."

I glanced around the darkened field and the sky above, billowing with clouds that seemed to grow more impatient by the second.

"Nope," I replied. "If we're doing this, we're doing it together."

"Fine," he said, his voice like a deflating tire. "Just stay close to me."

The Trails were as tight, confusing, and awful as ever, and we made our way through the tangle slowly and methodically, stopping every few feet to drop a jelly bean. Luckily, Andy's bag looked like it held hundreds, maybe even thousands, so we were never in much risk of running low. Before long, we were doubling back on ourselves, the ground lit by the multicolored markers. I'd been in the Trails plenty of times, but I'd never really studied them before that day. There was more to see than I ever realized or wanted to. We weren't in the wild, not really, as the fields that surrounded the trails were no more than a quarter of a mile away from a home, an easy sprint for a kid. Still, it felt like a desert island, a place so very far removed from the world of authority that it could have been Mars.

One trail led us to an open grove where dozens of baby doll parts were strung from threads that dangled from the low-hanging branches. I gasped when we stepped into it, certain that this must be the entrance to the Toy Thief's lair. Then we started seeing the pentagrams carved in the wood, and the truth became clear, though still frightful in its way. This was the work of teens, probably bored metal fans who thought this would be a funny way to scare one of their friends.

"It's fine," Andy said, poking at one of the dead-eyed faces with his machete. "Just wannabe devil worshippers."

I wasn't so convinced, and with one last glance at one of the eyeless heads, I ventured back into the brush. Once, we stumbled across someone's stash, a hastily covered-up trove that consisted of a single, half-full bottle of brown liquor, a pack of Vantage 100s, and half a dozen *Hustler* magazines. I watched Andy's reaction as he placed the cardboard and leaves back into place, and I was certain that he would make a trip back by himself whenever he had the chance.

"Shit," Andy said as we rounded a corner, tripping on a loose root. I could see it coming, almost in slow motion – the bag of jelly beans tumbling out of his hands, followed by the inevitable shower of rainbow colors. I must have been laughing, based on the way he turned his red-cheeked face toward me, eyebrows arched.

"Shut up," he said, shoveling handfuls of jelly beans into the bag. "Quit laughing and freaking help me."

I knelt down, and we both pawed around in the mud. Andy stood up a few moments later, and the candy spilled back out of a hole in the bottom of the bag. Once again, I laughed hysterically as he scooped them into the pockets of his cargo shorts. He was just about to say something back when he cocked his head and held his hand out toward me, trying to shush me.

"Quiet," he said, his own voice dropping, and all at once, I heard it too. I locked my hand onto Andy's shoulder and pressed a finger to my lips. Both of us froze, listening to the sounds of the woods and the strange noise that was drifting through it. It was a panting sound, a deep-breathing moan that my mind translated instantly to be the voice of the Toy Thief, no doubt in the middle of killing his latest victim. Andy's furrowed brow evened out as he listened. Then a half smile rose on his lips. With a single finger, he motioned for me to stay put as he glided soundlessly forward for a closer look. I refused to let him out of my sight, following along about ten yards behind, but Andy either didn't notice me or didn't care. Then, all at once, he held up his hand for me to stop, which, for once, I did without question.

The breathing was louder now, and I watched as Andy peered through a line of trees, out into a small bare patch. From where I stood, I couldn't see a thing, but Andy was apparently close enough to see it all. He stared for ten seconds, maybe less, and then turned back to join me.

"Let's go," he said almost silently in my ear.

"What is it?" I whispered back.

He placed an angry finger onto his lips and then pointed toward the trails behind us, motioning back the way we'd come. I pushed back against him, me being bullheaded for no real reason at all, and the two of us were locked for a brief moment in silent combat. Somehow, I lost my footing and stepped off the trail, onto a dried handful of branches. Andy grabbed my arm, helping to steady me, but it was too late. The crunching echo of branches rang through the Trails like an alarm being sounded, and the steady breathing stopped.

"The fuck?" an angry voice echoed from the opposite side of the tree line.

Andy pointed toward the exit and silently mouthed the word, *Run.* We were off. I didn't glance back, but I could hear the heavy footsteps behind us, the angry cursing, the promise to catch us and make us pay. I didn't recognize the voice, not at first, but after a barrage of curses, the voice came into focus.

It was Barnett.

I think I'd heard from someone in the neighborhood that his first name was Albert or Alvin. Something painfully uncool. So, after his first stint in juvie at age twelve, he started going by his last name: Barnett. He had always been big for his age, and now that he was seventeen, he was big for any age. He might have been six three or so, but it was hard to tell back then, as short as I was. It didn't really matter though. If half the stories passed around the neighborhood were true, he could be three feet tall and it wouldn't make a difference. Being a giant was only window dressing.

The stories. Jesus, those stories.

I knew it was him by that point, because I'd been around him on three or four different occasions. You'd forget about him while he was in juvie, or living with his uncle out of state, or shipped off to some boarding school, and then, all at once, there he was again, a giant standing among a group of children on the street corner. We'd be playing hide and seek or capture the flag or whatever, and he'd appear, expecting a welcome from the neighborhood. Why the hell a seventeen-year-old convict-in-training wanted to spend his time with kids ranging from eight to fifteen was beyond me. Now that I'm grown, he might not scare me as much, because I've realized that a hardass among children really isn't a hardass at all. Good luck telling me that when I was nine though.

So there we were, hauling ass through the woods with fucking

Barnett after us. I still didn't have so much as an inkling as to why the hell he was chasing us, but it didn't matter. When an elephant ran toward you, you ran away. That was just how it worked. The only good news about all this was that we were smaller, and when it came to the trails, smaller was better. We cut through the lines in the woods, jumping roots, never looking back even as his screams grew angrier and oddly desperate.

"Andy," I whined as I sprinted beside him, wondering what could possibly make Barnett so bloodthirsty, but my brother refused to explain.

"Go!" he yelled just over my shoulder. "Don't stop."

We finally broke through the wall of brush and into the field, the knee-high weeds whipping at my legs as I beat the ground with my tiny feet. We were out, but I didn't quite know if we were free or not. Being small was good for the trails, but out here, it was hard to say for sure. Barnett was bigger, and he was more athletic than either of us, especially Andy. In a straight shot, I wasn't overly confident that we could get away.

I realized quickly that none of that mattered. The familiar footsteps just behind me faded off, and I realized with horror that Andy had stopped running.

When I turned, I saw him, standing a dozen yards away from the mouth of the woods, machete held to the side, guarding the only way out.

"Andy," I yelled, but he didn't even acknowledge me.

And there Barnett was, a wall of flesh, shirtless for some reason, wearing nothing but jeans with grass stains on the knees. He towered over Andy, and I realized in that moment that we weren't dealing with a peer. We were kids, involved in silly kid shit. This was, by most measures, a man, a dangerous thing for kids to reckon with – and the look on his face told us he wasn't playing any games.

"The fuck is that?" he asked, his breath catching between words.

"Go back," Andy said, ignoring the question.

"What the hell did you say to me?"

He took a step forward, and Andy tightened his grip on the machete. It was still, even then, a pitiful weapon, but it was all he had, and he held it with a confidence that I didn't know existed.

"What did you see?" Barnett asked, his voice smoothing out, hiding something I couldn't quite place. There was anger in his voice, but desperation as well, the rage masking something deeper and much more dangerous.

"Enough," Andy said.

Barnett's hands balled into fists, and he stomped the ground with his boots. He began walking a tiny circle, his feet refusing to sit still as he pulled at the sides of his red hair like a crazy person.

"I'm gonna kill you," he said to Andy as he stopped circling and took a step forward.

"Try it!" Andy screamed. "You'll have to! Not just me either, but her too. Because we know. We *saw*. So unless you're ready to kill me or die trying, then you need to turn around."

"Why the fuck would I do that?" he screamed back, his voice containing more fear than anger now.

"Because that's the only way we'll never tell. If you lay a finger on me, she'll run. The cops will know. The papers will know. The whole fucking town will know. I might be dead, but it won't matter because they'll know."

Barnett fell down onto his knees and began punching the ground. I didn't understand, not then, what exactly was happening there, but I did know that Andy had him firmly in some kind of checkmate. Barnett's fit subsided, and he leaned back up like a man roused from a nap, his hair in messy curls on either side of his head.

"If you tell," he said, pointing at Andy, "if I hear from a single person that you told…I'll find you. I'll fucking kill both of you."

Andy nodded. "I won't tell. Ever. Now go back in there. Go on. You go your way, and we'll go ours."

It wasn't until that moment, as I dared to step closer, back to my brother's side, that I saw an amazing sight. There were tears on Barnett's cheeks. He wiped them away with a tired hand, skulking into the gloomy dark, utterly defeated. Just as we turned to walk away, the sky finally opened, and the rain began to trickle down, slowly at first, then in heavy waves. We sprinted the rest of the way home, and once we were safe inside, I turned to Andy.

"What was that?"

"Nothing," he said as he shrugged off his backpack and dropped it by the door. I followed him to his bedroom, where he stripped off his soaking-wet shirt.

"Seriously," I said. "What happened back there?"

"Don't worry about it," he said as he used the shirt to towel off his wet hair.

"How can you tell me not to worry about it? He could have killed you."

Andy stepped past me and slammed the door to keep Dad from hearing, and I assumed he was getting ready to spill it.

"You're right," he said. "He could have killed me. And you too. And for a second, I thought he was going to. That's why you need to let this go."

"But—"

"No," he said with finality. "I saw something that he didn't want me to see. That was that. I'm never telling anyone, and you know why?"

"Andy…"

"Do you know why?"

I shrugged. "No."

"Because if I tell anyone, even you, he'll kill us both. That's all the answer you'll ever get."

Unlike me, Andy had a tendency to keep his word. He never did tell me what he saw through those woods, but I have some hunches. I remember seeing Barnett a few weeks later, hanging around the block with a few of his friends. I watched them from the yard, me pretending to play in the dirt as I spied on them smoking and telling jokes with each other, passing the time until the streetlights came on. He was particularly close with one of the friends, a boy I recognized and whom I pegged as maybe fifteen or so. You could see it in their body language, the way they looked at each other, and I think, on some level, I understood. When I got up to go back inside, I noticed Barnett staring at me. The two of us shared a glance that lasted a few beats too long, but he never said a word. If things had gone differently, I might have been afraid of that stare, might have taken it as a preemptive strike, like him and his boys were casing our house. But I had seen worse than Barnett by then, and I knew there were other things to be afraid of.

★　★　★

"So, I'm thinking we get started earlier tomorrow. If we get at it before lunch, we should have plenty of time to check everything out. I'm thinking we go around the back of the Trails. I've never actually been back that far, but I'm pretty sure there's some—"

"Jack."

Once we'd dried off and the sun was down, I had walked back into Andy's room and just started prattling without taking a breath. He was sitting on the floor, staring at the TV, and in my excitement, I hadn't even noticed it wasn't on.

"Hold on a second. I was saying, there're some houses over on one side…I think it might be the back side of Mayer Street, but over on the right, waaayyyy past that field is where the old quarry is. That's what Robbie said, but of course, he never actually went back there himself. I'm not sure if I believe him about much of anything…"

"Jack," he said, standing up.

"…but a flooded quarry, now that's a good hiding spot.

Nobody goes back there, and if I was a monster that steals toys, that's probably where I'd—"

"Stop!" he screamed, staring me in the eyes.

"What?" I said, hand on my hip.

"It's over."

My brain didn't quite process the words.

"What is?"

"This. All this. I mean, jeez, we almost got killed by Barnett today, and he's just some dude. What's next? What if we actually find the damn thing? Do you think it'll just throw up its hands and give your bear back?"

His voice was getting louder, angrier, and he was scratching at his back vigorously, as if he had poison ivy.

"It's not just about the bear," I said.

"Of course it is!" he snapped back. "It's about you. It's always about you."

"Andy, I—"

"What, did you think you were helping me?" he asked as he crossed the room toward me, crowding me back against the door. "You've never helped me. Never helped anyone. If I have a problem, I deal with it myself. You get someone else to do it for you."

A look of pain was growing across his face, clouding his eyes as he dug away at the sore patch on his back.

"And another thing," he said, pointing his finger in my face. We both gasped at the sight of it, the scabby, old blood that he had scratched free, as if he had just killed something with his bare hands.

"Just…just leave me alone," he said as he pushed past me, throwing open the door and ducking into the bathroom.

I thought back to that afternoon, less than an hour ago, thought of the way he'd stepped in front a rampaging, desperate man to keep me safe. Why was he acting like this? He was always sullen, always just on the edge of some glib comment or outburst, but he loved me. I knew he did. And this thing between us, this secret that had sprung up from thin air, it was important. It meant more than just a teddy bear or a plastic superhero. The Toy Thief was threatening the last shreds we had left of our mom, and so it mattered.

I knew those things then as I do now, but I didn't have any fight in me. I was drained, wrung out, and I couldn't keep up this pace for much longer. So instead of waiting for him in his room, forcing him to see things my way, I dropped it. Tomorrow, the world might look different, as it often did after a night of sleep. I trudged to the kitchen and ate something, I couldn't tell you what, and before the clock struck eight, I was asleep, curled up in my bed, the dull pocketknife clutched in my left hand.

★   ★   ★

"Jack."

Confusion.

Dad shaking me awake.

"Wake up, Jack."

Sun streaming in.

Couldn't be. Just went to bed a few minutes ago.

"I said, wake up," he said, his voice growing harder, less patient.

"What?" I said, bleary as I sat up in bed, my eyes still closed.

"Have you seen Andy?"

"In his bed," I replied as I flopped back down onto the covers. Dad yanked them away, and when he spoke again, I heard an urgency in his tone that was so foreign it felt like a different language. He never sounded like that – so very afraid.

"I said...get...up."

Again, I sat up, and when I found the will to open my eyes, they found his eyes inches away. His fingers, like bands of iron, locked onto my shoulders as he stared at me.

"Andy," he said slowly. "Do you know where he is?"

"He was in his bedroom," I replied. "Last night."

"You haven't seen him?" he asked.

"No. Why?"

He closed his eyes and let out a deep, slow breath before saying another word.

"Your brother's gone."

CHAPTER EIGHT

We used to play a game in the neighborhood called capture the flag. The rules were pretty simple. Two teams would divide a section of the neighborhood into two more-or-less equal parts. Each team had a flag, usually an old towel or a t-shirt. Didn't really matter as long as it was white. Then the teams would split up and hide the flag somewhere on their half of the playing field, making sure that the entire flag was actually visible. No stuffing it in a trashcan or anything. After both sides were ready, the game began.

As soon as you set foot onto enemy territory, you were fair game. If they touched you, you were caught, and you had to freeze in place until someone from your side rescued you. That was one way to win the game: simply catch everyone else on the opposite team. But the real goal, the ultimate prize so to speak, was to sneak into enemy territory, find their flag, and get back to your side with it.

We always played at night, and most of us dressed the part, head to toe in all black. Some kids took it further than others, donning camouflage. This one kid, Donnie something, used to paint his face up with football eye grease, thinking it really gave him some kind of edge. It was, for a good portion of the guys in the neighborhood, a kind of fantasy, their opportunity to be soldiers sneaking behind enemy lines.

Those guys sucked at capture the flag.

I wasn't the fastest, and I didn't wear camo, but more often than not, I was the first picked when the teams were sorted out, because they all knew. They had seen it firsthand. You see, the game wasn't just about getting the flag or capturing the other team. None of that really mattered if you couldn't find the damn thing. We always stuck to the rules when we hid the flag, because there was no quicker way to get shunned from the neighborhood than to cheat. But part of the strategy was to hide it as well as you could without actually cheating. If there was a tree right next to a shed, you could hide it between the two, pinning it up on a low-hanging branch. It might be hard to find, but it was still legal.

It was a thrill once you made it onto the other side, with no one in sight, creeping forward in a crouch through creeks, ditches, patches of trees. But once you were over there, no matter how stealthy or fast you were, it didn't matter if you couldn't find the flag. That was where I came in.

I was smaller than everyone else, and I could move through the dead leaves with a lighter step than any of the hulking boys could ever dream of. But there was more to it than just my physical gifts. I knew to steer clear of the streetlamps, those little pools of light that would give you away in a second. I knew which houses had automatic lights that would flip on when you came into range, enough to paint a target on your back and bring the rest of the team running. I knew which of our neighbors raked their leaves in the fall, taking the crunch out of every step. But most importantly, I knew how the other teams thought, because I knew where I would have hidden something.

In short, I was a fucking bloodhound.

★　　★　　★

I was supposed to be in school that day. It was Monday, the last Monday, the beginning of the end of the school year. Half the kids were gone, and the others were watching videos and filmstrips, the teachers passing the time as much as the kids. I should have been there with my handful of friends, with Sallie and the rest, giggling, passing notes, our teeth practically chattering while the summer got its claws in us. Instead, I was watching Dad pace the room as he waited for the cops to show.

Once again, I had to give him credit. He stumbled through fatherhood, less with a plan than with a flashlight, but he did his best to hit the major milestones. Birthdays were good, if a bit underwhelming, especially compared to my friends'. Christmas was usually a nontraditional blast of junk food, scary movies, and as many toys as you could fit under a tree. I still don't know how he pulled that off year after year. And even though we didn't get the traditional tuck-in, kiss-on-the-forehead kind of good night, he still kept better tabs on us than I ever realized. Most nights, he was the first to bed, but, as I learned after Andy went missing, he would inevitably take a stroll through the house after we were asleep to check on us.

That was how he knew.

For the second time in a week, I stood just out of sight, spying as Dad talked to a pair of cops in the kitchen about Andy. Apparently we'd drawn the asshole card this go-round, as one of the cops, a big man with a buzz cut, rather stoically told Dad that that sort of thing was common among delinquents.

"Delinquents?" Dad asked incredulously.

"Yes, sir. I understand your son had a shoplifting incident just a week ago."

"Yeah. He did something stupid, but I don't think that qualifies as—"

"He has also been suspended four times from school for fighting, smoking, et cetera."

Dad sighed, but it wasn't a sound of exasperation – more of a plea to himself not to punch the cop in the face.

"What does any of that have to do with finding him?" he asked impatiently.

"Running away from home is also common among delinquents," the cop added.

"Don't fucking call my son a delinquent again."

Just then the other cop, a shorter, round-faced fellow, spoke up. "We'll do all we can, sir. You have to believe that."

I listened to them talking, considering all of the potential scenarios running through their heads. The unhappy home lives of runaways that made them feel as if life on the road was a better option. Most came back soon, so they said, but this was a small town, and every cop knew to keep their eyes out. It was all rather bland and prepackaged, but I listened along just as well as Dad. Soon they were gone, and I crept around the corner, a mouse uncertain if the cats were asleep.

Had my father ever looked so pitiful? His head was slumped in his hands, his thinning hair a mess from where he had run his frustrated fingers through it. From the side, he looked like an old barn about to cave in. The only thing supporting him was the kitchen table itself. He heard me walk in, and I saw his brows perk up, but he refused to look at first.

"You okay, baby?" he asked, still not glancing my way.

Hearing his voice, so broken, so desperately sad, sent a shock of heartbreak racing through my entire body. All at once, I couldn't even answer the question. Instead, I must have squeaked a little, some kind of pitiful excuse for a word. It was enough to turn those watery blue eyes my way.

"Oh, Jack," he said, sitting up straight and spreading his arms. I spilled into him and went boneless as he scooped me up as easily as he had when I was a baby. He told me it was okay, and he let me cry until I was just about empty. Once or twice, I could feel his tears drip down, mixing with my own, the two of us all but spent.

"He'll be back," he told me at the end. "Don't you worry. He's just a little upset, I'm sure, but he'll be back." We talked a bit longer before I sneaked back to my room and slid the door closed. Maybe they were right.

Dad.

The cops.

That little voice inside me, the quiet part that always told me what I wanted to hear.

All of them were saying the same thing.

He'll be back.

But I knew what they didn't. I saw the truth that they were blind to. He hadn't left. He hadn't packed up and strolled out. He'd been taken. Stolen by that half-formed, horrid creature. There wasn't any question in the matter. If my brother was ever to see our house again, it was up to me to make it happen.

★ ★ ★

I'm getting tired of writing this. I know that's a weird thing to say, especially from the outside.

Just quit then.

That's what I imagine most people would say, and my itching fingers tell me that would probably be for the best. They always itch when I'm doing something I shouldn't be. When I fucked around with Gabe Thompson after that football game when we were fifteen, they itched so bad I couldn't even feel what was happening below the waist. He didn't like me. He had all but told me as much in class that year. He always, more so than just about anyone I knew, made it a special point to terrorize me in class. People like him made my high school years a nightmare.

"I'll bet you don't even shave your bush," he told me once. "I mean, how would you hold the razor?"

I had ignored similar things for the better part of a month, but that particular sentiment was just too disgusting to ignore. I spit in his face, right in class, right in front of Mr. Pullman, and when he stepped over to split us up, Gabe started laughing. He'd broken me, made me give in to his awful impulses, and so he won.

I can still remember the grin on his face, even all those months later, when I bumped into him after a football game. It was homecoming. The stadium was less than half a mile away from the house, close enough to walk without much worry. Usually, a few friends tagged along with me, but on that night, I was going solo. I saw Gabe at the game, I always saw him, tracked him, kept an eye on him the way you might keep an eye on a rattlesnake that people let slither around their house. It was only really dangerous if you didn't know where it was.

I had a handful of friends at that point, weirdoes like me, people pushed out of the inner circles, hiding in plain sight at the edge of the crowds. There were plenty of us, and we were never really alone, but we never really mattered either. That was fine. Life on the inside of that glass globe looked awful by comparison. I caught glimpses of Gabe and his friends, the preppy, well-kept pretty boys in Dockers and tucked-in polo shirts, a wall of stinking, high-school-boy cologne enveloping them wherever they went. One of them had procured a bottle of liquor, some cheap, plastic-bottle vodka from the look of it, and they were passing it around, taking swigs whenever they felt it was safe to. They kept it hidden under a plastic megaphone with our school logo on it, the Green Bronco.

When the game was over, the crowd began to break up, splitting into subgroups for rides home with parents, older siblings, anyone that would spare a seat. I hugged my friends and set out down the darkened stretch of road lined with cars on their way out. There were too many people, and I began to feel itchy in my fingers, the way I always did after too long in a crowd, so I sneaked off onto one of the quiet neighborhood paths that would lead me home. I crossed around the edge of the field house, and there he was, stumbling along towards me. His house was also within walking distance, just in the opposite direction, heading for the nice part of town. He saw me, and I glanced down to the ground.

"Oh," he said, coming to an awkward halt. "You."

It wasn't the usual way he spoke to me. It was a tone of curious, almost playful surprise, like we were old friends stumbling across each other.

"Me." I stopped too.

He struck up a strained conversation, always careful to glance over his shoulder to make sure none of his friends were creeping up on us. So we talked, standing there, hidden in the shadow of the field house, and all of the things I hated to admit were impossible to ignore. He was handsome, almost painfully so, like a rower at an Ivy League school or a rugby player. Amazingly, he was actually being pleasant to me, making me laugh by making fun of himself, the same way he might act with the truly attractive girls in our grade. The ones who weren't untouchable. Before long, after the headlights had disappeared on the horizon, we began to walk toward my house, deeper into the woods, the pair of us swallowed by the dark. And then, without warning, I pressed him against a tree and began kissing him, and before I knew it, he was fumbling for his belt, dropping his pants around his ankles, practically begging me to get on my knees. Instead, I pushed him down onto his bare knees and pressed his face into my crotch.

It's important to understand that I wasn't some poor, pitiful girl who was swept off her feet by the prom king. *I* started the entire encounter, and I was the only one who got an ounce of satisfaction that night. After I dug my nails into his back hard enough to rip his shirt, I pushed his head away, picked up my panties, and left him standing there, his dick throbbing in the cool, open air. I couldn't help but smile.

When Monday rolled around, he refused to look me in the eyes, and from that point forward, he never so much as mentioned my name. It was a wonderful feeling, dangling our encounter over his head like a sword on a thread. From time to time, I would even slip him a note in class that read something like *Did you tell your friends yet?* or *When will you take me out to eat again?* Not once did he ever respond, but the fear of the world knowing what he had done, and more importantly, who he had done it with – ohhhh, that was absolutely delicious.

I was itching that night, and I'm itching now as I write all this down. Everything up to now has been tough to talk about. Mom. Dad. Andy. All of it.

But I'm itching now because I realize that everything up to this point has been treading water. The real story, the *bad* stuff, is just about to begin.

★   ★   ★

Dad paced around the house for the next hour or so, but he could only stand doing nothing for so long.

"Jack," he said, pausing in my doorway, "I'm…" He seemed at a loss for words, unsure of exactly what he was going to do.

"I'm going out for a drive," he added. "Just stay inside." He made it halfway out the door before I heard him turn back around and stomp down the hall. "And lock the door."

When he was gone, I sprinted to the front window and peered through the blinds as the truck pulled out. I figured he would circle the neighborhood a few times before heading deeper into town, widening his search. Regardless of where he went, I knew he wouldn't find anything.

I went back into my room and flopped onto the bed, staring at the ceiling, trying to figure out just what my next move should be. I had no idea where Andy had been taken, but I knew who took him. There was only one clue out of all this, only one thing that led anywhere: my path from the bus stop into the Trails and finally home the day before the Thief appeared. I had no doubt whatsoever that I had drawn the thing in, or my bear had. I thought of Barnett, of the strange, still-hazy scene, and the idea of going in there alone was enough to make me shiver. But then I thought of Andy, all by himself.

He was tougher than me by a mile, but he had been right. Neither of us knew what we were up against. If, by some chance, I could actually find him, I knew the odds of me getting him home were slim. I knew all of these things, but that didn't matter now. He was out there, and I would find him if I could, even if it meant the end of both of us.

I threw whatever I could find into my backpack. A flashlight. A bottle of water. A lighter. A handful of roman candles. I slung the bag over my shoulder and slipped the knife into the pocket of my jeans. I took one last look around the house, a curiously quiet place without Dad and Andy there. Had Mom stood here once, hands on her belly, a young, whiny Andy at her heels, and my father, nervous and jittery, asking if it was finally time? I wondered if she had taken one last, longing look at her home before she went to the hospital. Three left that day, and as far as anyone knew, four would return. The house must have been quiet then too.

Memphis prowled in and startled me back to the present, curling around my leg. He always seemed to show up, whether he was or wasn't needed.

"I'll be back," I told him, kneeling down. I scratched his head and rubbed the tears from my eye. "And I'm bringing Andy back with me. You hear me?"

He looked at me with his sharp, lazy eyes, and I ventured out into the day, alone. It wasn't three o'clock yet, but the woods between the neighborhood and the field were as dark as nightfall. The storm from the day before had broken, but the sky was still dark, still gloomy, and I knew it could rain at any moment. Every breeze through the grass, every crack and pop of branches, made me glance over my shoulder in fear. Monsters, both human and otherwise, seemed to lurk in every shadow, behind every scrubby wall of brush. More than once, when the wind picked up, I froze, the terror boiling up in my throat like bile, and I nearly turned and fled in the opposite direction. Each time, I would close my eyes, think of Andy, think of whatever darkness he was in, and the moment would pass, ruffling through my hair like the wind. So I pushed on toward the Trails, which stood like a monolith of dark green, and I shuddered as soon as I set my eyes on them.

I won't go in there. You can't make me go in there. Nothing can make me go in there.

One breath, then two. A step, small and pitiful, but enough to carry me forward an inch. The breeze was at my back now, urging me forward, inviting me in.

I opened my eyes, and there I stood, at the edge of the Trails. Without further hesitation, I stepped in. Had that place ever been so utterly devoid of light? Had the trees and branches and creepers pressed so far off the path the day before? It didn't seem possible, but once I laid my eyes on the first jelly bean, I felt my heart lift a bit. It was part of Andy, part of his own silly plan that made me almost giggle even as tears clouded my eyes. Deeper into the tangle I went, leaving the light farther behind with nothing to guide me but fluorescent bits of sugar. On and on I went, passing every turn, every corner, ignoring the parts I knew, leaving the relatively known for the vast expanse of unknown beyond it.

I hit the fork in the path where we had frozen the day before, and once again, I paused. I could still see it, the patch of grass where Andy had stood – spying on something he was never supposed to see. I knew that Barnett was gone. My brain told me he had to be, but it still took heaven and hell to get my feet moving once again. With a shiver, I reached into my pocket and drew out the knife, which I promptly flipped open. I edged close to the clear patch and peeked in, finding nothing but an empty patch of green. Then I took a few rubbery paces back to the trail, and I hesitated once again, this time not with fear but with confusion. I retraced my steps, back to where I had stood the day before.

I had been here.

Andy had been there.

Then we were running.

That was all. No time to mark a path. No time to bend down and drop a yellow or orange or pink jelly bean. And yet, there it was. Green. Shining like a neon emerald some ten feet to the left of where Andy had been standing the day before.

Nothing, I thought. *A bird moved it. Maybe a squirrel, or my imagination, or nothing at all.*

I thought of the downpour we had run through, how it must have cut lines in the slick dirt of the trails, little temporary rivers that would easily carry a jelly bean.

Yes, I thought. *Rain.*

I stepped over, my heart sinking a bit, and I reached down for it, and when I did, I noticed the next one a dozen steps down the path.

Calm down, I thought as I stared at it, listening to my heart pound. *It was the rain. Just rain.*

This one was yellow, and when I stepped over to it, I didn't have to pause for more than a second before I saw the orange one just a few short yards away.

I walked over and straddled the orange bean, staring at it like a bomb disposal specialist might study an unmarked box on a street corner. I stood in that spot, the little sliver of neon orange between my feet, and I began to slowly spin in a circle, looking for the next jelly bean, if indeed there was a next one. I was as methodical as I could be in my excitement, tilting my head from foot to sky with each half step, desperately striving to cover every speck of land, to find the next bread crumb that might reunite Hansel and Gretel. There were four different paths carved in the ancient earth, and they branched out in different directions like the points on a compass. None of them was well defined, and the longer I stood, the more certain I became that this was all just wishful thinking. I stepped away from the orange beacon and began to make small, concentric circles, radiating out from the center.

I kept my eyes down, focusing on the small patch of dirt or grass or leaves just between my feet, but after five minutes, I felt like a fool. There was nothing here, no perfect path, no 'aha' moment. Just rain picking up old, uneaten jelly beans. I was just beginning to lose hope when a red speck shined in the light just out of the line of trees. It was probably thirty feet or so away from the orange bean, and as I quietly waded through the grass, I was convinced it wasn't a jelly bean at all. Maybe a bottle cap or a candy wrapper, but certainly not a jelly bean.

Then I was on top of it, and my face beamed as the path forward became clear. There was a thin line in the tall grass of the field, just wide enough for people or deer to walk single file. On I went, one step at a time, and when I found yet another bean, all doubt was gone. I had no clue what had happened to Andy, whether he was hurt or tied up or even half dead, but I knew he was *alive*. This was, without any question in my mind, his path, the path that he knew I could find. One jelly bean at a time, I followed him like a bloodhound deeper into the suburban wild.

The field ended in another row of trees and a barbed-wire fence that hung limply in place inches above the ground. I climbed over it, following the sparse neon path, and a thought occurred to me. Based on everything I knew, the Toy Thief was nocturnal, even to the point of hating light. His entire existence seemed to depend on darkness, depend on never being found. I had no clue what would happen to Andy, what was happening to Andy, but I felt certain that the night would bring another trip into the Trails, back the exact way it had come. I was just guessing of course, but the odds seemed to be in my favor. The implications of this were clear. If the Thief found the trail of jelly beans, it would, without question, remove them. Then any hope of finding my brother would be gone for good. Even worse, he might choose to punish Andy for what he'd done.

I was stuck between two competing forces. My heart told me to run, to catch up as quickly as I could, but my brain said that every step was a risk, every movement a potential deadfall. I thought of my own pitiful traps the week before, and I didn't doubt for a second that the Toy Thief would be infinitely more devious and clever.

"Just imagination," I told myself. "Don't let it stop you from what you know you have to do."

Past the fence was a new wild I'd never even known existed so close to our home. I could still see the houses peeking over treetops in the distance, but I was far enough away that no one would ever hear me scream. The path was vague as I went, and I noticed smaller trails that shot off like rabbits in different directions, toward different neighborhoods and homes. I felt certain that any of these would lead me straight into someone else's backyard, and if I pried open the first window I found, I'd see someone else's bedroom lined with toys ripe for the picking.

I came into a tiny clearing and realized that these side paths were all issuing out from a central hub, extending like tributaries from a single river. I stood in the center, searching for the next colored checkpoint, and I found it. This particular path through the tall grass was more worn down than the others, a highway for the deer, the coyotes, and of course the monsters. Deeper and deeper I ventured, the day waning overhead, the distance between me and my house, my sanctuary, growing wider as the distance to Andy narrowed. Once, the trail moved close enough past the backyard of one of the homes that a dog stirred and began barking at me as I passed. But then the rows of homes ended, and I left the neighborhoods behind for good.

Beyond the cover of the woods, I found a small, ancient-looking road. I stumbled over the wheel ruts that led toward a low fence marked by a rusted chain that dangled across the weedy path. A yellow and brown *Caution* sign stared at me, mostly illegible through all the rust. I was at the old quarry, the place mentioned in whispers among the kids on the street, a place only the bravest actually laid eyes on.

Go back. Do it now while you still can.

For the first time since I had set out, I realized that the warning from within myself wasn't really me. It had a sharper, darker undertone that I couldn't quite place. Then it hit me: the dream from a few nights before. The dark, soupy blackness that formed itself into a man. The hollow warning it spoke to me before opening its bloodred eyes. What had it said?

No death for your brother...

Why did I have to remember that here of all places, now of all times? My mind, despite all the insanity of the past week, had made a special note of that dream, had locked it carefully away behind a rickety door that could be opened at a moment's notice. That dark tone wasn't quite like a man's voice, but something that might have once dreamed it was a man. I was trying to talk myself out of doing what I knew I had to do, but my mind had added this awful darkness to further dissuade me. It made sense, in a twisted way. After all, dreams come from within, and every grim moment, every curdled image is provided by our own subconscious. I didn't know any of this, not as a kid, but I did believe that somehow, my mind was using my fear against me, doubling, tripling my terror.

No.

Yes, of course it was just a dream.

No, it wasn't.

My voice now, all me, clear and vivid.

There was more to that dream, and you know it. No dream in your entire life ever felt like that one. And for good reason.

No. There was no good reason. Dreams were dreams.

Precisely. And that was no dream.

I clapped my hands to the sides of my head and went down on one knee. Maybe there was something there, some shred of truth about what I was telling myself, but it didn't matter — not now anyway. Later there would be time: time to sort all this out, time to make sense of the circus behind my eyes. But not now. Now only one thing mattered, and that was Andy.

"So stop," I said aloud, certain that every voice in my head could hear me. "And keep walking."

And I did. In an unbroken march, stepping over the low hanging fence, I went past the quarter mile of tall grass, past the jagged remnants of rock, the uncut pillars that seemed to rise from hell itself. On and on, until the ground began to slope downward, and I caught sight of it: the sheer face of gray granite, a hundred feet at least, ending in a bottomless well of dark water. I stepped to the edge, peered over, felt the world tilt underfoot. The path ended here, ended in a drop to almost certain death. I checked left and right, retracing my steps to the last marker I could find, but the trail had gone cold. For one desperate moment, I considered the possibility that the awful monster really didn't have any sort of lofty ambitions for Andy. It wasn't a kidnapping. It was merely a murder. I pictured it tossing him over the edge, maybe with a rock tied around his neck for good measure, his last pleas for mercy heard by nothing more than the passing crows.

"Andy."

I whispered his name, and the sound of my own voice made me want to scream. Down both sides of the canyon, the sheer cliffs were impossible for me to climb, and as far down as I could see, there was nothing but flat gray rock. Somewhere in that moment of final desperation, I realized there were tears streaming down my face. The dark clouds rolled overhead, but I was too tired to care, and I flopped onto the bare dirt and began to sob. I couldn't go back. There was nothing to go back to. But to stay here was to admit to myself that there was no hope.

Once I had just about cried myself out, I sat up and stared down at the black water. I hated the sight of it, so dark and full of secrets, and in weak, helpless defiance, I kicked a rock off the edge and waited. But instead of a splash, I heard the unmistakable crack of rock on rock. Once more, I peered over the edge, leaning as far forward as I dared to. There wasn't much to see, only the bulging wall stretching out before me. I had assumed, wrongly perhaps, that the rock wall was sheer, just like every other part of the quarry. Again, I found a small rock, reached out, and let it drop. It left my field of vision, and I expected to hear it splash down, but once more it cracked, stone upon stone.

Somewhere down there, just out of my field of view, was an outcropping. I scrambled to my feet and began pacing the edge of the cliff. I couldn't see much of anything until I had walked about a hundred yards to one side. The quarry wasn't exactly straight, and with the narrow, grading curve, I could just make it out: a flat platform of rock, maybe thirty feet wide, was hidden under the bulge of the wall. Even more incredibly, behind it was a hollow.

A cave.

I could even make out the remains of an old path to the bottom of the quarry farther down the right-hand side – a rutted trail just big enough for a single vehicle to drive down. In a sprint, I made my way to the narrow road, which hugged the side of the quarry and toward the rocky platform I had seen. I kept one hand on the wall as I stepped carefully down, unsure of how deep the water at the bottom was. It was a slow, awkward walk, but I made it without any issues, at least until I hit the bottom. At one point, vehicles could have easily been driven down here before the workers gave up on it. Now, with the floodwaters low, I could see the bands on the walls where the water level had gone up and down throughout the year. It was somewhere in the middle now, the washout from the day before bringing everything up a bit, but it had been as much as ten feet higher in the past.

The narrow road fed right down into the murky water, and I put a tentative foot in. There was no drop-off, just the continuous, gentle slope leading ever downward into the still, dark water. The road ended some fifty feet away from the entrance to the cave, and I began to shuffle in place like I was about to piss my pants. There was something about that water, so still and tepid, as warm as a bathtub. It felt dirty somehow, like wading through sewage. There was no way around it though, so I bit my lip and stepped in, clinging to the wall as I passed deeper into the murk. Past my ankles. Above my calves. My knees. The middle of my thigh. When the water passed my belly button, I stopped to reassess and sighed when I realized I was still thirty feet away.

But I was closer to the cliff wall now, and I could see it for the first time. It wasn't just some divot as I'd feared it might be. It was an opening, a gaping mouth that had once been cut into the earth, in search of granite or marble, before this place was given back to nature. I could see the opening big enough to drive a truck through, but the line of the water was just below the lip of the cave. And it was a cave. Man might have made it some long, forgotten years past, but this was no longer a place that men knew. I felt exposed and helpless splashing through that dark water, but I couldn't go back. This was it. It had to be, and so I hitched my backpack off and held it over my head, walking forward on my tiptoes until the water was up to my chin.

I wasn't the strongest swimmer in the world, but I was comfortable enough in water to press off the bottom and tread over the last few feet. I caught the edge with my left hand just as my face went under, and I sucked in a mouthful of that sour, tepid water as my feet found the sloping bottom once more. With a coughing spasm, I tossed up the backpack and scrambled up the slope, dropping like a rock once I was on the dry land of the cave entrance. With a glance up, I peered into darkness, wondering just what I might find when the light of the summer day died away.

CHAPTER NINE

I haven't been completely honest. I think you've probably picked up on that. You might not think there's a good reason to lie to you, but lying's all I know. Think back to that awful blind date with the chubby guy. No one bothered to tell me what he looked like, just like no one bothered to tell him the same about me. I have no idea what it's like to be him, but for me, the truth about who I am... well, it's the kind of thing I have to work up to.

I keep talking about my fingers. About how they itch all the time. They do. Wherever they are. You see, the last two fingers on my right hand. They're gone.

It hurts just to write that.

It hurts because this isn't who I am. This isn't who I was supposed to be. Can you remember what it was like for you in high school, or even worse, junior high? Maybe you were pretty or skinny or fat or tall or whatever. Chances are, you weren't perfect, and even if you were, you weren't *really* perfect. Sallie was pretty damn close. Blonde, tall, gorgeous. A cheerleader even. There was this group of boys who thought they were clever. They liked to come up with nicknames for all the girls, cutesy little labels with an edge of pure fucking meanness to them. Sallie had this tiny birthmark on her forearm, just a small patch the size of a dime that had just a hair more melanin than the rest of her body. They called her Shit Arm.

Clever, huh?

Now, imagine what it was like for an admittedly pretty young girl with a good sense of humor who just happened to be missing two fingers on one hand. I might as well have been in prison the way people treated me, boys especially. Prison would have been better, now that I think about it, because at least in prison, you knew where you stood. Every person I met, every conversation I had, every smile I got from a stranger, they all came with a ticking clock so loud I could hear it in my ear. How long would it take before I got careless, before I turned my hand the wrong way, before they saw who I really was? Who I had been turned into? My very fucking *body* was the prison, and I took it with me everywhere I went.

My fingers, still to this day, itch whenever I get nervous. The doctors call it phantom pain, sensations that exist in limbs that have long since rotted away. My brain, bless its heart, doesn't quite know that my fingers aren't still there, and in some strange way, they hang on to that last moment, a physical memory of the last time they were still attached. They were burning then, itching as if the skin were being peeled off of them, and maybe it was.

No, I haven't been completely honest. But I hope you can forgive me for that small transgression. If not, well…I suppose you can just go to hell.

★　★　★

The first steps into the dark mouth of the cave were a bit like stepping into a haunted house. It was dark, but not nearly as dark as I thought it would be – the sensation unnerved me more than I can really explain. It should have been darker, especially as I stepped deeper in, and my eyes and body were at odds with one another. It wasn't until my foot sloshed in the first puddle that I realized how much water there was in there, how much of the light it was reflecting back at me from the floor.

The walls and ceiling were symmetrical, carefully cut square blocks that had been carved out decades earlier. The floor was a bit bumpier, with small pools here and there from where the rain had been the night before. Somewhere behind me, miles in the distance, I heard a crack of thunder, and I shuddered to think how far the water could rise if a storm blew in suddenly.

There was only one path in, straight back up a gentle slope that rose toward the grassy ground I had been standing on ten minutes earlier. I followed the trail, clutching the wall one careful footstep at a time. It was an easier route than I had imagined, and before I knew it, I had traveled far enough up the slope to lose the mouth of the cave altogether. The previous sense that this was a well-lit place faded in an instant as I fumbled for my flashlight and the cheap little pocket knife. The beam pushed back the darkness, but not nearly as strongly as I hoped it would. It was a cheap plastic flashlight, the kind of thing you gave to a kid to play with – something you didn't mind too much when they broke it. Dad had a good flashlight out in the garage, a heavy metal one with half a dozen D batteries, and I cursed myself for not taking it.

A few feet later, the path leveled off and the room opened up on both sides, the walls expanding around me. They had been just venturing into this part of the mine when they abandoned it, and massive, angular slabs had been sliced out of the gray walls as if it were a giant cake. To one side, the room was even and square, ending in a bare hallway. On the opposite side, I found a stair step of sliced rock, uneven pieces that had been left when the work ended. I kept following the wall, checking this way and that, unsure as to where Andy and his captor could have gone, or if I was even pointing in the right direction at all. Moments later, I finished the circuit around the room and found myself staring back into the dimly lit hallway I had arrived in.

Go, that dark voice whispered. *Go now and forget this place.*

It was the same voice, my voice, but for the first time, it felt as if it were coming from outside of my body instead of within. Then, in a whisper into the cup of my ear, I heard it once more.

I'll kill you when I'm done with him.

I spun around, crying out weakly as I did. My pocketknife was at the ready, and I swung it, slicing out at whatever it was that could have sneaked so close so very quickly. There was nothing but open, black air, but I felt like somehow, some way, something was trying to stop me. If I hesitated for a single moment, I might have dashed back the way I'd come, but I refused to back down. I walked into the center of the room and shined the light on the nearest wall. Then I began to make a slow rotation, checking every inch of the room, scanning the corners for anything, any clue at all. There was nothing: no hidden alcoves, no separate halls, no branching paths. Nothing but dark gray rock.

No. There was…something. I noticed it next to the crisscrossed staircase, a patch on the back wall that was darker than the others. I had glanced by it once, thinking it was just a darker shade of rock, but suddenly, I wasn't so sure. Slowly, I walked over and realized what it was.

A hole.

It wasn't very big. Not much more than a child could fit through, and the odd shape told me that it hadn't been made by the miners. At least not intentionally. I never found out for sure why they closed the quarry, but in that moment, I had some ideas. The workers had come across a natural cave, and for some reason, they had to abandon their work. Maybe it had been a gas leak, or maybe they feared the entire thing might collapse. Maybe it was just something as mundane as the money running out. Whatever the cause, this tiny hole was all that was left, a tiny doorway from the world that man had built to the strange, wild world beyond.

I felt like a child slipping through her mother's womb as I slid into the darkness. The air was thick and cool, the musty smell of mold hanging all around me. My flashlight, seeming more pathetic than ever, sliced into the solid blackness, showing me a scene from one of our school field trips to Mammoth Cave. The walls were uneven, the floors bumpy and jagged, both a product of nothing more than the patient flow of water over thousands of years. Narrow rocks rose from the floor and dropped from the ceiling, and every inch of the gray rock seemed to hide secrets. A bony hand here. A deformed face there. A flap of loose skin draped over the rocks.

"Please," I begged my overworked imagination, "don't do this."

My mind refused to listen as it changed the drip of water into blood, the glistening rocks into eyes, and the slight breeze from behind me into faint, softly played music.

Music?

I closed my eyes, focusing all my energy on my ears, and as impossible as it seemed, I realized there was little doubt. A sweet, childish melody was drifting up through the black corridor like a lullaby. No. It wasn't *like* a lullaby; it *was* one. A delicate tune whose name I didn't know but whose words were instantly recognizable to just about anyone.

Go to sleep, and good night…da, da, da-da-da-da-da…

The sound of it transformed the barren crags into some obscure, faraway dream, a trip the likes of which I wouldn't experience for many years – not until I finally tried acid for the first time. It was all hopelessly unreal, and yet it made perfect sense. What else would I hear when I entered the lair of a monster that stole toys?

A foot at a time, I crept forward, and the music grew and began to blend with other sounds. I heard a twinkling music box, the kind that might have a ballerina twirling in the center. I heard a baby crying, a sound that sent shivers up my spine until I realized that it wasn't real. The repetitions were too similar, too exact to be anything other than another toy. I walked in silence as a quiet, gentle chorus rose from somewhere below me, echoing down the gnarled chamber, drifting like smoke. The farther I ventured, the more I expected to see it: a leering, glassy-eyed face staring back from the blackness with a baby doll in his hands. The more I imagined this scenario, the more I became convinced that I had to turn off my flashlight. At that point, I assumed Andy's captor already knew I was there, and all the music and crying were just part of some cruel game.

I shut it off and walked a few steps, then used it in short bursts only, just enough to get me the next ten feet. The chamber was still straightforward, with a few small holes here and there, each of them too small for even me to fit through, so I felt reasonably confident that the Thief wouldn't fit through either. Before me, the tunnel spread out into empty blackness that was cut only by the occasional stalactite. The path was also widening the farther I went, stretching out like the end of a cone. I could see the jagged floor ahead of me, and it looked as straight as it ever had for at least thirty feet. The music seemed to suddenly grow, and I flipped off the light once more and waited, blinking at the darkness around me.

I expected to hear footsteps slinking quietly toward me, but I heard nothing beyond the now-familiar sound of soft music. Frozen in place, I felt my eyes slowly adjusting, and I realized it wasn't quite as dark as I'd previously thought. Somewhere up ahead, glowing like a swarm of fireflies, I saw a dim light. It seemed to be bubbling up from the ground beneath me, a strange sensation that I couldn't quite place until I took a few more steps forward. In that moment, I realized that turning off my flashlight might have very well saved my life. The light was radiating up from a hole in the floor, a hole that was no bigger than a manhole. The light from my flashlight had all but drowned the glow out completely, and I gazed down, imagining how badly I would have been injured if I hadn't seen it.

Once I leaned down, I could see a sloping wall beneath me, a bit steeper than I would have liked, but angled enough for me to slide down. Had I tumbled in without readying, I would have at least hurt my legs, probably enough for me to break an ankle. I could picture the whole scene: me at the bottom of the slope, bone sticking out of my foot as I screamed and screamed, practically ringing the dinner bell for the Thief.

I stared down for a long time, measuring the distance in my mind before I dared take the plunge. I wasn't entirely sure I would be able to get out of there once I went in, but I was now more or less convinced my arrival had gone unnoticed. I had come too far, ventured too close to his lair for him to willingly let me any closer. In the distance, thunder boomed, and I shuddered, thinking how close it must be.

From my vantage point, the room below looked giant — a wide expanse of empty walls that dwarfed everything I had seen before that moment. An ember of light shined from a deep groove that glowed in the center of the room some hundred feet away. I couldn't make out any of the details, but from a distance, it looked like a maze of rocks — good hiding places for me and him.

With nothing left to lose, I eased down into the hole, adjusting my seat on the rocky slide and edging down as far as my hands would let me. It was cooler in the hole, the air drier than I expected, but I didn't have time to wonder much about this. The eerie music ringing in my ears, I loosened my grip, dug in my heels, and began to skid downward.

The slope wasn't as steep as it looked from above, and I slid down the incline, bumping and rattling my teeth here and there whenever I caught a rough patch. I slowed to a stop, and the vast expanse of the room became fully apparent. It was gigantic, a vista thousands of years in the making, the walls and ceiling overhead lit by the dim, glowing patch in the center. I wanted nothing more than to turn on my light, to really explore the amazing world hidden under the rock and dirt and grass, but I didn't dare. Instead, I ignored the stunning view and began to walk toward the strange, narrow path cut in the rock near the center. From this point, both the light and the music seemed to radiate out from a single point, somewhere still beyond my sight.

Each step was as quiet as I could make it, each breath held tightly, unsure of what the next moment would bring. The room spread out, an uneven and rocky floor arched with high, hanging rock formations, and there in the center was a neat, almost symmetrical aisle cut into the rock.

No.

Not rock.

I couldn't have dreamed to see it clearly, not from above, or even from the ground level so far away. The light was too weak, my eyes not yet adjusted. It wasn't a row of rock that I was seeing; it was two neat even rows of...something. They were, I could now tell, taller than they seemed from a distance. Indeed, as I stepped forward, I seemed to be shrinking as they rose before me. It wasn't until I was nearly in touching distance that I realized what comprised the giant, glowing aisles.

Toys.

Two careful lines of them, arranged in meticulous stacks from the floor to a height of some fifteen feet. I approached the first one and gasped when I saw the contents. A pair of eyes glimmered, black and glassy, and I saw the face of a tiger, stuffed, all but rotten after the long years in the dark. There were stacks of board games, action figures, vintage GI Joes, and Barbie houses. I saw a Mickey Mouse carved from what looked to be wood, the style of it older than anything I had ever seen in person.

Finally, I was able to wrap my brain around the strange geography of the place. The floor between the rows was flat and smooth, and it ran back into a deeper corner of the cave, a place where the dim light shined brightest. It was a fine spot for a nest, quiet and secluded, and the giant aisle of toys had been carefully formed around it, but for what purpose?

Safety?

Seclusion?

Or did all of those toys just remind him of something else?

Something he never had? A home perhaps? I couldn't begin to guess. The hallway between the stacks of toys was probably six or seven feet wide, and it ran straight back into the groove of the cave, and from deep within, the light shined. I checked the sides of the aisles, searching for a better way in, a sneakier path, but there was just this, a single road in and out. I slipped the flashlight into my bag, and with a careful step, I went forward, knife in hand.

Every step brought some new wonder, and I felt as if I were walking through a museum of toys. Artifacts from every decade made up literal walls of toys, some of them terrifying, if for no other reason than the fact that they shouldn't exist. This was a cave, a forgotten, hidden hole in the ground, and there was a child's skeleton mask, eyeless and watching, perched next to a wooden duck whose face was peeling. I saw rattles and mobiles, BB guns and slingshots, dolls' heads with eyes that rolled back like marbles. There was a puppet, sitting quietly, almost begging to be picked up and made alive once more.

About halfway in, the walls of toys began to come alive. A robot, head spinning, greeted me as I approached. I saw the baby that I heard earlier, making a whining cry accompanied by a heaving chest that puffed up and down. There was a glowworm, its head illuminated from within. Toys of all ages greeted me, shining, speaking, crying out in a cacophony of mechanical voices, some of which were older than my father.

As I swept my gaze across the spectacle, I realized that the Thief was responsible for stealing more than just toys. The batteries to keep this place running alone told me that my father's gripe about vanishing AAs wasn't just talk. The other thing I realized was that the majority of these toys would have stopped working long ago if not for clever hands that kept them running.

The closer I came to that core of light, the more jumbled things became. The smooth lines of the aisle became angular and broken, and I crouched behind a stack of board games and peered out. I was nearly to the end of the chamber, and I could, generally, see it all from here. I still hadn't laid eyes on either Andy or the Thief, but I knew I had to be getting close.

The glow, as I now realized, came from the myriad of light-up toys that surrounded the room: glowing eyes, beeping robots, animals that emitted beams of light that danced on the ceiling. There were dozens of them, all of them turned on at once, giving the room the appearance of a darkroom, full of light and yet half-visible at the same time.

As I surveyed the scene, I grew to think of the earlier, ordered aisle as long-term storage, whereas this section was more of the work-in-progress area. There were loose stacks of items here and there, labels and instruction packets stuck to the rocky walls. Along one entire wall, rocks had been arranged into smooth worktables where older toys sat in various states of dismantling. Tools lined the impromptu tables, everything from tiny screwdrivers to wrenches and a sampling of electronic pieces. Below the tables, plastic bins were filled with spare parts, including dozens of pilfered batteries.

Across the room, there was some kind of hand-built box, cobbled together with two-by-fours, about six feet wide and four feet deep. It was filled with stuffed toys, which glowed from within, and for the first time, I thought I had found the source of the music. One of the dolls was loudly playing lullabies in a loop, but I couldn't quite grasp what the purpose of the box was.

When my gaze first landed on the thing between the box and the table, I didn't recognize it for what it was. I'd simply never seen anything like it. It was a cage. There were bars, a grid of rebar, no doubt stolen from construction sites late at night. But the true horror was the decoration added to the frame. There were plastic baby doll parts that the Toy Thief had dismantled and attached to the metal, overlaying them in specific, insane designs. There were arms and legs running horizontally and vertically, and a single, wide-eyed head had been attached to each joint, forming gruesome columns.

I rushed over and knelt there, aghast, wondering what it all meant. Were the decorations supposed to be art? Something warm and welcoming to come home to? Who could say, but the effect in practice was horrifying, like a coffin built by the hands of a child.

All of it was too much. The spinning lights, the droning toys, the utterly mad cage of baby parts. My head spun, and I felt as if I would pass out then and there. I stared at a spot on the floor, forcing my mind to reset itself, to bring myself back into the moment before it was too late. Then, when my eyes rose back up, I saw it: the edge of a bare foot just visible inside the darkness of the cage. Andy was locked inside.

I clapped my hand over my mouth to keep from screaming his name when I realized it was him, and I was lucky I did. Across the room, the wooden box of stuffed animals began to stir and bubble, and I slid back, deeper into the darkness, watching, my heart beating wildly. I saw the hand first, black as pitch, as the Toy Thief emerged from his nest. The toys parted, rippling back like water as he slithered out, spilling over the edge and onto the cave floor, stopping only long enough to set something down on the edge of the box – some sort of globe. Even here, in his own domain, he walked on all fours, stalking his way across the room to the cage that held my brother.

From where I stood, I could hear the steady sounds of Andy's breathing, and I knew that he was asleep. I tried to imagine the night before, the screaming, the fighting, the constant rush of adrenaline-soaked fear, and I knew that it just had to have been too much for him. Something had to give. I wondered if that was exactly what the Thief had been waiting for, because he stepped soundlessly to the cage. Something was happening here. I knew it. I could feel it. But I felt beyond powerless to stop it. I knelt down, peering through a hole in the stack of toys, and watched it all unfold.

The Thief raised his black hand and began to pull at the tip of one of his fingers. The skin began to slide free. I shook my head. No, not skin. A glove, and beneath the black leather was a bone-white hand, thin enough to belong to a skeleton. He removed the next glove, and for the first time, I saw his palms. They were red and splotchy, covered in deep, ulcerous sores that glistened purple and red. One look, and there was little doubt as to how painful they must be, and I felt a sudden pang of guilt for hating this creature so. All that died away when he reached through the bars and placed his hand on Andy's leg. There was no doubt in that moment that my brother truly was asleep, but with a single touch of that wretched hand, he began to curl and moan, his body tensing like a knot as I heard him cry out, soft and pleading.

"*Nooo...*"

The sound of his pitiful voice clouded my eyes with tears, and I clutched at the knife, considering risking it all on a single, wild rush. It was foolish, but you can't imagine what it's like to hear someone you love plead that way. His eyes never opened, and he never fought back, but the moans continued for over a minute. I saw the Thief arch his back and grasp at the cage with his free hand as my brother writhed under his touch. I still didn't know what I was seeing, couldn't comprehend it, but I also knew I couldn't stand to watch much more. Just as I stepped out from my hiding place, intent on ending it, the Thief broke his grip and fell back onto the cave floor.

Andy's cries died away as sleep took him once more as the Thief curled on the floor, twitching. I dropped back down soundlessly, peering out from the dark as he slowly pulled himself up onto his knees. His head was swinging from side to side, his body slow and sluggish, and I realized what I was seeing. I wasn't sure then what the Thief's touch had done, though I have a better idea now, all these years later. In that moment, I could tell enough just from the language of his body. This was the look of a man who had consumed too much. Too much food. Too much wine. With a staggering gait, he moved toward his box of toys, stumbled to the floor, then pulled himself back into his nest. There was a shuffling within as the stuffed animals swirled a bit before settling, still and quiet once more.

After that, the cave was silent. It took a few minutes of waiting and watching before I worked up the nerve to venture out. There were no more places to hide in this chamber, and once I was in that inner sanctum, there was no getting out. With that realization in mind, I slipped around, hugging the wall and checking each footstep as quietly as possible. Moments later, I was back at the edge of the grim cage, peering down at Andy. My first instinct was to reach through the bars, to shake him awake, but I knew that would be the end of us both. I had to figure out how to get him out first.

I ran a hand over the top of the cage, shivering just to touch the doll legs and arms that lined it. I was expecting to find a heavy padlock, but all I could feel was a series of tightly wrapped coils of metal wire. I knelt down, investigating the bottom of the fence, and I found a hinge that would drop the front of the cage down to the ground if the wire was unspooled. Could it be that easy? I tested the wires and found that it wasn't quite as simple as I thought it might be, so I turned my attention to the stone table and began searching for something to get Andy free. In the clutter of dismantled toys, I found a pair of pliers that looked like they might do the job. I was just ready to go to work when my eyes came upon the faded photograph that was stuck under a rock on the back of the table. It was so out of place in this horrid hole that it caught my attention at once. It was of a boy, no more than eight, posing next to his mother. It was summertime; she was in a 1950s-style one-piece bathing suit, he in a pair of checkered swimming trunks. They were both smiling, she the sweet, caring smile of a mother, so very proud, and he the forced, slightly silly grin of a boy who doesn't want his picture taken. Before I realized it, I was holding it in my hand, staring at the fraying print, enthralled by the strangeness of it. Without another thought, I slipped it into my pocket.

I went straight back to work, bearing down on each wire until it snapped free with a little *plink*. After the first one, I stopped, waited, watching the box full of stuffed animals, certain that at any moment, the calm surface of cotton would open and he would spill out. He never did, so I focused on the cage, snipping each and every wire without delay, refusing to look back because I knew that would be the end of it. If I had seen so much as a single toy shift in that pile, my resolve would have broken. One after another, the wires fell away, until after one last snip, the front of the cage fell down onto me. It was heavier than it looked, but I caught it in the crook of my arms and gently set it down.

And there he was. Andy. My Andy.

His legs were covered in the red handprint sores, and I was almost afraid to wake him because I knew how badly it must hurt. Even so, I couldn't wait, not any longer, so I leaned into the cage and brushed my hand against his cheek.

"Andy," I whispered.

Once more, he moaned, and I instantly had a vision of the creature shambling out from his hiding place. I dared a single glance back, seeing nothing but shadow.

"Andy," I said a bit louder as I cupped my hands around his face, shaking him as I covered his mouth. He tried to twist away from me, and I pressed my fingers tighter against his mouth. It wasn't working, this back and forth, and both of us were making too much noise. I had to end it, had to get us out of there, so I mashed my right hand against his mouth and grabbed his ear with my left and began to twist it. His eyes shot open, and I tried to silence him as quickly as I could. It was only half a scream, and all I could do was pray that the droning toys were enough to cover it.

There was fear in those eyes, the terror of someone waking from a nightmare only to find they were still dreaming. Then his gray eyes refocused, found mine, and began to water. I took my hand away from his mouth.

"Jack," he whispered.

"Shh," I said, motioning to the room around us.

I helped him sit up, and I realized, for the first time I could remember, my brother was crying. "How?" he said. "How did you find me?"

I didn't have time for this, neither of us did, but I dug into my pocket just the same. I found the orange jelly bean and held it in front of his eyes, a tiny pearl in my hand. He took one look and nodded, tears streaming down his cheeks. Then he buried his face in my shoulder and began to softly sob.

"Andy," I said, finding the sides of his face with my hands. "You have to listen to me. We have to get out of here. We're not safe. You're going to have to walk—"

That was all I got out before the pain took over and the ground dropped away under my feet. It was an instant agony beyond compare, a pain in the roots of my brain, like my skull being ripped apart. I couldn't see. Couldn't think. Couldn't focus on anything other than the pure misery. There was a laugh somewhere in front of me, and I caught a glimpse of the Thief standing upright, peering down into my face with a grin. The metal crown was gone now, as were the glass lenses, and his blank, pink eyes leered into mine. I realized where the pain was coming from. He was lifting me off the ground by my ponytail, his toothpick arms stronger than I could even begin to comprehend, as he held me like a fish on a hook. Who knows how long I would have stayed there, dangling and kicking as my scalp ripped free from my head, but a voice, weak but resolved, ended my misery.

"Put her down."

It was Andy. I couldn't see him. I could barely see anything, but his voice somehow reached me, brought me back from the awful brink of misery. Then my feet found the floor, and I fell, dropping like a bundle of clothes. My eyes were pricked with tears, but when I glanced up, I saw enough through the blurry haze to catch a glimpse of Andy, holding something out in front of him as the Thief loomed over him, covering him in a gaunt shadow. I squinted, unsure of what he held in his hands. Then the light caught it, and I knew. Andy had snatched up the globe that the Thief had set down, and he clutched it to his chest like…like a child with his own toy.

"You want it?" Andy asked, and the ghoulish thing began to reach forward. "Don't move!" Andy screamed. "You take one step and I swear to God I'll fucking shatter it, you hear me?"

My eyes were clearing, and though the back of my head felt as if it were bleeding, I found my footing and stood back up. I still had the pocketknife, and I almost, in a fit of silly anger, lunged forward and began stabbing the Thief. One look at Andy told me how foolish my plan was. We were in control, but only just. Any wrong move and we might not ever see the sunlight again. Far off, I heard the rolling bass of thunder, and the Thief cocked its head, seemingly hearing something that I couldn't. Then he turned his pink rat eyes back toward me, his brow furrowed as if he were considering his chances. Andy read the whole scene like a page from a book.

"Try it, motherfucker!" he screamed as he held the globe aloft. "It's yours, ain't it?" he asked, shaking it lightly. Flutters of light caught in the center, and all at once I realized it was a snow globe. "It's important to you, huh?"

The Thief nodded slowly.

"Just like that Superman. It probably wouldn't have looked like much. I mean, a burglar would have just gone for a TV or jewelry. But you. You knew. Somehow, you knew."

I slid next to Andy, quickly putting distance between me and that thing, and the Thief made no move to stop me. We had him now. As absurd as the whole thing seemed, we had him. He was as much our hostage as Andy had been his, all because of that simple white globe. I still didn't know as much as Andy did, but I was certain that toy would be our ticket out of this place. All we had to do was play it smart.

"Let's go, Andy," I said, placing a gentle hand on his shoulder. "While we can," I added in a whisper.

"No."

I was already backing away when I heard it, when the enormity of what he had said set in.

"Andy. Let's go. Now. Right now."

He turned, stared me in the face, and repeated, "No." Then he took a step toward the lanky ghoul. "We're not going anywhere until we get back what belongs to us."

"No," I said in his ear. "We can't stay here, do you hear me?" Another low rumble shook the ground.

"We're not going anywhere!" he screamed as he shoved me behind him, sending me reeling, stumbling onto the ground. I fell on my ass as new tears pricked the edges of my eyes. Andy glared at me, but he never once dropped his hand to me.

"Get them," he said to the Thief. "Hers and mine. Or I'll make you regret it."

The creature stared, seeming unsure of this new turn. Then he slowly slunk away into the darkness.

"Why are you doing this?"

"Because they're ours. He had no right to—"

"No," I said, cutting him off. "Why are you acting like this?"

He said nothing at first, just stared at me, confused. Then, like a switch had been suddenly flipped, his eyes grew dark and guilty.

"I don't know," he said, his breath quickening. He was shaking his head back and forth, his chest heaving like a man on the edge of a panic attack.

"Calm down," I told him, reaching out to him.

"No," he said, swatting my hand away. All at once, he was on his knees, scratching at his raw legs. "That thing," he muttered. "That fucking thing. It thinks it can do whatever it wants."

"Then let it," I cried. "I just want to go home."

There was a shuffling behind us, and we turned to find the Thief slithering down the wall above us, his head twitching, pink eyes glistening. With his head turned down like a scolded child, he approached us and opened his mouth. I knew it was coming. I had wondered if it were possible. But knowing did little to prepare me to hear that voice as he spoke.

"Y-yours," he hissed. The word was choppy, broken, something that had been forgotten and remembered. The pitch was high, like a toddler who didn't know he had long ago grown up. There was a sense that this creature had passed adolescence and manhood, straight into old age, all beneath the earth, surrounded by other people's toys. I remembered the picture in my pocket, and I wondered.

He opened his sore-infested hand and the plastic Superman spilled out onto the ground. Then he raised another hand from behind him and showed me the bear. Part of me wanted it, begged for it, longed to be back in my bed curled up with it. Then I saw the red, scabbed hand that held it, and I felt a sudden desire to draw the lighter from my bag and send it up in flames. But either way, it was mine, and I was leaving here with it.

I kept waiting for him to drop it like he had Andy's toy, but he didn't. I noticed his hand was shaking, and a thread of saliva was dripping from the side of his mouth. I remembered how he had found me after I went walking in the woods with my bear, remembered Andy's theory that the Thief had tracked me like a bloodhound. Then I remembered the way he had acted after he laid those horrid hands on Andy's skin, and I knew, somehow, that the two things were the same. He was feeding on Andy, taking something from him, just as he fed on the toys. I thought of Andy's other forgotten toys, the ones the Thief had left behind, focusing only on the most important, the most delectable treats.

Whatever this…feeding was, it was happening right there in front of me, to my bear, and it must have been a wonderful sensation. Even here, with Andy clutching what seemed to be the Thief's most prized possession, he still couldn't easily let go. I couldn't stand it anymore, so I reached forward and snatched the bear away. It felt suddenly dirty in my hands, and I just didn't want to touch it, so I scooped up Andy's Superman and slid them both into my backpack. The Toy Thief closed his eyes and sighed, the moment of ecstasy broken.

"Now," I said as I zipped the bag closed. "Please. Let's go."

Another rumble of thunder, this one even louder than before, seemed to wake Andy out of the haze he was in. Slowly, still holding the globe in front, he began to shuffle back down the hall.

"M-mine," the Thief said, pointing. "Pleassse…"

"No," I whispered. This thing was pitiful, an awful, bent creature that shouldn't have existed. And there was pain in that horrible face, miserable pain that might be temporarily quenched by that snow globe. I glanced up at it, saw the tiny family within, saw the silver flakes dancing around them, thought of the boy in the picture. I wanted to give it back, to leave this awful creature to his own devices, but I knew we wouldn't make it far without something to ensure our safe passage.

"Not until we're out of here," I said for Andy. "We'll leave it outside. You can get it when we're gone…"

"Puh-puh-lease…is mine. F-from her…"

Was that her in the picture? The thought made my heart break a little, but Andy had different plans. He was shaking, that strange look washing over his face once more.

"Your mother?"

"Yesss…"

"Did you love her?"

The creature nodded.

"Good. That means this will hurt."

With a single, swift motion, he raised the globe and threw it down onto the rocks, shattering it into a million glittering pieces.

CHAPTER TEN

Dad died about six years ago. I was grown by then, on my own, self-sufficient more or less. It was a punch though. One I didn't see coming. Those are always the ones that hurt the most.

It was his heart, because of course it was. Decades of fast food will do that. He had a massive heart attack on…a Tuesday, I think. Then, on Thursday, when he was waiting on surgery, he had another one. They thought everything was stable, but his ticker was just a bit weaker than they thought. He wasn't that old, after all. Men his age run marathons and climb mountains nowadays.

I didn't know what to do. I can be honest about that. I was working nonstop at the time, fresh out of college, carving out a shitty career for myself. All of it, rolling along without a care in the world, when boom, the call came in. What are you supposed to do? What can any of us really hope to do when that call comes in?

You go. You sit. You talk.

"They'll get you fixed up," I told him about twelve hours before he died. "They know what they're doing."

I spent the entire day sitting next to his hospital bed, occasionally holding his hand when he cried here and there. He didn't think it was the end. Neither of us did, but he had passed beyond something in his mind. The days of living one moment to the next were over, because he knew that soon enough, there would be no more moments. The last day would be two days away, then tomorrow, then today. I could see him working it out in his mind. I won't say his life flashed before him, but he was more wistful than I could ever remember him being. Growing up, it had always been about pushing forward, charging into the next moment, making sure that Andy and I were full of food, that the lights were still on, that the bills were all paid. Now bills didn't mean anything. I was paying my own way and Andy was…well, he was behind bars, the family secret that everyone knew about.

We talked about Mom, and he told me about meeting her, the way she laughed at all his jokes. He told me about what a wonderful mother she had been, and he made sure to change the subject when he saw how uncomfortable it made me. And then, as I knew he would, he talked about Andy.

"I don't know what I did wrong," he said, tears on his cheek. "If I had it to do again, I…I just don't know what I could have done different."

I never told him about what happened that summer, beyond what he already knew, what everyone knew. There were parts of it that he surely guessed at, the secret that Andy and I shared, but he never knew the truth. How could he? But in that moment, for the first time, I came dangerously close to telling him everything, because I wanted him to know that it wasn't his fault.

"Dad…what if I told you that there wasn't anything you could have done?"

He turned, stared me in the eyes, the look of an expectant child waiting for you to give them the answers to every question they've ever had.

"What do you mean?"

I stumbled, unsure of how to answer. "I mean that…what if Andy was…too far gone? What if something…changed him?"

The grief in my father's face deepened. "I know what you're thinking. And you're right. I feel like my life has been a jigsaw puzzle, and every time I move a piece, another one falls to the floor. Gone."

"No," I said, realizing where he was going.

"Yes," he replied, shushing me. "If your mother had never died,

Andy might not have turned out like he did." He raised a hand to my cheek and added, "But I never would have gotten you."

I let him cry. Let myself cry. Then I let the moment die and fall into the rearview mirror of the past. Maybe, when we were both old enough to believe in crazy things again, I'd tell him the truth. Maybe I'd get Andy to help me. Between the two of us, we might even convince him.

'Maybe' never came, and Dad was dead the next day. They buried him beside Mom. Three times a year I put flowers on their graves: once on each birthday, and then on their anniversary.

⋆ ⋆ ⋆

The shattered pieces of the snow globe flew, raining down upon the stones like springtime hail. All I could do was watch the glistening shards of glass as they tinkled to rest on the cave floor. I couldn't quite grasp what I was seeing, and from the look on his face, neither could the Thief. Only Andy seemed in complete control of himself as he defiantly sneered at the creature, whose chest was heaving, his nostrils flaring, his mouth open and soundless. That sight – of a hopeless, desperate thing staring at the aftermath of Andy's temper – that was what brought me back. I didn't say a word. I only grabbed Andy's sleeve and began dragging him back down the hall of toys.

For a moment, Andy resisted, keeping his eyes locked on the Thief, the grim, awful satisfaction of what he had done shining on his face. Then, like cutting a thread, whatever held sway over my brother released its grip, and he turned to run.

The glowing, multicolored eyes of a thousand toys stared at us as we clambered back toward the exit, while behind us, the Thief's deep, ragged breathing was beginning to break. The sound changed, morphing into something else entirely, a whine that rose to a whistling, high-pitched scream. It reminded me of a mother bird watching her eggs being devoured. I risked a glance back, just enough to see it frantically scraping the pieces together, pulling them into a pile even as they sliced into his bare hands. It was useless of course. What Andy had done would never be fixed, and the whine broke into an insane cry of miserable pain and anger. It would be coming for us, very soon and very angry, and I knew we'd never get out of there unless we did something to slow it down. We hit the edge of the aisle, back into the gloom of the cave, and I grabbed Andy and spun him around next to me.

"Why?" I said through my teeth as I slid off my backpack. "Why? Why? Why?"

"What are you doing?" he asked as I dug frantically through my supplies.

I ignored the question and continued asking my own. "Why, Andy? Why? Why? Why, Andy?"

I kept asking it, over and over, my voice like a record stuck on a scratch. I didn't want an answer, not yet at least. I just had to ask the question. It was as if my body were filling with pressure, a frustrated steam that could only be released through my mouth.

"I don't know," he said, peering back down the aisle. "I don't know. I really wish I knew." His voice was on the edge of breaking. "Just hurry. We have to get out of here."

The Thief was screaming now, a wild yowling like something out of a horror movie, and I knew our time was almost up.

"What are you doing?" Andy asked, but I already had the answer in my hands, the bundle of roman candles in my left, the lighter in my right.

"No!" Andy hissed. "He's already mad enough to kill us." His voice was as frightened as that of a child who had broken his first rule. "If you do that—"

"You smashed it!" I barked. "If I don't do this, we're already dead."

He opened his mouth to say something else, but the first wick was already lit. I turned toward the stack of toys and mashed the roman candle into a hollow of board games and began to light another. This one I tossed on top of the pile. Andy had stepped to the edge of the aisle, and he grabbed me just as I lit the third.

"He's coming!"

I turned into the aisle and aimed as the sparks began to fly. The sight of the ball of white flame flying toward it made the Thief dive instantly into the row of toys for cover. I didn't see where he went, but I let the candle finish as I showered the path in front of me with sparks. Beside me, the first two had already burned out, but I could feel the heat as the wall of ancient toys began to catch fire.

"That's enough," Andy said, pulling at me. "Please, let's go."

I couldn't see the Thief anywhere, but I doubted my attack would be enough. There were three more candles left, and I evaded Andy's grasp, rushed to the right-hand stack of toys, lit them, and mashed all three candles into a pile of dried-out Beanie Babies. By the time I stepped away, the cave was glowing as the right-hand stack caught with a *whoosh*.

I knew how old this stuff was, knew how amazingly dry this section of the cave had been, but nothing could have prepared me for how quickly it all went up. Suddenly, we weren't trying to stoke a fire; we were trying to escape one. I slung my backpack across my shoulders, and as one, we turned and dashed up the slope toward the exit. Pieces of old cloth, bits of paper and burlap, and flaming wisps of cotton began to rain down on our heads and shoulders. Andy was in front, and once, a withered slip of baby-doll pants landed smoldering on his shoulder. I had to slap it out.

We hit the steep slope that would lead us out, and both of us began to clamber up. That was when I heard the screams. They were no longer screams of fear or anger, but of pure anguish. They were the screams of an old man watching his childhood home burn. I turned back just long enough to see the Thief silhouetted against the blazing fire. I can't imagine how he could stand so close to it, how it wasn't charring the flesh from his bones, but he refused to leave. He was crying, wailing, begging for the flames to recede as his clothes caught fire. It was a purely pitiful sight, and the only thing that took my eyes away from it was the smoke. It was building up overhead, billowing across the roof above us and pressing down like a wall of black death. I swooned and coughed, threatening to pass out on the spot, but I refocused on the climb, reaching for a solid handhold as Andy caught the lip of the tunnel overhead. He was able to pull himself up, and then, after balancing on one foot, I caught his outstretched hand. As he dragged me to the relative safety above, I heard a deep breath of air from behind me, and I dipped my head to see both of the giant stacks tumbling into a flaming heap where the Thief had been standing. I didn't see the body get swallowed up in the wreckage, but I felt certain that it had been.

We fell on top of each other in the tunnel, faces slick and black with soot as the thunder rolled outside and within. Neither of us had the energy to move for a moment or two, but the growing stench of burning toys finally got us on our feet.

"You okay to walk?" he asked.

"Yeah," I gasped. "You?"

He nodded. I wanted to ask him what had happened down there, why he had acted the way he did, what the last twelve hours had been like. But that was a conversation for another time.

"Let's go home," he said.

"Yeah. Dad's waiting for you," I felt compelled to add.

The tunnel was lighter now, thanks to the flames, and though the smoke was beginning to rise, it would be some time before it filled the tunnel completely. We moved carefully, watching our steps, so as not to twist an ankle in one of the knotted holes.

"You shouldn't have come for me," he said after a moment of silence.

"You don't mean that," I replied.

"I do," he said without hesitation. "We shouldn't have made it out of there. I think you know that." His face in the semidarkness was wracked with a mixture of relief, fear, and something I couldn't quite place. "I can't believe you found me," he added, his voice breaking.

"The jelly beans," I said. "They were in your pockets, weren't they?"

He didn't speak, but he nodded his head, sniffling. He reached for me, and I did the same, and all at once, I realized that look on his face had been pure, unabashed love for his sister.

A charred hand shot up from a hole in the rock just next to my feet and grasped my ankle. I screamed, shook free, and fell to the cave floor as it swiped the air blindly for me. I didn't need to see the white, scabby hands or the fresh burns to know who it was. I tried to shake him off, but he had me, his grip like cold iron. Andy was yelling something, but all at once I couldn't hear him. My ears were filling with the sound of that voice, the one from my dream of the man made of darkness.

You…

There was a pressure on my leg, a warmth that spread up to my knee, that grew and bloomed, changing from a gentle heat to a fire, a blaze within my skin.

It's you…

It was baking me, singeing the flesh off my muscle, the muscle off my bones, and boiling the marrow within. Somewhere high above me, I could hear Andy screaming – far off, inside of a tunnel miles away, as I swirled into a murky pit of darkness. I sank into it, and shapes seemed to rise in the blackness: silhouettes of people, moments frozen in time.

Children, reading an ancient book, something they know they shouldn't, making a game out of it as they speak the old words aloud. What are they doing? Why are the shadows upon the firelit wall moving, almost dancing? One of the boys, a blond, shaggy-headed preteen, begins to writhe as one of the shapes solidifies and slips from the wall, a shape like a half spider, half rat spilling into him, covering his face with black tendrils before disappearing behind his grim smile...

Another scene rises from the dark, this time an old man, hunched over a table, his son watching him paint the faces onto wooden toys, his hands careful, dexterous, and clever. The boy wants to be like him, and he will be, but not in the way he imagines. Something is watching them, a weak, gangly creature that hides in the planks above like a giant spider. It wants the boy, needs the boy, because the body it hijacked, the body that's been its home, is giving up, even after the changes, even after the long dark of the cave it calls home...

Now a boy with a soft face, listening to his mother read him stories as he gazes into a snow globe, her gift to him, the only possession that he can remember. Neither of them sees the face leering from the window, another body now spent, used up, ready to be discarded. In a flash, the mother is gone, and the boy is lifted from the bed, never to be seen again...

"No," I heard from some far-off place, the voice of a girl's brother fighting for her life across some unimaginable gulf of space and time. But his voice pales in comparison to the voice within that blackness – a rumbling hum that is all around her, inside her, *is* her.

This feeling, the voice moaned with obscene longing. *After all this time. I've never known this feeling...*

It was me. I was that feeling, something ecstatic to taste, something unknown and new after countless years of boredom. I was nothing more than a new prize.

Pressure. A light hand on my face, pulling me back from that edge, and another voice.

"Let her go!"

Never, it moaned. *Such possibilities…*

"You son of a bitch, let her go!"

Your brother bores me. I think I'll have you instead…

The grip on my bare leg was broken, and I shot back into reality so fast my head spun. My first concern was my leg, and I looked down, afraid to touch what must now be bare, empty bone. But I saw nothing more than my own skin, spotted with a light red handprint. Andy was holding a rock, and the skeletal white hand was bleeding from where he had been pounding on it. Andy slid under my arm, lifting me, and the two of us limped farther up the tunnel, away from the small hole, which was now filling with black smoke.

Just once, Andy and I looked back to see the Thief pushing his head through the hole. He was red, half-covered with horrific burns, the skin peeling around the pink eyes. All that was bad, but it paled in comparison to the mouth. The lips were gone, burned away, and all the madness in that thin frame seemed driven into that gaping wound of a mouth. We both gasped aloud as the arm receded and the face pushed forward, but there was no way he could make it through a hole that size, a hole smaller than a basketball.

Then an awful thing happened as the face crept closer and closer, edging through the impossibly tiny hole. The shoulders, wide and bony, seemed to hinge and split, slipping through – first one, then the other, as if the horrid creature were being born before our eyes.

I remembered a strange thing in that moment, one of those weird facts that kids pick up from their parents, the kind of thing you stow away and forget that you ever knew. My dad had told me about mice one year. We had found a bunch of little brown pellets in the pantry. Mouse shit. It looked just like rice. We were laying traps out, and he told me about mice and rats, how they could sneak in just about anywhere. Their bones were flexible, and they could shift them around if they needed to fit into a tiny space. Ribs could flatten out; shoulders could float freely. Basically, if they could fit their heads into a hole, they would figure out a way to get the rest in too.

I didn't know if it was true or just another one of Dad's stories, but when I saw the Thief squeezing through that hole, his face a ragged mess, his eyes filled with murder, I knew it was the truth. Bit by bit, he was making it through, driven by sheer, unparalleled malice, and the sight seemed to lock every one of my joints in place. Once again, it was Andy who peeled me off the floor, got me moving, got me out of the side tunnel and into the cooler, fresher air beyond. We tumbled out of the cave and landed on the carved stair steps of the mine, and for the first time, I actually heard the drone of the storm outside.

"Come on," I said, my senses finally returning to me. I led us down the darkened stair steps of rock, taking them two at a time. Andy tumbled down behind me, catching one of the steps wrong, and we both fell down the last one, expecting to break a rib on the rock floor. Instead, we splashed into knee-high water that drenched us from head to toe. Sputtering, we helped each other to our feet, and I saw the absolute amazed confusion on his face.

"Where the fuck are we?" he screamed.

"The rain," I answered. "Flooding the place. We gotta hurry."

I clutched his hand and pulled him down the slope, into the dark, deepening water. The stone-cut room, half-lit to begin with, was now nearly black as the rising water blocked both the tunnel and the light outside. The water passed our waists, and I felt Andy pulling me back.

"No," he said, a look of pure terror in his eyes. "I can't."

He'd never liked closed places, a fact that I used against him on multiple occasions, daring him to go into closets or to get into a car trunk. The thought of it alone was enough to make him violent, but this wasn't the time or place to hesitate. I could hear the Thief somewhere in the dark behind us, spitting and shrieking. If we waited for another minute, we'd both be dead.

"You *can* do it," I assured him. "All you have to do is hang on to my hand."

"Please," he begged, "there has to be another way."

"It's a straight shot. One path. And you're a better swimmer than me. All we have to do is stick together."

"No! *No!*"

I grabbed both sides of his face, forcing his darting, nervous eyes to lock onto mine. He wasn't a person at that moment; he was some kind of animal that had just realized it was locked in a cage.

"You can do this," I told him. "Just hold on to me."

I felt him easing a bit under my touch as some of that wild animal energy drained away. He was nodding, but he never said a word when I grabbed his hand and plunged into the rising water. We half walked, half swam toward the exit, which appeared to us as a narrow line of daylight just ahead. With each step we passed deeper into the murk, the water hitting our chests, necks, and then faces. Soon, we lost the floor entirely, and so we swam toward that narrow line, which seemed to be dimming by the moment. I wasn't sure how deep it was, probably seven or eight feet, but in my fight to stay above water, our hands drifted apart.

"Jack," he said pitifully as the water carried us back and forth in gentle waves.

"I'm here. Just keep swimming."

He did, and I did, and the rainwater filled our mouths, eyes, and noses. I became aware that the ceiling, once a good twelve feet above, was close enough to touch. The line of daylight was close now, less than ten feet away, but it had narrowed to a sliver that blinked in and out of existence as the water lapped against the ceiling.

"We're almost there," I was able to blurt out before I heard the hiss just behind me. The Thief was climbing on the ceiling, his eyes a sickly pink, his mouth an open pit lined with jagged rocks.

"Mine!" he shrieked as he grabbed at Andy's back, twisting his long fingers around his t-shirt. "You took mine. I'll take yours."

Andy pushed off the roof with his hands and dove under the water. The grim hand followed him as the Thief continued hissing and spitting, but he soon pulled his hand back, clutching only a swatch of dark cloth he had ripped away. I stared, dazed, desperately treading water. There was a moment, just a few seconds, where I saw that insane anger melt into something else – a look of misery, of fear, of outright terror.

"Ohhh...he won't be happy..." the Thief whispered, his pink eyes pleading with me.

Then I felt Andy's hand on my leg, and I shot underwater as well. We swam, eyes open, but blind to all but the hazy blue light that beckoned us toward the exit. The pair of us beat our hands, kicked our legs, driving farther and farther away from the mouth of darkness, lungs burning, but refusing to surface until we were absolutely sure we were free. When we finally did come up for air, we arose into a torrential downpour under a dark blue sky, but none of that mattered. We were out. Andy looked at me, confused as to just where in the world we were, and I pointed toward the ramp. Moments later, we were on dry land, clambering up toward the flat field that had carried us both, so long ago, to that nightmarish place.

That was when he hugged me, for the first time I could ever remember. He was crying again, and I think I understood. That place had broken him, changed him, made him walk into a corner of despair and hopelessness that a thirteen-year-old shouldn't have to. He had been, for the first time in his life, certain he was going to die. And now here he was, in the open air, standing on grass, safe in the knowledge that a dark cave wouldn't be his tomb.

"Thank you," he said quietly.

He wasn't one to say thank you very often, and I wasn't one to make a big fuss about it, so I just stepped back, looked him in the eye, and nodded. We could see the smoke now, a dark cloud that might have been lost in the storm if we hadn't been standing so close to it. It rose from small places here and there across the field, tiny holes that only smoke could find a way through. We walked most of the way back holding hands, not because he was weak or tired – just because he wanted to.

CHAPTER ELEVEN

Dad only dated one girl that I can remember. Not *remember* exactly. I can picture her face. Scraggly red hair. Dark blue eyes. Always wore sandals. And though I have no evidence to back it up, she just seemed like the kind of woman who would smell like incense. I have nothing against incense, but I did have something against her. She was, after all, moving into an open space that had always been there, a vacant parking spot with the words MY MOM written in yellow paint. How could I like her?

Her name was Carla, or Carol, or who gives a shit?

I was fourteen at the time, an especially prickly age, and she hit just about every prickly button that I had. She always wanted to talk, always asked how things were going, and one time she even called me *girlfriend*. Can you imagine?

In hindsight, she probably wasn't so bad. If I had given her a chance, maybe she would have been my girlfriend. But she would never have been my mom. I'm not sure if that's what she wanted or not, but it didn't matter. What did matter was Dad's face whenever he saw the two of us talking. He would get this quiet little grin, and his eyes would get all misty. I knew, even at my most prickly, what he was seeing. The potential. What it could have been. She might just be a cardboard stand-in, but even that was more than he had ever seen face to face.

There we were. His girls.

It only made me hate her even more.

The whole thing lasted about a year before everything started to fade out, little by little. There were never any big blowouts, no screaming matches, not even an honest heart-to-heart between the two of us. Without me saying a word, he just knew, which made sense. He always was the one who knew me best. So, one day, she was just gone. Dad and I were both in the kitchen, making separate, unrelated lunches, when he told me. I nodded.

"Why?"

He sighed, the tone of his breath telling me how close he was to letting it out.

"Just...wasn't working," was all he said.

I've never stopped wondering about that moment, and to this day I feel horribly ashamed of myself. He had that chance at happiness, but I was too damned petty to see it. After that, he never, as far as I knew, even tried to find another mate. So, just like that, Carla/Carol slid quietly into the history books, more or less forgotten. Except for one thing. She raised koi.

Dad took me to see them one day while he was still with her. At the time, I didn't even know what koi were, but I recognized them from the zoo. There were several huge pools in Carla/Carol's backyard, like above-ground swimming pools with blue liners all hooked up with pumps and filters. The orange-and-white and black-spotted fish, which were as long as my forearm, swirled and danced beneath the surface.

"Aren't they like goldfish?" I asked.

She laughed, and I found room in my heart to hate her just a bit more.

"Sort of. They're a different breed of fish. These are a breed of carp."

Dad was smiling at the two of us. "I always heard they can't grow any bigger unless they get into bigger tanks. Like, if you put a goldfish in a swimming pool, it would get to be as big as a shark."

She laughed, that silly, schoolyard giggle, as she slapped at his chest. "That's not true either."

They kept talking, Dad making silly jokes, her bubbling stupid little chortles at every opportunity, but I ignored them and stared into the blue water. I didn't care if it was true or not, because in that moment, what Dad had said was all I could think about. Imagine it, growing along with the tank you were put into. Never getting a bit bigger than whatever cage held you. I thought of it the rest of that night, as I ate dinner, watched TV, and finally slid under my covers. At any moment, I could venture out. Down the hallway. Out the back door. Into the yard to stare up at the starlit sky.

And what about Andy?

How often did he get to see the sky? Did he ever see the stars anymore? How much could a person grow inside a concrete cell?

I went to sleep that night hating that stupid woman, hating koi, hating myself for being free.

★   ★   ★

"Wait."

It was still pouring on us, but we had made it all the way to the edge of the woods that led back into the neighborhood. Both of us took turns checking over our shoulders, but now that we were nearly back into civilization, my heartbeat had started to return to normal. Andy, on the other hand, was as squirrely as ever, and he eyed the dark horizon behind us as I talked.

"We need to talk about our story," I said.

"Story?"

"Yes," I said, frustrated. "Dad's lost his mind since you left."

"I know," he said, still looking over my shoulder, seeming to barely listen. "I figured he would be after all that time."

"It wasn't that long," I said.

He finally turned and looked at me, that fresh panic rising in his eyes. "What do you mean?"

"I mean, Dad freaked out, but it was only a few hours so—"

"Hours?" he said, his whole body shivering. "No. It was... days. Maybe even a week."

"No," I said. "It wasn't."

"It...it had to be..."

I shook his shoulder, trying to shake him out of it.

"It's the truth," I replied with finality.

"In...in that place...I couldn't tell what was going on. It was constant. Just, pain. Confusion. And that voice."

A chill ran up my spine, because I knew exactly what he was talking about. I ignored it, for now at least.

"We can talk about that later, tonight, once everything's calmed down. Dad called the cops and everything. We have to get back."

He turned away from me, staring behind us, his head darting left and right.

"It won't follow us," I said with confidence, even if I wasn't sure of the fact. I believed he wouldn't follow us out here, but there was no way to know for sure. The Toy Thief didn't strike me as the kind of creature that would fight unless he had no other choice. The night in my bedroom had proved that. But it had passed beyond what was normal for such a monster. It was mad. What Andy had done had thrown it into a fury of utter insanity. So all bets were off now. I thought we'd be okay, until the sun fell at least, but I also wouldn't have been overly surprised if it sprang around the corner and tore into both of us on the spot.

"We have to get home. Everything will be safe once we get home." Another lie, but one I desperately wanted to believe.

"Yeah," he said, his eyes lost between me and the field behind us. "Home."

In that single moment, what I had already known about Andy's kidnapping came into stark focus. He was changed. Altered. Maybe even broken. I knew, even then, that something so awful would have changed anyone, made them as gun-shy as a wild dog. But this was something else entirely. One person went into that cave, and another came out. I glanced down at the handprints on his leg, and wondered to myself if he would ever be the same.

We talked through our story, how Andy had been picked on by some older kids around the neighborhood the day before. We never said who, not specifically, but if pressed, I'm sure we would have said the same name. He'd left the house the night before, intending to get some payback by vandalizing the bully's house. The only problem was, Andy got caught in the act and had to run. He evaded them, but by then, he was miles away from home. He hunkered down in an alley and waited for morning, dozing off for a few hours.

It wasn't a good story, but we both knew it didn't really matter. He was home, and that would be enough. Once all the questions were asked, it would have to be enough. Satisfied and ready for dry clothes, we left the woods behind and made our way toward our house. There was no one in sight. No one ran out and scooped us up. No cops appeared, lights ablaze, to escort us home. It was just two kids with questionable decision-making skills taking a stroll in the rain.

I stopped Andy next to the backyard and pulled him over to the shed, out of sight of any windows. "You good?"

He nodded, seeming to barely hear a word I said as he scanned the path we walked up on.

"Knock that off," I said sharply.

"What?"

"That. Staring. Looking around like a bird or something. Dad won't buy a word of it if you keep acting like that."

He was breathing hard all of a sudden, and I realized he was swinging again, his mood shifting from one pole to the other like a human pendulum.

"Fuck you," he said abruptly. "Quit acting like you're my mom. You always do that. You're not. So fuck you."

I tried not to show how deep his words had bitten into me, and

I choked back my natural reaction to slap him.

"I don't know why you're doing this," I said slowly, "but I'm the only reason you're out of there. You said so yourself."

His eyes darted left, right, left again, all in the span of less than a second. "Right. Good. Fine. It's fine."

I didn't dare press him any further.

"Then let's get this over with."

As we walked those last few feet up to the house, I felt as if I were walking next to a bear or a mountain lion. He was my brother, and I loved him, but all at once, I didn't trust him. He felt like a walking, talking, loaded gun, the sort of thing that had to be respected, handled carefully, but never truly trusted. I could see it as clear as the rain clouds overhead, but the question that pounded away inside my head was whether or not Dad would see it as well.

We opened the sliding glass door, and I stepped in first. Only silence. The house breathing. The rain falling. Thunder crashing in the distance. For a moment, I feared the worst, feared that somehow the Thief had found his way here, had already taken something much more precious than any toy. Then I heard the footsteps, heavy, leaden, the unmistakable trundle of my dad.

"Jack," he said from down the hallway, and I stuck out my hand to hold Andy in place for a moment. I felt him push at me, trying to swat my hand away, but I didn't back down.

"I'm here," I said as I pushed my brother further back into the rain.

"Where the hell did you go?" he asked, storming into the kitchen. "I told you not to leave the—"

"Dad," I said in a quiet tone, forcing him to drop his voice and listen.

"You're all wet. What have you been into?"

"I found Andy," I said as I stepped aside and let him in. I'm not sure why I did it that way, but I wanted to be the one to let him back in, to be the one between the two of them if things went bad.

Andy stepped in, his clothes and face dripping onto the linoleum floor. I never looked back at my brother, because I was too busy staring at Dad, watching him, figuring out what he would do.

"Andy," he whispered, and I knew it was all going to be fine. He crossed the room in two long strides and wrapped his son up in a bear hug, squeezing the water out of him as he clutched Andy's head onto his massive shoulder.

"Oh God, Andy," he pleaded as his voice died down to a near whisper. "Thank you, thank you, thank you…"

"I'm okay, Dad," Andy said when he had finally had enough. "I'm fine."

Something in his voice snapped Dad back to reality, and he took a step back, grabbing the collar of Andy's shirt. "Where the hell were you!?" he demanded. "I called the cops. I was worried to death. Why the fuck did you do that?"

I could see it in Andy's eyes – that wildness creeping back in, brought on by having another person scream in his face. For a moment, he reminded me of a soda can being shaken up, and I just knew he was about to burst. Then he blinked, and the other part, the real part of himself, took control.

"I…I just walked off. I was…having trouble at school…"

It sounded fake, sounded like a lie, and I jumped in and took the wheel.

"There were some bullies at school," I said. "Older guys fucking with him, he said."

"Watch your mouth," Dad said, never even glancing at me. "Is that true?" he asked Andy, loosening the grip on his shirt.

He began to blink quickly, but he nodded as well, and the two gestures together made him look more like an embarrassed teen than a lying one. That was good.

"But where did you go?"

"I left last night. I was…going to get them back. Maybe egg the guy's house or something."

For me, it would have sounded fake, a half-baked lie that wasn't ready for primetime. But for Andy, it sounded genuine. Dad knew, just as well as I did, how little he thought things through when he was mad.

"So," Dad said, urging him on, "what happened?"

"They came out. I don't think anyone saw who I was, but... they were yelling." He looked down at his soaked shoes, and inspiration seemed to strike. "I think one of them had a gun."

"Jesus, Andy," Dad said, shaking his head. "You could've gotten killed. What happened next?"

"I just ran. I ended up in town," he said nervously. "I was just wandering. I...I got lost. I ended up sleeping next to a dumpster off the square."

"God," Dad moaned. "How did you get home?"

"I walked," he said, his voice suddenly breaking. "I...I tried to get home...I tried, I really did. I just...it was so dark..."

At first, I thought he was just finding the thread of the lie, taking it and running, the way I always did. Lying was like breathing to me, a second language I was born with, but Andy never was a good liar, and I realized he was telling the truth. He was back there now, back in that nightmarish cave, hidden in some dark corner of the earth as a creature that had no right to exist fed on the best parts of him.

"Hush," Dad said as the first tear rolled down his cheek. "You're home. That's the only thing that matters." Dad turned and looked at me with tired, watery eyes.

"What was your part in all this?"

I was as quick as ever. "I was down by the creek, just messing around. I saw him coming, so I ran up and helped."

It wasn't much of an explanation, but I knew it would work well enough. Dad was too beaten to dig much deeper. He led Andy back to the bathroom himself and began to help him out of the wet clothes.

"No," Andy said, pushing him away. "I...I got it. I need to take a shower first."

Dad didn't fight him, but he did wait patiently outside the door. I had a sudden image then, of a man, a father, tapping his toe nervously outside the maternity ward as his wife was giving birth to their second. I imagined his face when they told him the news, and before I had a chance to change out of my own clothes, I rushed over and gave Dad a hug.

"It's okay," I said, parroting what he had said moments before. "He's home, so it's okay."

"That's right."

So much had happened, so much that would make a parent half-mad with concern, and yet Dad didn't know one-tenth of the truth. I could hear the doubt in his voice when he told me it would be okay, and I think he heard the same in mine. We loved each other. We loved Andy. And both of us, in different ways, knew it would have to get worse before it ever got better.

When Andy was finally out of the shower, Dad went to the kitchen to make some calls: to friends, cops, whoever else needed to know. I found my brother in his bed, curled up as far back into the corner as he could be, and draped with a heavy comforter. I sat on the edge of the bed, slow and careful, as if my brother were as fragile as an egg.

"You okay?"

He opened his eyes and stared back at me. "I...I don't know." It was the truth. I could see it all over him. "Do you think... he's dead?"

I surely wanted to believe it, but I wasn't any more certain than he was. Even so, I nodded. "He has to be. He was burned all over," I said. "And even if that didn't kill him, he probably drowned."

He was staring at me, deep into my eyes, past them, through them, into something else entirely. "You saw him. You know what he can do. And you don't believe that any more than I do."

There were questions, things to talk about, but I didn't think either of us could do it, not that night. We were spent, the pair of us. The sun was setting in the stormy sky, and soon I wouldn't be able to hold my eyes open if I had to. In the other room, I could hear Dad on the phone while banging some pots together with one hand. He was cooking – what, I couldn't guess, but it was more than he had done in years. Such was the plight of my family at that moment. I looked back at Andy, whose wild eyes were darting around the room, checking every corner. There was no point in lying.

"You're right. It might not be dead," I said directly. "But we hurt it. *You* hurt it. That means it's weak. That means we can kill it."

I wanted to say more, but at that moment, Dad burst in with a pair of plates loaded with slightly too-done grilled cheese sandwiches and Doritos. I was still wet, still soaked actually, but I slipped down onto the floor and tore into mine then and there, without another word. Despite how different Andy might have been, his hunger was unaffected, and in less than five minutes, we had cleared the plates, along with a glass of milk each. Dad flipped on the TV and we sat there on the floor, the three of us in Andy's room, like we hadn't done in years.

"You want more?" Dad asked when we were finished, and we did, both of us. Minutes later, we had fresh ones, these a bit more golden than the first round.

"You know," Dad said as we ate, "the police will probably come by tomorrow. They'll want to talk to you. Both of you, I imagine."

I glanced over at Andy, who, after eating, had begun to look a bit more like himself. "Okay," he said in his usual quiet tone.

"That's fine," I answered.

He patted Andy on one knee and patted my damp shoulder. "Look," he said, "I don't care what happened. I really don't. And I know that I ain't been the best dad ever."

I opened my mouth to correct him, but he raised a hand.

"No," he said. "Just hush and listen. I didn't know how to be a dad. Not by myself anyway. And if I had anything to do with this, I mean anything, I want you both to know I'm sorry for it."

He wrapped his arms around our shoulders and started squeezing us, his voice growing a bit shaky. "I hope you know how much I love you. And whatever…this was all about, I don't ever want it to happen again. Do you both understand?"

"Yes," I said.

"Yeah," Andy said.

"Good," he answered. "Now get some rest."

He left us alone, and I considered shutting the door and hashing everything out with Andy. It had to be done, we both knew it, but one look told me all I needed to know. Now that his belly was full of the first food he'd eaten in a day and a half, his eyelids were turning into lead. I knew he was on his way out, so I stood up, leaving a damp spot on his bed and the floor.

"Wait," he said quietly. "Don't leave."

I went back over and knelt down so we were eye to eye. "We're safe," I told him once more.

"Please," he said again. "Just until I fall asleep."

I couldn't argue with him. I was tired myself, and ready to get out of the wet clothes, but there was no use in fighting. He was shivering, even under the comforter, and I realized it wasn't because he was cold. He was back there, back in the cave again, and there was nothing more frightening to him than the idea of being alone. So I leaned against the side of the low bed and watched him, waiting for his eyes to close. My hand was resting across the bedrail, and I laid my head against it, refusing to let my own eyes close until I got out of those damn stinking clothes. A minute later, I felt his hand sneak out of the covers, across the sheet, coming to rest under my own. I gave it a gentle squeeze, and I waited. A few minutes later, I heard his breathing slow, and

I raised my head up. He was out, and for the first time in several days, he looked at ease. I crept out of the room, carefully shutting the door behind me as I left.

I went into the bathroom and sat on the toilet with the lid down. I listened to the familiar drip of the leaky faucet – one of Dad's to-dos that never quite got done. The sound was almost reassuring somehow. It had been dripping for years, and it was as much a part of this place as the rattling air vent in my room or the chorus of cracks and pops when you walked down the hallway. With a slow hand, I stripped out of the wet clothes and dropped them in a pile on the floor. It was, quite possibly, the most wonderful shower I had ever taken, even if I kept glancing at the frosted window in the center of the wall, certain that I heard something just outside.

I got out, slipped into an old, too-small robe Dad had bought a few years before, and sat down on the toilet once again. I turned the hair dryer on the lowest setting, letting it warm up the room as I brushed the tangles from my hair. My mind was swirling with everything that had happened that day, but my sleepiness was beginning to overtake me minute by minute. Thunder rolled somewhere in the distance, and the familiar sound of rain on the roof was too soothing, too wonderful to even consider staying awake. I barely had the forethought to flip the hair dryer off before it slid from my hands, and I let my head drift back onto the wall, so very comfortable in that moment.

I knew the instant the dream began, but I could never be sure of when it ended. I opened my eyes and stared into the gleaming bathroom mirror, confused and surprised that the normally beige wall behind me had gone slick, inky black. The wall pulsed, moved, shivered as I stared at it, and I realized with utter horror that my head was touching it, resting against that awful, slimy surface. It wasn't blackness; it was something deeper, something that ate the light itself, and though I tried to move, my body was locked up, each joint refusing to bend.

I'm in here, he said, the surface of the wall shimmering as he spoke. *I'm in you.*

The smell of smoke filled my nostrils, a pungent odor of burned flesh that entered into every pore on my body.

I was weak. That body was nearly spent. I thought your brother would be a fine fit, but then... He paused, and I could hear the anticipation in his voice. *But then...you.*

I tried to move, tried to wake myself, tried to scream. But I became more and more aware that this wasn't a dream. It was the same as before, only that time I had been lying in my bed, staring at the shadow that shambled toward me.

I'm coming for you now. You can't stop me. Your brother can't stop me either. I'll hurt him before it's over. He's half mine already.

My ankle was burning once more, and I had to glance down to be sure there wasn't a hand gripping my leg.

Oh, you think I'm mistaken. I can see it all over you. You think he'll come to save you. That you'll be able to change him back.

A mouth rose in the liquid layer of darkness, a pair of lips close enough to kiss my ear, and a simmering, hateful laugh split the lips.

What is it? Love? You think that's enough to save you? I was called into this world by children just as foolish as you. I knew the rules, knew what would happen when that body died. I come from a place where there is no love, no light, no hope, and I'm never going back. I broke the rules. I've been doing it for longer than you can possibly imagine, and I'll do it until the sun dies and all of you cattle are nothing more than dust.

I tried to speak, tried to wake myself, but I no longer held any illusions that I was the one in control.

Struggle, little one. It will only make the end that much more delicious.

I awoke with a choked breath in my throat, something that might have been a scream at the end of any other dream. My hair was dry now, matted and tangled on my forehead. I couldn't stand, not yet anyway. My ankle was still burning where the Thief had touched me, and I wondered what that touch had done, what it truly meant for both me and Andy. I had only a glancing sense of it, but I could feel something inside of me. The black thing, that darkness that whispered in my dreams – it wasn't just talking to me, and I was more convinced than ever that it wasn't my overburdened imagination. It was *inside* me. It had been injected there, shot into my skin by those deformed hands. I could only imagine what Andy was feeling at that very second.

I leaned forward, resting my face in my hands, breathing deep, realizing that parts of the dream hadn't left me just yet. I could still smell the scent of burned flesh in the air, still imagine that something was breathing just over my shoulder. I opened my eyes, stared into the mirror, and watched the boring, beige wall behind me. I reached back without ever turning around, felt the drywall under my skin, tapped it, made certain it was real. All of it was real. This wasn't a dream, not any longer. This was my house.

The toilet seat still creaked underneath me.

The fan still droned overhead.

And the familiar drip of the leaky faucet...

I sat up a bit, tilting my head to one side. I listened. Second after second, moment after agonizing moment, I heard nothing but my own heart pounding, my own breath coming in and out in sharp, wheezing spurts.

No.

Not my breath.

I closed my mouth to be sure, wanting to scream when the ragged sound continued from somewhere close. Behind the curtain. Something was there. Something that kept the water from dripping into the drain. I stood up, quietly reached for the handle of the door when it spoke.

"P-please..."

Every muscle in my body froze, and my stomach rolled over itself, tumbling like a gymnast. The days of pissing myself felt like sweet, lovely memories, and I was quite certain that shit would run down my leg any second. The voice was weak, ragged, and pathetic, and I instantly felt an unexpected pang of sympathy when I heard it. I began to turn the knob slowly, and again he spoke.

"I-I know you're there. P-please..."

I turned back, staring at the shower curtain, my bowels like fire in my belly. Then I saw it. A hand, red and black, with specks of bone poking through the skin here and there. The curtain drew back slowly, and I saw him, curled into the corner of the tub, the leaking faucet dripping onto his shoulder. I wanted to scream, wanted to run away, but I felt almost instantly that there was no need to. He was nearly dead. I could see it in his eyes, the pink edges curled with black-singed fur. His mouth was open, his lips dark and dead. His body was a ruin, and the simple act of living seemed like an almost unbearable trial. I tried to imagine the horrible fury that had driven him this far, only to fall limp just as he reached his goal.

Behind him, the frosted window was still cracked open a bit, and I could see that the night had fallen quietly, the rain no longer pouring. He could have killed me by now, could have choked me while I slept. But he seemed to know what was coming, seemed to know what the near future held, and I could only imagine that realization had drained the fight out of him. Revenge didn't mean much when you would be dead yourself before the deed was even done. I looked back into the pitiful pink eyes, and against my better judgment, I sat back down on the toilet.

"What can I do?" I asked, instantly becoming a caretaker.

He shook his head, not quite sure how to answer. "Nothing," he said finally.

"Who are you?" I asked.

Again he barely shook his head. "Not sure. Used to have a name. Can't remember. So long ago."

I remembered the picture I had stolen, the one of the boy and his mother, and I fished it from the pile of my damp jeans, careful to keep the frayed picture from ripping into pieces forever.

"This," I said, holding it gingerly out in front of my face. "Is this you?"

I couldn't be sure, but I think I saw his pink, ruined eyes water a bit, and a grim little smile appeared. It was almost enough to make him momentarily less gruesome.

"Me," he said wistfully. "I was gone. Long time, gone."

"How long?" I asked.

"Not sure."

"Do you remember this? When you took this picture? You were probably my age then."

He closed his eyes, cringing as the singed flesh cracked and wept. "Yes," he said finally. "I remember. She gave me that... my own toy. A globe. Snow. Never had seen snow. She said we would go somewhere white. One day."

I leaned closer on the edge of the toilet seat, close enough for him to rip out my throat if he chose to. "What happened to you?"

The pink eyes opened once more. "Him," he replied, confirming what I already believed to be true. There was something darker, some evil force that had been controlling him, and for the first time in countless years, the human being inside was peering out.

"He came to me. In dreams at first."

"Dreams!" I blurted. "Yes, in dreams. A shadow with bleeding eyes."

"You see him?" he asked.

"Yes," I replied.

There was a look of pain across his face, and I felt horribly humbled and frightened by the fact that this dying creature was pitying me.

"Bad."

"What do you mean?"

He took a deep breath, but not nearly as deep as he had before. "He's not from...here."

"What do you mean?"

"Someone…brought him here. Gave him a body. He shouldn't be here…shouldn't be alive."

"Like, a ghost or something?" I asked, confused.

His answer was short, but clear.

"Demon."

There it was. This thing, whatever it was, had no business even existing in our world, and it was being passed from person to person, a disease intent on keeping itself alive by finding another host. Andy was supposed to be next on the list, but now there was little doubt that I was the one caught in the crosshairs. How many missing children were turned into these things, pawns in some game they didn't understand?

"How did he…do this to you?" I asked.

He swallowed and I could see that speaking was growing harder by the second. "I woke up in a dark place. The cave," he added with a slightly bitter look at me.

"What did he…do?" I asked.

He swallowed like an old man swallowing a dry pill. Then he held up his impossibly thin hand, showing me the red sores that were now charred and black. "He touched me. Each day. Over and over again."

I pointed at the gruesome hand and asked, "Why? What does it do?"

He smiled, the idea of it still, even at the end, slightly alluring. "I never eat. My last meal was with her," he said, pointing at the picture. "No food for me. Only this."

He held both hands up, and I could picture Andy writhing underneath him, could feel my own ankle burning and itching.

"You feed off people?" I asked, and he nodded. "Feed on what?"

"Goodness. Innocence. The best parts of them."

Again he smiled.

"When I was done with them, there was nothing good left. It

took weeks. Months. Years sometimes. I visit in the night. Touch them. They dream. When the sun rises, I'm gone."

Any pity I had known had faded, and my hands were little balls of white knuckles. I wanted to kill it, wanted to go into the kitchen and slide the biggest knife I could from the block and bury it in that grotesque neck. It wouldn't change anything. Even then I knew it. But it would make me feel better.

"Why?"

He looked confused.

"I want to know why," I said, leaning even closer.

"Because that is what *he* wants."

In my mind's eye, I saw that shimmering black reflection, felt the pursed lips at my ear.

I'm coming.

"What does he want?" I asked.

"I don't know," he answered. "To plant seeds, I think. Something inside of us, all of us. Something waiting to be awoken. Killers. Abusers. Men and women that ruin themselves, and in turn, ruin others."

"Is that what he did to Andy?"

He shook his head, but barely moved as he did. His words were slowing to a crawl.

"No. Andy. Was the next. The replacement. He wasn't taking out. He was putting himself in. Soon, Andy would be pushed aside. He would take control."

"That's why you're dying, isn't it?" I asked. "Whatever it was that kept you alive is half gone. It's just you now."

"Yes," he said. "He makes them...makes us...more like him. Changes us so we can do our new job." He held up his hand. "I didn't always look like this," he added as he brushed his fingers across his ruined face.

"So Andy was going to be the next one? The next Thief?"

"Not anymore," he said quietly. "You."

I felt my temper swelling once more, but sheer willpower kept me on the seat. "No," I answered through my teeth. "I won't be."

Once again, I saw a miserable pity in that face, his brows arching down, his eyes growing watery. He could, for the first time perhaps, see himself in me. Who knew what sort of torture it took to create this awful thing, but I knew that I was the first person he had spoken to in years perhaps. If only this had happened sooner, with someone else, in some other time, how many people could have been changed? How many families might still be intact, still unbroken?

"You don't understand," he said with teary eyes. "Not yet. But you will."

"How can I stop it?" I asked.

"You can't," he said.

"There has to be a way," I said, more to myself.

"No. He's ready for something new. He wants you. Wants to wait until you're old enough. And then…"

"Then what?" I asked, my voice quivering.

"He wants to take the next step. A child. Something none of us could give him. Only you. One touch, and he knew."

The pink eyes drifted closed, and I let him be. We had gone through so much, and I feared the worst for Andy. Even now, with no more surprises, I wasn't sure if I would ever really have my brother back again. And now this. Something else. Something worse, coming for both of us, bent on revenge.

"One more thing," I said.

"Tired," he answered.

"You'll sleep soon," I said. "I promise you that." The eyes slid back open and locked on mine.

"Why the toys?"

He looked surprised, as if the question itself had never even occurred to him and he had to think about his answer. Then the ragged lips parted in a weak, barely audible voice.

"Hands," he said slowly. "They take from people. Feed on them. But the toys…they are different. They soak up all the good things…happiness…smiles…laughter. They are in here…all of them…all he has stolen…the dreams…children's dreams…they love toys…"

His hand opened, reaching for something I couldn't see. "With people, I always felt…wrong. Like I was taking something…something they would never give. But the toys…the toys…they reminded me…"

"Of what?" I asked in a whisper.

"…of her…of me…of a better time…"

My own eyes were watering as he spoke, and I knew that this pitiful excuse for a man wasn't any more to blame than Andy was. We were, in our own ways, all broken, as chipped around the edges as an old plate. His hand sank back to the edge of the bathtub, to the picture, which he picked up and clutched to his chest. Finally, those awful eyes closed one last time.

"Stay…" he whispered as he curled into the cold sides of the tub.

"I will." I sat for a moment, watching him. Then I held out my hand and said, "I'll be right back." It was foolish, leaving him there like that, but I knew what I had to do. Besides, it only took a second to find the bear. It was still damp, but when I wound the metal clasp on the back, the familiar tune started tinkling. He smiled when I set it down on the edge of the tub, but the smile quickly faded into a look of uncertainty. A look of guilt.

"It's okay," I said as he stared at the bear. "I promise."

He reached for it then, and I knew in that moment that everything he had told me was true. He wasn't in the bathtub anymore, not really, not in the way that counted. I can't say where exactly he was, but I remembered what he had told me. About how the toys soaked up all those feelings, all those good emotions. When his hand touched that bear, was he me? Was he lying in my bed, dreaming of my mother? Or was that glow off the toy just enough to make him remember his own bed and his own mother? I never knew the answer.

Over the next half-hour, I listened, as each breath grew a bit shorter than the last. I thought of Andy, of Dad, of my own mother, whom I'd never really met. Then, when the breathing stopped, I pulled back the curtain. No one used this bathroom but me and Andy, so I figured it would be okay, at least until morning. Either way, I was too tired to deal with it. I set an alarm to get up early, before anyone else, and I finally slipped into bed to quietly cry myself to sleep.

CHAPTER TWELVE

Dad's funeral was such a blur, that long, arching day that didn't ever want to end, no matter how badly you wanted it to. There were friends, a smattering of relatives, passing faces that I barely noticed. He looked peaceful. It was odd that he was almost smiling.

People say that the pain goes away when you lose someone, that every day it hurts a little less. That's only half true. The pain doesn't actually change. Pain is just pain, but you build up an immunity to it, like an alcoholic. It doesn't really hurt less; your heart just gets a bit more numb with each passing day.

It hurt, not just because of him, but because of Andy too. I tried to get them to give him some kind of provisional pass, a day out under supervision. They didn't allow it, of course. I had to tell him face to face, a wall of glass between the two of us. I can still remember it like it was yesterday.

"Did anyone tell you?" I asked him, speaking into the old plastic phone.

"Tell me what?"

He had a beard. It had been a few months since I had come by to visit, and I was shocked by how old he looked, like an honest-to-God man, the years just piling up like dominoes. There were even patches of gray in his whiskers. How the hell had it come to this?

"Dad," I said quietly, refusing to look at him.

"Dead?" he asked. If it had come from anyone else, it would have sounded cold, but from Andy, the single word spoke volumes. Apprehension. Fear. Pain. And most of all, the stark realization that he didn't even have to ask the question to know the answer.

"Yes."

Dad had never been to see Andy, not a single time. I never talked much about him when I visited, mainly because I didn't want to flaunt my relationship with Dad in his face. It seemed too harsh to mention him, like Andy telling me how much fun he and Mom had. It might have been true, but that didn't make it a good thing to say.

"How?"

"Heart," I said, and Andy laughed a bit.

"Could have guessed that. Too many cheeseburgers."

"He never was much of a chef."

"He had his moments," Andy said. "Grilled cheese."

"Yeah," I said with a smile. "Good grilled cheese."

Andy rested his head against the glass, his eyes drifting closed. He looked like he had something he wanted to say, but it was hard to get it out. Finally, he lifted his eyes to mine. "Did he... ever say much about me?"

I stared at him. It was the first time he had ever asked me anything about Dad.

"Do you really want to know the answer to that?" I asked him.

He let that marinate for a minute.

"Yeah," he said finally.

"He did. He talked about how much it hurt to think about you. About how he was never disappointed in you. Just in himself."

"I wish I could have told him," he said. "About what happened. About...everything from that summer. Maybe he wouldn't have been so disappointed."

"You won't believe me," I said, regret twisting my stomach, "but I almost did tell him. More than once, actually. I couldn't stand it. The thought of you, stuck in here while I was out there. Living."

He glanced down at my right hand. "Probably not the life you wanted."

I stood up and gazed down at him. "It could be worse. We both know that. It could have been either of us in a cave. Any life I have, I owe it to you. I wish Dad had known that."

"When's the funeral?" he asked.

"Friday."

He nodded, his face suddenly working into a grimace as he wrestled with the weight of what I had just told him. He didn't say anything, so I started to lower the phone back onto the cradle. A light tap on the glass made me pick it up again.

"Do you still have my old stuff?" he asked.

"I got a couple of boxes."

He nodded. "One of them's got a tin lunchbox. It's the *Ghostbusters* one Dad got me when I was, I dunno, five or six."

"I remember that one," I said with a grin.

"Inside it, I got a couple old things. Baseball cards and shit like that. Somewhere in there, wrapped up in a bandanna, is that Superman. You remember the one?" he asked.

"I think so," I said, the words catching in my throat.

"Find it. Take it with you tomorrow, and if you get the chance, slip it into Dad's pocket."

He wiped a tear from the side of his nose before setting the receiver down. He walked away without another word.

★   ★   ★

I was up early on Tuesday morning, earlier than I could ever remember getting up on a weekday. Thankfully, Dad was caught in his own morning rush, too busy to notice much of anything we did. There had been times in the past when I looked at the live-and-let-live policy in our house as a negative thing, another symptom of our odd family, but on that morning, I saw it as a blessing. Regardless of all the forces moving against us, I had a more pragmatic problem to deal with. The Toy Thief was gone now, and all that remained was a body left to rot in our bathroom.

Dad never used the middle bathroom, but he did stop and check on me and Andy on his way out. Some days, he had to drag us out of bed himself, but we were pretty self-sufficient once our eyes were open. I knew that this problem wouldn't wait, and that school had to be on the back burner today. With that in mind, I prepared myself mentally and stumbled into the kitchen. I heard the fridge open.

"There she is," Dad said in his usual tone. Out of the three of us, he was the only morning person.

"Hey," I moaned.

"You all right?" he asked as he popped a frozen sausage biscuit into the microwave.

"Sick," I said.

He frowned. "Doctor?" he asked.

"Maybe not," I replied. "Just out in the rain too long yesterday. Probably just need some rest."

He nodded.

"Andy up yet?" he asked.

"Haven't seen him." I reached into the fridge and poured a glass of orange juice, never making eye contact, when I added, "He might need to rest some too."

There was a long pause, but I refused to look back. Instead, I took a long sip from my juice, making sure that everything looked just as it should. Another day. Just a sick daughter and an exhausted son. Nothing to be worried about.

"Did he tell you that?" he said, an edge of suspicion in his voice.

I finally turned around, my brows creased. "No. He's just usually up by now. I know yesterday was a rough day for him."

I was on the attack, but subtly so, and I kept my tone in check. Dad wouldn't be suspicious if I got snippy, but he might if I *didn't* get snippy at all. This was me we were talking about.

"School's pretty much done anyway. Everybody's just floating this week. I'm sure it's the same for Andy too. Even the teachers got one foot out the door."

Dad chewed on it and finally said, "Fine. Keep an eye on him. We need to sit down and talk when I get home from work." He pulled his breakfast from the microwave and pecked me on the cheek. "Be good."

I sat at the counter, sipping my juice, never looking up at him until the door shut behind me. I heard his truck start up, and I dashed to the window just in time to see him pull away into the rising sun of a clear day. I took a deep breath and readied myself before I pushed open the door of the bathroom.

The door creaked open, and I expected the smell to knock me down. I had left the frosted window cracked the night before, just in case, but now I wondered if it had been necessary. For a long while, I stood there, watching the shower curtain and listening to the sounds of robins chirping outside the window.

"Okay," I whispered with my eyes closed. "You can do this."

I reached for the curtain and pulled it back, hoping that maybe last night had just been some awful dream. I knew at once that it hadn't been. He was still there, still leaned back into the corner of the tub, his pink eyes dry and cracked, his lips pulled back strangely over his teeth. His mouth looked as if he had died in the desert while searching for water, so dry and desiccated. That awful burned hand still rested on the edge of the tub, gripping it as if it might get away from him otherwise. In the other hand, close to his sunken chest, he held the bear. I stood there, staring, wondering if I could smell anything rotten or if I just thought I did. No. Nothing yet. Just the familiar scent of burned flesh, not unlike a barbecue. The realization made me kneel down to the toilet and retch up the few sips of orange juice in my gut.

I slumped back against the wall, and once the world stopped spinning, my mind went back to more pragmatic things. I...we... had to get him out of here. We had all day to do it, but I didn't have the slightest inkling as to how we could ever hope to accomplish this task. He was bigger than either me or Andy, and even though he was as thin as a rail, I figured he probably weighed more than he looked. I spent a moment or two trying to make a plan. Then I realized I was getting ahead of myself. The first thing to do was to show Andy.

Andy.

The Thief's words from the night before rang in my mind once again. This entity, this *demon* as he called it, wanted Andy's body, and it had already begun to push Andy's personality aside to make that transition happen. I remembered the way he'd acted, his normally calm, hard-to-ruffle personality suddenly swinging from one extreme to the other. Glancing down at the dead body, I wasn't sure if it was all over now or not, though I certainly hoped it was. All I could do was take it one moment at a time and hope for the best.

Whatever the final goal had been, Andy's transformation wasn't complete. He was still my brother, still good – of that I had little doubt. Even so, I didn't fully trust him. If you beat a good dog long enough, he'll learn to bite. That was my brother now, and I wasn't sure how he would react when he saw the Thief dead in our own home.

Andy was still sleeping, still curled into the corner like a puppy in the back of a kennel. I kept waiting for his eyes to open and lock onto mine, but they didn't. He was truly out, but there was an edge to him, a sense that he wasn't really resting, not the way he had before he was taken. He shifted uneasily, and more than once he spoke to himself – tiny, sharp whispers that I couldn't make out. I quietly sneaked over and sat gently on the edge of the bed.

"Andy," I whispered, afraid to actually touch him just yet. His eyes were darting from one side to the other behind his closed lids, and I knew he was dreaming. I couldn't imagine that it was pleasant.

"Andy," I said a bit louder as I tapped his shoulder. "Wake up."

I had to shake him several more times, but he finally awoke with a start and immediately sat up, drawing the covers up to his chin. His eyes, as mad as blue hornets, were dancing from side to side, scanning the room.

"Andy," I said once more as I placed a hand on his shoulder. "You're home. It's okay. You're back home."

He looked at me, and his grip on the blanket began to loosen. "Home," he said, nodding.

"Sorry," I said, and he looked at me, confused. "For waking you, I mean. We need to talk, though."

He never stopped nodding, and I wasn't sure if he was agreeing with me or if he had just temporarily lost control of the muscles in his neck.

"We need to talk about everything that happened." I waited for him to reply, and when he didn't, I added, "Talk about what's still happening."

He cut his eyes at me, and I knew he had heard the message. "What?" he said frantically. "What's happening?"

I wasn't sure where to start. For one thing, I still had questions, and even though I was fairly certain that Andy didn't have the answers, at least not all of them, I figured he could get me closer.

"When you were back there…in that cave…what happened?" I said, wanting to get some things straight first. "I mean, what did he do to you?"

He cast his eyes down to the bed, his face flushing red with either shame or embarrassment.

"It's okay," I said. "I mean, you didn't do anything wrong."

"You know," he answered, finally glancing up. "He did the same to you when he grabbed you."

I remembered it well, but I still wasn't sure what it all meant. "I saw him grab you too," I said. "Before I got you out. I heard you…in pain."

He nodded and scratched at his leg before holding it out for me to see. "It's already healed," he said. "In just a day. It heals so quick. The kind of thing you wouldn't even notice if you weren't paying attention."

I nodded. "Yeah. It's supposed to be like that. Something you don't ever see. Don't question." I waited for him to add more, but when he didn't, I went further. "When it grabbed me, it felt like I was sinking. Like I was drowning in ink. Everything was just pure blackness."

He didn't answer, but I could see him back there in his mind. "There was a voice," he said finally. "Something that whispered to me. Told me things. Made me promises. It told me it would make me better. Make me happy. That I'd live forever."

I listened, breathless as he talked. Then I asked, "Did you believe it?"

"I don't know," he said. "Maybe. Part of me. It wasn't just what he said. It was…this pain. All I could think of was…her."

"Her?"

He looked up at me, staring right through my eyes. "Mom. I kept seeing her. Her face. She'd be smiling one second. Then she'd be melting. Her skin falling off her bones."

I could see from the mad glare in his eyes that he was seeing it again, that these images were as real now as they had been then.

"She would talk to me," he said, his voice cracking. "Tell me she didn't need me anymore. That I was the reason she was dead. That being in a hole in the ground was better than being my mom. And just when I thought I couldn't stand the pain any more, I'd hear his voice, telling me that he would save me. He would change me. *He* would be my mom and my dad."

Again his eyes caught mine.

"And if you only knew how bad it hurt. If you could only imagine it. Then you'd know that it was easy to believe."

"It wasn't real," I told him. "You know that. Mom loved you. Dad loves you. I love you. There's nothing here that can hurt you."

"Maybe," he said, wiping his eyes. "But we weren't supposed to see what we've seen."

"I saw something too," I said. "I mean, there was the pain, but...something else along with it. People. Kids. The others that he's taken over the years."

"Yes," he said, reaching for my hand. "I-I didn't know if any of it was real, but they were still in there. Still inside him. Like a parasite that killed whatever it latched on to, but they never really died. They didn't *get* to die because he took part of them." He stared down at the floor and added, "Forever."

It confirmed everything that I had feared: that this creature was keeping itself alive by kidnapping children and warping them into that foul Thief, swallowing part of their souls in the process. Losing my toys felt suddenly like a small and pathetic thing to even be concerned about.

"We know his secrets now," Andy said fearfully. "We know, so he'll be back."

I nodded. "You're right."

I walked him into the bathroom, making sure to stay in front of him, easing him forward the way you might coax a frightened dog. "Now listen," I said, turning my back to the shower curtain. "This will be a...shock."

"What are you talking about?"

"Last night. I took my shower. Then I fell asleep in here. And then I...found something."

I gave him a few more words to explain what had happened,

but his face was already tightening as he sensed what was coming, what was hiding just behind us. I could imagine what he felt, the same way I had felt the night before, but multiplied and magnified. Still, the sun was shining, the birds were singing, the rain had finally died away. This was our home, our safe place, and the darkness that had locked him away couldn't reach us here. The very thought felt like some kind of violation.

"No," he said, cutting me off midsentence. "Not here."

"It's okay," I told him once again. "He can't hurt us. Not anymore."

"He?"

"You just have to see it for yourself."

With that, I drew back the curtain and listened to Andy half scream, half moan when he saw the crumpled, burned body. My brother, who was bigger, stronger, braver than me, actually dropped as if someone had cut his legs out from under him. There seemed to be a dread inside of him now that was infinitely deeper than any I could imagine. The sight of the Thief scared me, filled me with revulsion and loathing, but it simply broke Andy.

"No," I said, reaching down. "He's dead. I promise you. I saw him die. I was in here with him."

"No, no, no, no, no," Andy kept repeating, shaking his head from side to side.

"Stop this," I said firmly, but he ignored me. "I said stop it!"

I drew back my hand and slapped him across the face hard enough bring tears to his eyes and send ripples of shocking pain up my arm. He stopped shaking his head long enough to glare up at me, wounded.

"Now listen to me," I said. "He's dead. I don't know if the rest of this is over or not, but his part is. He's gone, and we have to do something about it."

Andy's mouth was half-open, and a thread of drool dripped out from his bottom lip like a nearly invisible fishing line. The perfect outline of my small hand was clear on his cheek, a sight that sent a pang of guilt through me.

"Do you understand?" I asked him. "I can't do this alone. I need you. I need my brother."

In that moment, I could see that he was more or less divided, split down the middle. Somewhere inside was Andy, the one I knew and trusted and loved. Sure, we fought, and between the two of us, we had enough issues to fill the bed of my dad's truck, but he was whole. He was something I understood. The second Andy, the one who had dropped to his knees in a heap at my feet, was something that had been infected, used, and shredded into bits. A patch of his heart had been scorched and salted, and it felt likely that nothing would ever grow there again. Nothing good at least. In time, that dark patch of himself might give birth to something, but only if I did nothing.

His behavior ever since I had rescued him was nothing less than these two forced in a struggle to the death. As I stood there, the internal conflict inside him seemed to shift, and the better part of him emerged. He looked up at me, and I could see it all over him: his eyes focused and clear, his body at peace with the awful scene before us. He was scared. We both were. But he was, just maybe, equipped to deal with it.

"I think so," he said.

"Good," I said, pulling him back to his feet. "I think maybe it's time to get Dad involved."

"No," he said, his voice suddenly panicked.

"Why?" I asked. "I mean, he wouldn't have ever believed us before, but look. We got proof now."

"No," he said, even more forceful. "We can fix this. We *will* fix it."

"But we don't have to do it alone—"

"I said no!" He looked down and suddenly realized that he was holding onto my arm, squeezing it hard enough to turn his knuckles white. He pulled away, and a look of shame and fear rippled across his face. "I...I don't want anyone to know..."

I couldn't quite imagine what those lost hours must have been like, but I thought I understood.

"Okay. We'll do it your way."

Neither of us had any good ideas, at least none that we could pull off easily. The quarry was the safest bet, but even that was over a mile away, and neither of us had any great ideas as to how to move a seven-foot-long body in broad daylight. We immediately settled on waiting for nightfall, though we didn't have any great way to move him. We didn't know, not yet at least, how heavy he was, but we figured that just carrying him would be out of the question.

"We need something big. Something with wheels," I said.

"The garbage can?" he said without much confidence. I brushed off the suggestion at first, but the longer we circled the idea, the better it became.

"It might be a little loud," I said, picturing the noise it made on the driveway.

"Maybe not," he said. "If we take it slow, through the grass maybe, it might work."

"What if somebody drives by?" I asked.

"Simple. We stick to the main road pretty much the whole way. No cutting through yards or anything. Anybody shows up, we just park it next to the closest mailbox. As far as they know, we're just getting it out a day early."

It seemed risky, but what other choice did we really have? "Okay," I said. "But what about him?"

"What about him?"

"What are we doing with him until then?"

"Well," he said, surveying the body up close for the first time. "We need to get him out first. Any ideas?"

"Out where?"

He scratched his head for a moment, then snapped his fingers. "The basement."

Our basement wasn't really a basement at all in the traditional sense. It was completely unfinished, more of a high-roofed crawl space. The floors and walls were dirt, and there was a cinderblock wall in the center that divided the room in two. It was isolated and close at the same time, and best of all, the only door was on the outside of the house, tucked away on the far side of the back porch. If we got the body down there, it would be a cinch to sneak him out once night fell.

"Yeah," I replied. "It would work. I really think it would work."

Andy turned back to the body and stared at it. "Now," he said. "Getting it down there..."

"Yeah..."

We both sat there, just staring.

Then Andy said, "Sleeping bag."

Dad had bought him a real heavy-duty one a few years ago, and with some work, we could probably fit the Thief all the way inside. While Andy went and dug it out of his closet, I searched around in the utility room for some thick, yellow rubber gloves. I felt guilty for refusing to touch it, especially after the little bit of bonding we had done the night before. Even so, the thought of putting my skin against it filled me with a revulsion I couldn't begin to explain.

"You ready for this?" I asked tentatively as I re-entered the bathroom.

"Not really," he replied.

Together, we stared down at the thing in the tub.

"What about that?" he asked, pointing to the bear.

"I don't know," I said truthfully. "I want it. I really do. But I don't even know if it's mine anymore."

"Leave it," he said. "It won't ever feel the same again."

It was true. I knew it was, but it felt like losing the single thread that still attached me to Mom. The only thing that was ever truly from her. I imagined what she would want me to do, how she would feel about all this madness. In the end, I decided to let it go, and we went to work.

In minutes, we were both slick with sweat, and more than once, each of us had to step away and cover our mouths to keep from gagging. We threw the window open the rest of the way and turned on the overhead fan, neither of which seemed to help much. It wasn't the smell of rot or decay that you might imagine. Instead, it was the scent of a slab of ribs left on the grill for too long, burned until the good smell of food turned pungent and sharp, twisting into something beyond foul. There were hints of other things too: dark, moldy smells that baked out of the old clothes, as if they had been buried in black dirt for years. We tried to feed the body into the sleeping bag headfirst, working it down an inch at a time. Once, when Andy tilted the head back, the mouth yawned open and an ancient, dry smell drifted out, like old grass clippings in the sun.

The Thief was lighter than we thought, his skin and body almost crisp to the touch. When he'd told me he never ate or drank, I hadn't believed it, but now I understood. He really hadn't been alive, not in the traditional sense, and I imagined that if I pressed hard enough, I could sink my hand into his chest. He reminded me of a mummy, something that had long ago lost whatever made him human, driven forward by some dark energy – hatred maybe.

By the time we had him halfway in, Andy stepped back and said, "I need some air." He walked straight out of the bathroom and out the back door, standing in the clean, open air with his nose to the sky.

I followed him out, saying, "It could have been worse."

"Yeah," he replied, eyes squinting. "I know that's true.

But it doesn't seem true. The whole thing smells like a nightmare cookout."

We sat there on the edge of the porch for a moment, just resting, watching the leaves waving on their branches. "I wonder what his name was," I said finally.

"Who cares?" Andy replied.

"I do. You should too."

"He tried to kill me. Or change me. Or whatever."

"Yeah," I answered. The real Andy was back now, and it finally felt like the two of us could talk.

"You know, I talked to him last night."

"You *did*?" he asked, incredulous.

"I did. I think he knew he was dying. Something about how weak he was. It was like he was back in control again."

Andy kicked at the dirt around his foot. "What is that supposed to mean?"

"I think you know. You're part of the reason he's in there right now."

"I didn't fucking start this," he spat.

"No. No, you didn't. But you broke that globe."

"Oh, come on…"

"No," I said. "You could have gotten us both killed. We were almost out when you pulled that shit."

The other Andy, the wild one, would have yelled back, or slapped me, or maybe even worse. But this was *Andy* Andy.

"I don't know why I did it," he said furtively.

"I think I do."

"Well then," he said, "tell me."

"When you were…dreaming. When that voice was talking to you. Did it feel like it was trying to change you?"

"I dunno," he replied. Then, after a pause, he said, "Yes. I think so. No. I know so."

"I thought so. He," I said, pointing behind me to the open

window, "used to be like you. The last Thief snuck into his house while he was asleep, took him away from his mom, locked him in a cage, and sucked out everything good."

"What are you saying?"

I glared at him. "I think you know. You were the next in line. If I hadn't found you, then in a few weeks or months or even years, it would have been you sneaking into houses."

I think he already knew this, at least in some way. But hearing it laid out like that, the logic of it was impossible to deny. It floored him, and I could see the other half threatening to burst out and have his way. He closed his eyes, and he seemed to be fighting with himself, like a sick man wrestling with his urge to vomit. The moment faded, and when his eyes opened again, I knew Andy was still in charge.

"There was something else," I added once he had calmed down.

"What now?"

"Me," I said plainly. "I mean, when he touched me, there was something he liked. Something…new. I think it was because I'm a girl, but…I'm just not sure."

"Come on," he said, standing back up. "We can't change any of this, not yet anyway. So let's just get this over with."

We slipped the rest of the sleeping bag down over him quickly, both of us pretending not to notice when the zipper rubbed the flesh from his arms, peeling it off like a layer of old onion. He was, as I feared, too long to fit, but he was thin enough to fold up at the knees. We shimmied the bag the rest of the way and zipped it closed. Then, with me on the back end and Andy on the front, we lifted him out. It was a slow, messy trip through the house, mainly because of me. I was, without question, the weak link in the project.

"Just drop it," Andy said halfway down the hall after I struggled to pick our load up for the third time.

"I can do it," I said through gritted teeth.

"Just drop it," he barked. "I can just drag it."

The sleeping bag left lines in the carpet which I followed along and scuffed up with my shoe. I considered getting the vacuum out, but me cleaning house on a sick day would have sent up about a dozen red flags. When Andy had dragged him to the back door, he stopped to catch his breath.

"Go on," he said between huffs. "Check it out. Make sure there's nobody out there."

It was a school day, so the coast was clear from kids, and pretty much all the adults would be at work. Down the clearing of the backyard was a small creek, and just past that was the set of apartments. Only a few of the windows pointed our way, but we knew at least a few parents who worked the night shift. That, along with mailmen, deliveries, and stuff like that, meant there was no way to be truly sure it was clear.

"It looks good," I told him.

"Looks good or is good?"

"I think it looks good," I said.

He stomped past me and peeked out the door himself. He knew I was right, of course, but he just had to check for himself.

"Come on," he said, picking the bag up. "No stopping. Just move as quick as you can, and if you have to rest, just drop it and I'll drag it the rest of the way."

Never in my life had I felt so visible and open, as if there were spotlights on both of us. I'm not sure how long it took us to make the dash from porch to basement, but it couldn't have been more than ten seconds. But those ten seconds were enough for my imagination to conjure up dozens of scenarios, each worse than the last. Patrolling cops. A concerned dad. A nosy neighbor. Any of them were enough to shut us down.

A small part of me welcomed the idea of being caught. Simply thinking about it was inviting, because it might mean we would finally have some help with this absurd turn of events. We were, despite everything that had happened, still just kids, and I relished the daydream of a grownup stepping in and telling us what to do. But that was just my daylight voice, the energetic, glass-half-full voice that told me all of this would be okay in the end. The other part of my mind, the realist if you will, told me that the more people involved, the worse for everyone. I would have loved Dad's help, but the second he knew, his life was on the line as well.

"Shit," Andy said a few feet from the basement door.

"What?" I asked, glancing around for whatever it was he had seen.

"The door!" he barked. "Why didn't you open the fucking door?"

"You didn't ask me to."

About three feet away, Andy dropped the sleeping bag with a thud as he scrambled to get the basement open. It wasn't locked, mainly because there wasn't anything in there worth stealing, but it did have a jerry-rigged handle made of wire and a length of wood, just enough to keep the wind from blowing it open. Normally, it was the sort of thing you could flip open with your eyes closed, but now, in this pressure cooker of stress, Andy couldn't find a way to open it. He was cursing under his breath, his face was turning red, and I realized, almost too late, that the other Andy was about to appear, threatening to burst through the small cracks in my brother's resolve.

"Move," I said from over his shoulder, but he pushed me away with a single strong arm. He was shaking the door now, pulling it like a wild monkey trying to break out of a cage.

"Stop."

He didn't hear me. He didn't hear anything. All at once, he gave up on the handle altogether and began punching the wooden planks with his bare knuckles, each blow echoing through the neighborhood.

"Jesus, Andy, stop it!"

His knuckles were red, cracking, bleeding, and with each new punch, he left a bloody print. In seconds, there were three knuckle-prints, then six, then eight, all as I grabbed at his shoulder, pulling him, trying and failing to draw him away from the edge of madness, to drag him back to me.

"Dammit, stop, please, just stop!"

Before I knew it, I had hit him on the back of the head, reaching up and swinging my fist down like a hammer. It shot a bolt of pain up my elbow, but it at least got his attention. He turned, his bloodshot eyes locking on mine, and he swung. The world went spotty as I heard the crunch in my jaw. There was the ground, the gravel, the dirt, rising up to meet me. I hit hard, but I didn't feel anything other than the slight humming throb in my ears. For some strange reason, I remember seeing an anthill just in front of my eyes, and in my swirling, woozy confusion, I worried that they might try to crawl into my mouth. There was a voice, distant, like it was speaking through a pillow, saying the same panicked thing over and over again.

"No, no, no, no, no…"

On and on. I didn't care though. The world was too vague a thing to care about. I must have rolled onto my back at some point, because I remember the blue sky dotted with black clouds. Not clouds. Just black dots that danced around the edges of my vision, bubbling, growing, and eventually consuming the blue altogether.

The cold of the frozen bag of peas was what finally woke me up. I don't know how long they had been resting on my cheek, but from the numbness, I would have guessed several minutes. I was on the couch in the living room, and when I sat up, a pain raced through the front of my head. I stumbled into the bathroom, both eager and fearful to see what I looked like. My face in the mirror wasn't nearly as bad as it felt. It was swollen, sure, but not so bad that I couldn't make up a good lie. A neat, bloody outline of knuckles lined my cheek, and on my forehead, I had a bit of gravel still half stuck, half buried in my skin. The sight of myself made everything instantly hurt more than it had just seconds before, and I spent a few minutes washing the dirt and blood away. Once everything was clean, I realized I had a handful of scrapes across my brow. Still, not too bad considering. But certainly enough to have to explain when the time came.

Before I left for good, I checked behind the shower curtain once more. The smell of smoke was still hanging in the air, but the bits of ash and skin had been washed away, and a sharp smell of disinfectant permeated the space. How long had I been out?

I met Andy in the kitchen just as he walked in through the back door, soapy bucket and a rag in one hand. He took a deep breath before walking over to me. I could see in his eyes that he was back to himself once more, but I cringed all the same when he moved closer.

"No," he said, stopping short and touching my shoulder, awkward and unsure, like we were on a first date. "You don't...I don't...I'm so sorry. I didn't mean to..."

I let him babble like that for a minute, mainly because I was pretty certain that talking would make my jaw hurt like hell. I knew what had happened to him, knew what had been done to him, but was still unsure how deep my brother's change really went.

"Stop," I said finally through my half-open lips. "Just stop."

"B-but..."

"No," I replied. "I know. You didn't do that. You wouldn't. I know that."

"Yes," he said in a relieved tone. Years later, when I learned more about the world, I would think of that moment often – the way he apologized, the sharp guilt in his eyes, the way it burned him to realize he had done something so awful. I've known drunks, alcoholics, junkies, cheaters, just about everything you can imagine, and I've seen that look on all of their faces. Their regret is so real, so powerful that it nearly consumes them whenever they go too far. And yet they seem completely unable to stop.

"The body?" I said, my jaw too sore to ask the entire question.

"In the basement," he said, his tone like that of a dog, so eager to please, to fix what he had broken. "I washed the blood off the door. And I cleaned the bathroom. And the peas," he said, looking around for them.

"In the living room," I answered.

"Yeah, yeah. I got those for you too. I thought it would help… you know. With the swelling."

He was right. The peas had helped. And he had done a good job of fixing everything else. Now if only he could stop breaking things.

"Anyone see you?"

"No," he said, his tone suddenly less confident. "I mean, no one that I know of."

I checked the clock on the front of the microwave. It had been nearly an hour since we stepped out the back door together. If anyone had seen a teenage boy beat the shit out of his sister, we'd know by now. So I sighed, breathing somewhat easy despite the pain I was in. Our plan, despite the roadblocks, had worked up to this point. Now all we had to do was get him to the quarry tonight. I imagined the dozens of ways that could go wrong.

"What happened out there?" I asked.

"I dunno. I just lost it when I couldn't get the door open. And then one thing led to another, and—"

"No," I said. "Not that. I saw that. How did I get back in here?"

I knew the answer, or at least part of it, but I wanted to hear it from him. I wanted to know what was happening inside his head.

"I came back," he said as he stared at the ground.

"Back?"

"Yeah. That's the only way I can describe it. It was like I knew what I was doing, but I wasn't really the one doing it. I knew it was wrong, is what I mean. But..." he glanced back up, "I didn't want to stop. That door. It was like it was alive. I felt like it was laughing at me."

"That's ridiculous."

"I know that!" he said in a sudden rush of anger. "I'm not stupid. That's just what it felt like."

"So what made you stop?"

Again he stared at the tops of his feet, an embarrassed look in his eyes.

"You," he said finally. "I saw you. What I had done. And it brought me back."

My head felt suddenly heavy as a dull throb grew behind my eyes. "You got this?" I asked.

"Yeah. We're good."

"Good. I'm going to lie down. Wake me up by four," I said. "We need to think what we'll tell Dad about...all this." I motioned to my cheek.

"Okay. I'm sorry. I hope you know that."

My head was hurting too bad for me to really know anything. "Sure. Four. Got it?"

He nodded and I slipped away. Despite everything that had happened in my room, I still felt safe once I was under my sheets. It wasn't the room, or even the bed. It was because I was alone. Andy was out there, and a thin, hollow door separated the two of us. That alone was enough to put me at ease, and I slipped quietly into sleep, leaving the pain safely behind.

CHAPTER THIRTEEN

They let Andy out about five years back. He told them how sorry he was for everything he'd done, about how it was all a mistake, even the stuff with me, which couldn't have been an accident. They knew all about his troubles at school, the outbreaks of violence before and after his arrest. There was quite a list. Still, he'd been a boy when it happened, and he was in jail for a long, long time. I don't know that anyone in charge actually believed he was what you would call rehabilitated, but it didn't matter. He'd served his time, so he walked out.

They started him out in a halfway house, a little shithole with four tiny rooms, each home to a pair of work-release guys. There were drug addicts, DUIs, wife beaters, the whole deal, but only Andy had nearly killed anyone. That made him sort of a twisted little celebrity, at least that's how he told it. I was there when they let him out, and I drove him to the house. He asked, in a roundabout way, if he could live with me.

"I mean, I have to spend six months here," he said. "I'm dreading it, but I've done worse. Lord knows that. When my six is up, I'm not sure where I'll go…"

Just fishing really. Too afraid or proud to ask, and me not sure if I trusted him, even after everything. I dodged the question, and on the way over, I stopped at the cemetery.

"Where you going?"

"To see Dad."

"No," he said with a blank face.

"I thought you'd just—"

"No. Just no."

We drove on, and he got out of the car at the halfway house without another word. He called me a few times, letting me know how things were going. It didn't sound too bad, considering all he'd been through. They set him up with a job working a fryer at some chicken joint within walking distance. He said it was nasty work, that the fryers had burned all the hair off his forearms.

"Beggars can't be choosers," he added.

"I suppose not."

Most of our calls were a mixture of general chitchat – the whos, whats, wheres, and so forth – combined with awkward silence. Neither of us knew what to say. We were strangers, and that's just how it was. About five months in, he told me he had a place lined up to stay.

"Her name's Kirstie. She works with me. She's sweet. I guess you could say we're dating."

I could hear the excitement in his voice, and I realized that he'd never had a girlfriend. He'd been thirteen when they locked him up, and he'd probably never even kissed anybody. The idea made me equally bitter and sad.

"Good," I told him. "I'm glad to hear that. I'd like to meet her."

I tried to imagine the kind of girl who would want to move in with a convict whose only career prospects included working his way up to the cash register. That thought made my fingers itch, and I realized my own love life wasn't much to be jealous of.

"Yeah," he said, the smile clear through the phone line. "I told her 'bout you. She'd love to meet you."

We never did get together. I still don't know all the details, but I do know that Kirstie had problems of her own – drugs, to be specific. Meth, I believe. She was a mess from top to bottom, and the two of them never really had a chance to make anything work. The next time I heard from Andy, he was out on his own, living in a little apartment. He didn't mention her, and I didn't ask, and that's how it went, for a while at least.

Then Andy found out he was a father.

★   ★   ★

I dreamed again. A real dream this time, not a vision or a message from beyond. It was a simple one. Just me, sitting in the bathtub with all my clothes on. I smelled like a campfire. I glanced down at my hands, expecting them to be charred and burned, but they were the same hands I looked at every day when I sketched in a notepad or scribbled down my homework minutes before class started. I don't know why I was so afraid, but I kept waiting for something to happen, waiting for a moment that never came. The moment seemed to linger, stretching out like taffy, far beyond when it should have ended. No blood, no monsters, no writhing pool of blackness, just me in a bathtub, the smell of smoke in the air, staring at my hands without blinking.

Andy didn't wake me up until nearly five, barely long enough to get a fresh bag of peas on my cheek before Dad got home. The swelling was noticeable, but not so bad as to be overly concerned about. If I played it right, he might not even see it.

"What if he does?" Andy asked. We were both standing just inside the bathroom as I turned my head this way and that, trying to assess the damage.

"I slipped getting out of the shower," I said. "Bumped it here," I added with a slap on the bathroom counter.

"Will he buy it?" He sounded more concerned than he had all that day, and I realized how guilty he felt about the whole thing.

"He will."

And he did. He came in, same as he always did, and though he seemed a bit more attentive than normal, checking on both of us multiple times to make sure all was well, he didn't quite notice the obvious things that mattered. Not my swollen jaw. Not Andy's red, blurred eyes. Certainly not the strangely clean bathroom. Looking back, I don't blame Dad. He was, just as much as the two of us, trying to keep it together. There was no doubt that he noticed some things, but I'm sure he thought there was more time. Why wouldn't he? He didn't want to push too hard on me or Andy, because he didn't want to make things any worse. I don't think it would have made any difference even if he had known. We were too far gone by then, by the night when everything finally went down.

I think I knew it was coming, at least in one way or another. The dreams. That feeling of something large and unstoppable rolling toward me. That hopeless feeling in the pit of my belly. All of it only grew, changed, becoming deeper and more powerful as I waited for the sun to finally drop. I wouldn't sleep. I honestly didn't know if I would ever sleep again, at least not while the sun was down. We ate a quick bite in the living room, pizza coming around in the rotation once more.

"Everyone have a good day?" Dad asked.

Andy couldn't even muster so much as a sentence, and I jumped in to save him.

"Yep," I said cheerfully.

"Did you do anything?"

I scanned the question, scrubbing it for any hint of distrust, but I found it clean. "Not much. Watched TV. Andy played games mostly."

"That right?"

"Yep. How's work?"

He glanced from Andy to me, watching us with cocked eyebrows. Then he fell right in. "Pretty good. Got a lot of work to get done before the end of the month…"

So the moment passed without another word from us, and within a few hours, the house fell silent once again. I waited until

Dad drifted away, back to his room, and I found Andy. He was in his own room, the TV off as he sat at the edge of his bed. He was staring at the floor, and he didn't seem to notice me when I walked in.

"Can't sleep?" I asked.

He raised his eyes. "Oh. You."

"Yeah. Me."

I plopped down on the bed next to him, not waiting to be asked. We sat there, my legs dangling, his feet brushing across the carpeted floor. The Nintendo sat across from us, and I briefly considered turning it on and playing something. I never got to play much when he was around because he stayed on it 24/7. I don't think he would have stopped me.

"What are you thinking?" I asked.

"Nothing. Everything."

"You worried?" When he didn't answer, I answered for him. "I am. I keep having dreams. They keep getting worse, and they seem so real, I don't think they're dreams at all."

When I finished, I realized he was looking at me.

"I dream awake," he said. "Does that sound crazy?" I didn't answer. "Maybe that's how you know it's not really a dream at all. He's still in here, you know. He's part of me. I can't…find myself in there. Does that make any sense?"

I wasn't sure what he was asking. "I don't know."

He pressed a hand to his head hard enough to turn his knuckles white. I could see veins in his forehead, tears in the edges of his eyes, and the wild, darting back and forth that never seemed to end.

"I need you to tell me what to do," he said, raising his eyes back to mine. "The voices keep getting clearer, and I hear something under my skin, telling me what to do. How to think. The things I need to do to feel good. The people I need to hurt."

He was leaning into me now, pressing closer to my face.

"He wants me to hurt people. The people closest to me."

I was standing at a crossroads. I could feel it, like my entire life hinged on how I responded in that single moment. Everything that came after would depend on how I reacted to this news. An idea flashed: me running from the room, grabbing Dad, calling the cops, doing whatever it took to keep me, and by extension Andy, safe. This was what my brain was thinking when my heart took control of my body and placed my hand on top of his.

"No," I told him. "You're not going to do that."

His eyes were watering, and I could see him fighting back the urge to strike out at me, to hurt me, to choke the life out of me.

"You're my brother, and you're not going to hurt me."

"I...I..."

"Say it," I demanded. "Say it now."

"I don't know what—"

"I want to hear you say it." I wasn't asking anymore, and his wild eyes met mine.

"I'm your brother," he whispered, the voice of a child. "And I'm not going to hurt you."

"I believe you," I whispered back, and I meant it. "Let's give it another hour or so. Make sure Dad is really asleep. We'll carry it down to the quarry, and that will be the end of it. For good."

He was nodding along with the words, but his eyes were staring off at something else, something I couldn't see.

"Andy," I said in a sharp tone, "be ready."

He nodded, and without another word, I walked out of his room, leaving him to sit quietly on the bed. I went straight to my own room and locked the door behind me before slipping between the sheets and pulling them up to my chin. I watched the shadows on the wall, the leaves filtered through the blinds, fluttering in the wind, moving like something alive. They looked like they wanted inside, with me. I listened to the wind, to the house popping, for the sounds of footsteps that might be creeping down the hall. More than once, I held my breath, wondering if the awful thing that jumped from body to body would ever even have to lift a finger to kill me. Why put any effort forth when my brother could do it for him? At some point, I began to drift – not quite asleep, but close enough to wander, glide above my conscious mind, see things, hear things, feel things that were both real and in my mind.

Footsteps.

Whispers.

Voices from within.

Andy's voice.

Dad crying.

None of it real. All of it real.

I must have finally drifted all the way off. I heard the tinkling sound of music. Familiar, but hard to place. It came from somewhere just far enough away to be a dream. Faint, growing, fading, and growing once more. It was 'Twinkle, Twinkle Little Star.' Everyone knows that song. After all, that song had eased me to sleep when I was a baby. It was a memory written in my DNA, the kind of thing I would recall on my deathbed. A sweet sound. A sweet memory.

I could still remember the time I found it. The first time since I was a baby that I had heard it, but even then, I'd known. It was my song, written for me as far as I knew. A song about the stars, something lovely and sweet. I had been in the garage then. It was the first time I found the bear, the ratty green one, and I found that metal clasp on its back and spun it around with my small fingers and listened. There it was: a clear sound, a real sound, not something in my mind at all, but in my room, rising from the floor, from the carpet, from underneath, lower, under the wooden joists and layers of plywood.

From the dirt.

I opened my eyes and listened.

It was faint, but there was no doubt. It was real, as real as the wind and the shadows on the wall, and it was moving. Heart racing, I slipped out of bed and followed it on hands and knees, creeping across my room, keeping pace with the odd trail it seemed to be making. I hit a wall and nearly screamed, because I knew something was down there, some new horror, and the only thing that could hope to give me peace in that moment was to stay on top of it, to know where it was. Not knowing – that was the true nightmare. So I fumbled my door open and spilled into the hall, ear to the floor.

I found it again, halfway down, curving toward the back door. It was wandering, fumbling in the darkness, carrying my bear. Was something toying with me? It felt likely, and that question itself was more important than even the bigger, more obvious questions, but none of that mattered when I was that damn scared.

I imagined the crawl space, open and dark, the musty, murky smell, the spiders, the centipedes, and God only knew what else. What sort of thing would dig around there? I knew where the bear had been, wrapped in the sleeping bag and still clutched in the Thief's dead grasp – still clutched by the penitent, pathetic creature that died the night before.

I thought of Andy again and wondered if he would even be any help. I didn't think so, and the realization that I was on my own made me sick with fear. The tinkling sound led me into the living room, over to the far wall, where it halted, hovering, waiting.

Then the music stopped, and I froze.

I held my ear to the ground, listening for footsteps, music, stumbling feet, just about anything that would give me some sense of where it was. Then I heard it: a shuffling that seemed to vibrate the floor itself, the sound of something being fiddled with, shaken loose. I could feel the tremors of it in my hands, and I feared it was trying to tear through the floor right then and there. I sat back, afraid that a knife or a hand might shoot up through the floor.

That was when I heard the rattle of metal, no longer in the basement but in the room with me somehow, and I nearly screamed.

I scanned the dark edges of the room, and I saw it – the floor vent, rattling in its slot. Just a few taps here, then a pause, then a few more. It could have been a mouse walking over the vent's surface, so gentle and subtle. Memphis had joined in the hunt by then, and he slunk along behind me, back arched, seeing, hearing, maybe even smelling more than I could. He looked curiously at the vent, hissed, and dashed away. I crawled over, close enough to get a good look. That was when I saw the pink eye staring up at me.

CHAPTER FOURTEEN

Kirstie, the cash girl at the chicken joint, had been pregnant when she ran off out west. Andy didn't know that, not until about a year later, when he got a message saying that he needed to pick up his son. A boy named Andrew. Andy ended up going out there for a few weeks, spending time with the boy, getting to know him. Andrew was still just a baby, but from the way Andy talked, the boy seemed to know his daddy.

"He smiles whenever he sees me," Andy told me over the phone. "I can't really explain that. I spent most of my life in jail; now I work a fryer all day. And he still smiles at me."

"You're his daddy," I told him. "He's supposed to like you."

The idea was so very foreign to him.

"I hope I can do it," he added.

"Do what?" I asked.

His voice sort of faded in and out, and he seemed to lose his train of thought. "I…I dunno. There's just…I hope I don't mess it up."

"All new dads feel like that."

"No," he said sharply. "It's not just that. I can't explain it, but…I just hope I can do it."

He changed the subject after that, jumping to Kirstie. It turned out his former fling hadn't just looked him up out of the kindness of her heart. Their little relationship had been short and rocky, especially at the end, and she wanted to be closer to her family. That's what had sent her back out to Colorado, where she grew up. That, and the cancer.

"She's...she ain't going to last very long," Andy told me. There was sadness in his voice, but a bit of fear as well, and I knew what was coming before he said it.

"She wants Andrew to be with me. Her mom's losing her shit over it, telling her I ain't worth a damn. I was holding him in the other room, and I don't think she knew I could hear. Or maybe she did and just didn't care. Either way, she says, 'You'd be better off pitching that boy in the damn river.' That's how highly she thinks of me."

"She doesn't know you," I said.

He thought about that for a long while and said, "What if she's right? What if I only make things worse for that boy?" I could hear his voice getting watery. "I love him. That sounds weird. I don't know him, and he don't know me, but I love him."

"That's not weird at all."

We talked circles around it, and by the end, Andy had made up his mind. He was a dad now, and he'd try his best to make it work. He came home for a bit, then took another trip out a month later. Kirstie was nearly gone by then, so he spent the better part of that week with her, letting her hold little Andrew and say goodbye. When it was all said and done, they were back here, and I finally got to hold my nephew for the first time. He looked a bit like Dad, a bit like Andy, and, surprisingly, a bit like me. I didn't see it at first, but it was right there in his eyes, a sharp edge to them that told you this boy might be cute, but he might not take shit either. That made me smile.

* * *

The eye receded into the darkness of the floor, and I fell to my knees with a moan. I couldn't do anything more than shake my head and stare at it, wondering how much longer I could go before madness took me over for good. The metal vent cover shook again, and I saw it rising, slow and steady like a boat on high tide. It rose and rose, inch by inch. Then it fell to one side with a clatter.

That was when I saw the hand, that same burned, skinless hand, still moving, still alive somehow. I thought of how much of a husk it had seemed, how bloodless and desiccated. It wasn't alive, not in the way that everything else on this entire planet was alive. I knew then that I hadn't watched it die, not really. All I'd seen were the human slivers that still remained curling away like dead leaves. Now the only thing left was the seed in the middle, the dark, twisted part, planted half in Andy and half in that awful frame.

The hand receded, and I heard something clicking, whirring down in that black, mouth-like hole. Then the teddy bear rose up, tinkling the same familiar little song. It floated, hovering, held aloft by a red-black hand, which gripped it by a single ear. He swung it left and right, almost playfully, before dropping it onto the carpeted floor. A gift. Something just for me.

Then I heard the laugh. Giggling. He knew exactly what he was doing to me. He was breaking me, weakening me, putting small cracks throughout my psyche. It was brilliant in a way. Something was coming for me, something that had tasted me, tasted my essence. He wanted more. I knew that now. He had a choice between me and Andy, and he had chosen me. All he had to do was soften me up enough to finish the job for good.

I was on my feet, dashing back down the hall toward Andy's room, falling through the door and tumbling onto his bed. I was so hysterical that I didn't even notice he wasn't in there. I checked behind the doors, under the sheets, under the bed, but I couldn't find him. He had sneaked off somewhere in the night, and though the idea terrified me, it didn't really surprise me.

"What are you doing?" I heard him say from behind me.

"Jesus, where were you?" I said with a little shriek.

He stared me up and down, untrusting, unsure how to handle the way I was acting.

"I was outside."

My eyes swelled in their sockets.

"Why?" I said, trembling.

"I couldn't sleep," he replied. "What's with you?"

I'd slipped off the bed, making my way toward the door now, unsure of everything. "What were you doing out there?" I imagined him opening the basement door, imagined him being called out there by his master, under some dark spell.

"Just walking," he said quietly. He had that same shifty look about him, that same hollowed-out stare.

"You didn't see anything?"

He froze, and his eyes locked onto mine.

"You're my sister," he said with a bit of surprise in his tone, as if he had just remembered the fact. "I'd never hurt you."

No sooner had the words passed his lips than he grabbed my wrist, twisted it to a near-breaking point, and kicked my legs out from under me. I tried to scream, but he had stuffed a pillow over my face. I felt something sharp biting into one wrist – a cord from one of his games, binding me to the foot of his bed by one hand. Then a belt wrapped around my mouth, choking me, keeping me from screaming. It wasn't until all of this was done that I saw his face, saw his bloodshot eyes rimmed with tears.

"I'm sorry," he whispered. "But you don't know how much it hurts."

He dashed from the room, and I heard the back door slide open, and I knew it was back. The Toy Thief was inside my house once more – only this time, there was no need to sneak in. Andy rounded the corner first, and it followed on shaky legs, barely able to walk any longer, a newborn fawn with a nightmare face. The head lolled, the pink eyes were dry and unblinking, and the mouth was a black nothing lined with yellow teeth.

Hands, gangly and burned, were opening and closing, driven by some awful hunger to feed once more. The boy who'd smiled in swimming trunks, who had cherished a tiny snow globe with every ounce of his heart, was gone, and all that remained was death incarnate.

I tried to scream, to beg, to plead with the only part of myself that could still hope to gain sympathy. My eyes refused to look at the ghoul that shambled toward me, and instead, I looked to my brother, my only hope, my Andy. I pleaded with my eyes, but he refused to look at me. He kept his face glued to the floor as the voice rose from that gaping hole of a mouth, speaking in tones of utter hatred and disgust.

"*You furssttt...*"

"You'll get it out of me?" Andy asked. "What you put there? And then it'll be over?"

"*Yesss...yourrr handdd...*"

Andy raised his palm and looked away as the bony, spidery fingers enveloped it. Something was happening now, something different, something that few living had ever seen. Andy was quivering, his entire body shaking as the skin around his wrist and forearm began to turn black. I thought it was killing him, injecting some poison into his skin, but when I saw the pink eyes begin to water, I realized I was wrong. It wasn't injecting the darkness in — it was drawing the darkness out, undoing what it had already begun back in the cave. Andy's skin grew more and more pale, the inky color receding, and he slipped to his knees, his body waving from side to side. Only then did the Thief release his grip on my brother.

"Yes," the Thief said in a clearer tone. "Whole again. It takes time to travel from one body to the other." He glanced at me. "To pass from one to another. I like to make them weak first, to make the transition easier. But with you," he said, smiling, "I'll make an exception. I'm ready for you. For something new.

And when you're old enough, who knows…I might have a son of my own…"

He reached for my free hand, and I pulled it away at the last second, but not quickly enough. He was able to snag the last two fingers on my hand, and that was all it took. In an instant, I felt my consciousness slip – not into sleep or fear, but to be swallowed by something greater than myself. I was part of something large and dark and evil, and it was consuming me piece by piece. I would be changed, I realized that, and in time, my eyes would go blind and pink, my teeth would become fangs, and my body would shrivel and stretch as I became more and more like my master. Most of all, there was not a single shred of hope to be found.

That's right, he whispered inside me. *Let it all happen. Watch it, this old, pathetic husk die, and know what's waiting for you.*

It was true, all of it. I saw the Thief shriveling before my eyes, the pink globes going dimmer and dimmer as the hatred that drove them spilled into me.

No one can help you, he proclaimed. *No one. You will spend eternity inside of me, and when I'm done with you, you will…*

Pressure.

A grinding, blinding sort of pain that I was only dimly aware of. The sound of meat slicing, tendons tearing, bones separating.

And finally, my eyes opening.

Andy was in front of me and the Thief, holding something that glistened in his hand. A butcher knife, slick with blood and something black that sizzled in the open air. The liquid bubbled, hissed, and vanished in the span of a few seconds. Then, for some reason I couldn't understand, I fell backward, away from the iron grip that held me. My body was my own once more, but I was at a complete loss to explain how.

I saw the Thief, still withering, still dead on his feet, and within the bony grip of his charred hand, I saw the red stumps of my fingers poking out. Blood mixed with blackness dripped onto the carpet, and I caught a glimpse of the other half of my fingers, still attached to my hand, but equally red. A black, misty fluid pumped from the holes where my fingers had been, and with each beat of my heart, I saw the essence of the Toy Thief go airborne, sputter, hiss, and disappear.

No! I heard the voice say, loud and strong within my head.

"No," said another, this one weak and pitiful, echoing from the Thief's throat. I realized what I was seeing. A fish, caught from a pond and thrown cruelly onto the dry bank to die, and all the flopping and thrashing in the world could do nothing to save it. The Thief reached for me, for my neck, trying to choke me as he screamed both within my mind and without, but the once-iron fingers were weak and helpless, and the hands fell limply away, shriveling, turning to ash on my skin. Blood spewed from the stumps of my fingers, coating my chest and neck with a thick red stream stenciled with a black essence that dissipated as I watched, both curious and detached.

"No," Andy said desperately. "Please, no."

He was doing something, digging around behind me, but I was too mesmerized by the sight of the Thief to notice. He was almost deflating, the eyes falling in on themselves, the lips receding, the already crisp skin tightening. He was, before my eyes, going from alive to dead and beyond, all of those years hitting him in the span of a few seconds. The skin shriveled, cracked, and sloughed off in tiny pieces, dead leaves falling away. Soon there was no skin at all, and even the bones seemed to shrink as what was left of the creature fell to the carpeted floor in complete silence. It was impossible – the years, decades, all of it passing in the span of ten seconds, reducing the once terrifying Toy Thief to a pile of ash and old clothes.

My other hand fell free as Andy cut me loose, and I felt a rush of warmth as the blood pumped back into it. Then the belt was gone, and I could breathe and talk, even though there wasn't much I wanted to say. I was floating, hovering above the carpeted floor, and my body didn't feel a single sensation beyond quiet peace. I could have died then, probably should have died, and I wouldn't have given the matter another thought. Dying would have been just as pleasant as anything else. There was Andy again with one of his t-shirts in hand as he took my mutilated fingers and squeezed them tight. That brought me back – the pain of my brother saving my life.

"How?" I asked him. "How did you know?" My voice was like the tread of boots in a gravel pit, but Andy understood.

"He told me," he said as he tended my deformed hand. "He didn't want me to know how vulnerable he was when going from one person to the other, but I saw it all the same. He wanted you, but he had to be whole to do it. Half was in me, half was in him."

"But how did you know...my fingers..."

A guilty look swept across his face, and I knew. He hadn't had some grand plan. He'd only wanted it out of him. And once it was, he was enough himself once more, and he found his will to fight back. It wasn't romantic or brave, but it would do. He bound my hand up and wrapped the belt around it as tightly as it would go. The pain was real now, almost blinding, but I came to long enough to see him staring at the empty clothes, the last remnants of the Thief. He looked back at my hand, then down at the knife, and I saw the truth in his eyes before he even said a word.

"I...I've got to go," he said as he reached down and began to gather the clothes.

"No," I said, already crying. "You can't."

"I have to," he replied, and I knew it was the truth.

"We could...make something up. I can do it, I can fix it," I said, blubbering.

"No," he said honestly. "You can't."

We were just kids, and no story we could make up would save my brother. He had sliced off two of my fingers. That was the only truth that mattered. Any evidence that might have saved him had shriveled up and disappeared, and a wad of old, dingy clothes wouldn't change anyone's mind.

"Andy," I begged. "Please."

He shook his head. "I might not see you again. Maybe not for a long time. Maybe never."

I nodded, because there was simply nothing else to be done. This was the end of the lives we knew, and there was no fighting it.

"I'm sorry," he added, gathering up the musty black clothes and holding them against his chest. "Sorry I wasn't myself. Sorry I wasn't what you needed."

"You did your best," I said. "That was pretty good."

"No, it wasn't," he added, but there was no fight in his voice. "But I'm glad you said it."

"Just go," I said through my teeth. "Go while I'm still awake."

"Goodbye then," he said weakly before kissing me gently on the cheek. Then he was gone, leaving nothing behind but a blood-soaked carpet and a warm spot on my cheek. I heard the steps down the hall, heard the door slam shut, and listened to my own labored breath coming in harsh wheezes. Andy was gone, his last bit of work still ahead of him, and now it was my turn.

I drew myself up, stumbled into the hallway, and walked to the door to Dad's room. I never went in there, but on this occasion, I let myself right in. It was always darker than the rest of the house. I flipped on the light and saw him there, looking small and strange curled up in his bed. He stayed on the left side, keeping the right side more or less untouched. He was on his feet in less than two seconds, the skill of a longtime parent. Then he stood there, blinking, seeing me but not really seeing anything.

"Jack," he murmured. "Whatissit?"

I knew the lie, knew what I had to say, but I faltered.

"Daddy," I cried, holding my hand in front of my face, and finally, he saw.

"Oh God," he said, grabbing my wrist carefully. The t-shirt was red now, lighter on the outer edges and dark crimson in the center. One look and anyone could see that it wasn't doing much to stop the bleeding. I'd never before or since seen Dad so speechless.

"What did you do?"

I?

The question confused me, but after a few seconds, I understood. This was an accident. It had to be. Daughters could scrape knees, burn themselves with hot cocoa, get beat up or knocked up. They could do these things and a million other things that fathers might fear, but they didn't get attacked in the night in their own house. That was unimaginable.

"It wasn't me," I said, the guilt rising like bile in my throat as I anticipated the moment that had to come.

"What?" he said. "What is it, baby? Tell me."

I shook my spinning head and blinked my welling eyes.

"It was Andy."

CHAPTER FIFTEEN

I woke up in the hospital, surrounded by beeps and the smell of piss and antiseptic. I remembered everything almost at once, and I raised my bandaged hand in confirmation. For the longest time, all I could do was stare at it.

"Easy," the nurse said as I inspected the almost spherical ball of white. "Don't move it. Everything's patched up, but it will take a good while to heal."

I was still woozy, feeling drunk from the morphine that had kept me sedated while they patched me up.

"Id idges…idges."

I held my free hand up and pretended to scratch my mangled paw.

"Oh," she said. "Itches?"

I nodded.

"Yes, that's a common thing. They call it phantom pain. You'll probably be able to feel those fingers for a long time. Years even." I rolled my head to one side and stared at the wall, disgusted.

Most of the other facts are out there. The news picked it up. The papers printed it. A writer in town even wrote a book about it. True crime, she called it. I looked it up one time and found out that she'd only sold about seventy copies. That made me smile.

According to the news, Andy tied up and attacked his sister. That's me. There were dozens of theories as to why, the most popular being that media had had some sort of effect on his mind. Metal music, videogames, horror movies. The unholy trinity. It could have been a dabbling with satanism. After all, he had tied me up and sliced off two of my fingers. It sounded positively sacrificial. After the deed was done, he stole my father's truck and tore out across the neighborhood before, thankfully, wrecking it a few miles away. The old truck was found in a ditch next to an abandoned stretch of field, the tailgate dropped, the radiator smoking. It only took the cops a few minutes to find it after Dad called them, but it took the better part of an hour for Andy to come marching out from the woods beyond the field, finally giving himself up. And that was that.

They missed plenty though. They missed the fact that he cut me free after cutting off my fingers. They missed that he helped to bind my hand, and probably saved my life in the process. And most important and unsurprising, they missed why he took the truck in the first place. He didn't know how to drive, at least not very well. But it was a long walk to the Trails and the quarry beyond. Andy, for all his efforts, succeeded at three things.

He saved my life.

He got rid of the evidence.

And he got himself sentenced to fifteen years in prison.

The almost ritualistic brutality of the crime ensured that he was tried as an adult. The prosecutor made a big, splashy show of the whole thing, questioning what it could have been that drove this child to commit such an evil act. Dad made me go to the sentencing, even after he let me stay away from the entire trial. I objected, but he swore it would be for my own good.

"You need to see him," he told me as I scratched at my nonexistent fingers. He was right of course. I did need to see Andy. I needed to thank him. I needed to tell him I was sorry for the way everything went. I needed to give him a hug and a kiss on the cheek, to tell him I loved him. But I didn't get to do any of that, not on that day at least. I sat there, quietly watching, pretending to ignore the eyes that gazed back at me with dark curiosity, wondering if anyone knew the truth of what happened.

I didn't even get to speak to him that day, or any other day. Not for a long time. I was sixteen when I finally did go see him for the first time, and by then, whatever warm brother-and-sister love we'd shared had cooled, hardened into odd awkwardness. I wasn't the same tomboyish little sister he had saved, and he wasn't the gangly, handsome boy who had saved me. He was taller by then, over six feet if he stood up straight, which he never did. His complexion had gone sallow and dull, and his eyes seemed to sink into his cheeks, receding from the light. He was only twenty, but I swear, his hair was beginning to thin.

No, I didn't tell him how much I loved him then, because you don't say things like that to strangers, talking to each other through a sheet of wired glass. We talked small talk, and he told me it was good to see me. That shifty, bird-eyed look would come over him here and there, but it wasn't a steady thing, not like it had been before.

"You look good," he said without ever looking me in the eye.

I slid my shirtsleeve down over my hand. "Thanks. You do too," I lied.

Maybe we thought we were being recorded, or maybe we just didn't want to say anything out loud to each other, not yet anyway. Either way, we never spoke a word about what happened, and that's just how it went. We warmed up a bit over the years, and after a decade or so, we even learned to laugh here and there. It was a long, tough road that none of us ever wanted to be on, but we walked it as best we could.

Who knows how long things would have gone on like that if he hadn't gotten paroled? I've already told you about Kirstie and Andrew, the next generation in a long, unbroken line of fuckups. I had hoped that his son would be the thing that set Andy right. Made him whole. Fixed what that awful thing had broken. At first, when the pair moved in with me, I thought it might just do the trick.

They say having a kid does strange things to a person – that for some people, it brings out the worst in them. They see that little version of themselves, still perfect, still scar-free, and they lose their minds a bit. All of their own wasted potential becomes an open book in front of them, and instead of facing it, instead of sitting down and reading it line by line, they slam it shut and walk away. *There's still time left for me*, they tell themselves as they leave and never look back.

Andy seemed, at least at first, to be cut from different cloth. Some folks see their children, and they realize that there is only one true path to immortality. That crying, shitting ball of skin they cradle in their arms is a link in a chain that connects them back through the ages, and in that chubby body, they see the lives of their most ancient relatives. All the lives they lived, all those paths converging, all those random chances, realized in your own child. In that moment, their life's work becomes clear. Protect them. Guide them. Teach them to not make the same mistakes that you did.

That was Andy in the early days. Me, him, and Andrew, making a strange house in the same town we grew up in. We might have made it, and I thought, or maybe just hoped, that we would. But it didn't take long to realize it was just a dream, something whispered in my ear when I was half-asleep.

It wasn't Andrew. He was a baby then, little more than a mouth to stick a bottle in, or a body to cuddle up with under the covers. And it wasn't me. I was half-curdled, sure, but I always had been, and that boy, that little thing I never asked for – well, he made me feel something I hadn't known for a long time. Dad had needed me. Andy, in his way, had needed me. But for years, no one else in the world did. That little Andrew though, he needed me like he needed oxygen. He needed me to feed him, to warm up that bottle to stick in his mouth, to rock him whenever he woke in the middle of the night. I did these things, and a thousand others, grudgingly, or so it might look from the outside. But I was always good at keeping secrets. The truth was, I loved it.

No, it wasn't me who unraveled. It was Andy. He just wasn't there. He was hollowed out, like a pumpkin scooped out and filled with nothing more than air and candlelight. It was the Toy Thief of course. I imagined what it might do to a person, to have someone else inside them. Did it leave a hole? Was there an empty spot where they pushed part of you aside to make room for themselves? Or was it even worse than all that?

Maybe it wasn't an empty spot. Maybe it was, quite simply, a dead spot. That everything that horrid, low darkness touched had gone terminal and just crumbled into dust. That when Andy cut it out of me, it wasn't just that creature that was dying in the open air, flailing like a fish out of water. It was Andy as well. The best part of him, disappearing like so much smoke. God, it makes me cringe just to write it.

It was there though, clear, bright, easy to read. It was in the way he would scrunch his face up whenever Andrew wouldn't stop crying, as if his body were incapable of patience and understanding. It was in the way he would hold the boy, his boy, and stare out into the yard, watching birds like a catatonic old mutt, never noticing when Andrew was awake, was crying, was threatening to roll out of his lap and onto the floor. It was in the way he would sneak into the boy's bedroom at night and stand there, staring at his crib. I'd watch on a monitor, breathless and exhausted, wondering when, *dear God when* would he finally go to sleep? He wasn't safe around his own son, and as much as it killed me, I couldn't deny it. I told him as much. I always was the first to talk, never one to keep my mouth shut, even when I should.

Why?

Why am I like that?

Why have I always been like that?

"You're going to hurt him," I said.

I can still remember the day. Andy was sitting in a rocking chair, staring at the TV, not watching it, just gazing right through it. *Wheel of Fortune* was on. I think it was the wheel that had caught his attention. The way it spun and spun, clicking like some kind of…

Like some kind of toy.

He was giving Andrew a bottle, and the boy was finished. He kept pushing it away, his fat fingers struggling to get air, and I stood there, watching, letting it go further than I should, because I needed to see. I *had* to see. The milk was running down his cheeks, over his chin, and then, without warning, up his nose. He was coughing, choking, unable to even cry, and I reached for him, snatched him away.

"What the fuck is wrong with you?"

I stormed out of the room and left Andy sitting there, his eyes watching me, half-glazed.

I didn't see him again for a few hours. Andrew was sleeping, and when I realized how long it had been since I laid eyes on Andy, I went looking for him. He was still sitting in the rocking chair, but the TV was off. So he just stared out the window, dead to the world as far as I could tell. A man might make it through prison like that, might even make it through a simple, dead-end job day after day. But a father can't be dead inside, not without someone getting hurt.

"I know you're there," he said, proving me wrong.

I walked in and sat down across from him. "What is it?" I said bluntly. "What is…all this?"

"Whenever I hold him," he said, "something's…off."

I shook my head in frustration. "Everyone says it's hard at first. I mean, it takes time to learn how to be a dad."

"No," he said softly. "I love him. I know that. But something isn't right."

I shifted in my seat, wondering why he refused to look at me, to actually see my eyes.

"What is it?"

"My hands," he said, holding them plaintively before him. "They can't...they don't work right. I touch him. I feel his skin. But I can't..."

"Can't what?"

He turned toward me now, grief and fear blooming in his eyes. "I can't hurt him. I'm *supposed* to hurt him. My hands," he said, pleading. "They can't do what they're supposed to do. I'm not supposed to be...*this*." He motioned to his chest, staring at his skin. He quivered and rocked, scratching at his skin the same way you might scratch at a wool sweater, rubbing his knuckles like his bones were uncomfortable, like they wanted out. It was a painful, awful, and miserably pitiful thing to see.

"Fix me," he said, reaching for me. "Please, you have to fix me. It's gone. The dark. I know it is. I felt it die that day."

My fingers itched, and I nodded. "I know it is too, Andy. I felt it too. So all of this," I said, touching his chest, "it's all you. You can beat this thing. I know you can."

The tears on his cheek were the first real signs of emotion I had seen from him since he moved, and somehow, they made everything worse. I could have dealt with the anger, the blind fury that had made him smash the globe so long ago. Anger was something that made sense to me. But this. This pathetic thing in front of me was too much.

"He needs you," I said. "Out of everything else on this planet, he needs you."

"No," he replied, his voice rising and hitching. "He needs Andy. Andy would be a good father. Andy would know what to say. And Andy wouldn't expect to feel anything more than skin when he touched his son."

"That's you," I said. "It's all you."

"I don't know what I am. I don't quite think I'm a man. But I don't think I'm a monster either. I don't know what I am."

He let his eyes drift back down to his lap. Then he said the last words I ever heard him speak.

"All I know is, Andy's dead."

I tried to talk to him after that, but he wouldn't say another word. I watched him the rest of that night, keeping as close an eye on him as I could while still taking care of Andrew. But I was only one person, just a girl. Girls get tired.

When Andy got into his car and drove several miles away before killing himself, I like to think he did it for us. He wouldn't have wanted me to find him like that, his eyes glazed, a pair of empty bottles on the floorboard, whiskey and pills. They'd given him the prescription when he got out. Said it would help him sleep.

Once, in the early days after he got out of jail, he told me that he had never left that cave, and he was right of course. All those years later, he was still in there, still locked in that cage. Then again, another part of me thinks he was already dead on his feet long ago. The moment my mom left, she took a good part of him with her. The pictures showed that. The Thief took a bit more, and jail a bit more. The sleeping pills just finished the job.

That was about three years ago now. It scared the hell out of me at first, the idea of taking care of Andrew all by myself. Then I remembered the few months we had already spent together, the two of us like awkward roommates, me single-handedly taking care of the baby, and I knew it would all work out. He's a sweet kid, running around now, rough and rambunctious, but with a quiet streak that surprises you. I've never told him to call me Mom, because I never wanted to be anyone's mom, and it just felt wrong to try and make him do something like that. The questions are coming though. I can feel it.

He doesn't ask about his dad, but you can see him working it all out now and then. I showed him some pictures, hoping to put him at ease, to make him feel just like everyone else at daycare

— the mom, dad, grandparents, all of it. One of those quiet spells came over him then, and before I knew it, he had sneaked off and I couldn't find him for a half-hour or so. I finally found him under the cabinet in one of the bathrooms, tucked back in there like an animal or something. Just like a cat.

That was how we first found Memphis. He'd been hiding in the shed out back, desperate and tiny, ribs showing through his short fur. I fished him out with a can of tuna, parsed out a piece at a time. He was rough from the start, always skittish. The kind of cat you couldn't quite trust not to eat your food whenever you left the room. Still, he was the best damn cat I'd ever had. He lived to be fifteen, and he was just as mean as ever on the day he died. Some people might hate a cat like that, but I think we understood each other. Maybe that's why I was able to coax Andrew out just the same way.

Just this year, a few months after he turned four, I took him to the Trails. We live on the other side of town now, and I don't have much reason to go back to the old stomping grounds. The whole place was built up, sliced into small lots where the Trails used to be. We drove around the new subdivision, crisscrossing our way through each of the different side streets, my hands shaking a bit on the steering wheel.

"This place," I told Andrew. "They called this the Trails."

"What's trails?"

"It's…hard to explain. It was like, woods. Forest. With all these little paths cut in it."

"Why?"

I laughed. That was his new favorite word.

"It just was, baby."

I tried to mentally pinpoint the landmarks I had known, based on the houses that rested in the same spots. A two-story house of dark red brick was probably the place where we stumbled onto Barnett. A little roundabout marked the spot with the tree etched in pentagrams. If only these people knew. This side of town has changed so much, especially since we left. Did we take the bad parts with us? Or was it the Thief?

Bit of both, if I had to guess.

We drove to the far side of the neighborhood and found it fenced off, the chain link hidden behind a wall of greenery, much less offensive to the eye. There was a small turnaround in front of the gate, and I stopped there, almost certain that someone would ask me to leave. I didn't care. Even if a cop showed up, I was going in.

"What's this?" Andrew asked.

"Just a place I want to see, baby. Just to make sure I wasn't dreaming."

I pulled back the chain around the gate, enough for him to shimmy through, and I slipped in behind him. It was lovely back there, just as it had been before, that last time I'd seen it. I'd never come back before then. For most of my adult life I couldn't have even imagined setting foot here. But there I was again, a woman grown, awestruck by the place, by how small it all looked, how the spans between tree lines seemed so very close. I thought once more of Andy, who had taken one last trip back this way. It had been in the dead of night then, and I wondered if the moon had been out for that last stroll.

The quarry came into view, wide and lovely and silent. For all its beauty, it was an ominous place, the sort of place where a hand might shoot up from below and drag you down into the angular, man-made caverns, and to the wild caves beyond.

"Careful," I said, pulling Andrew far away from the edge.

"What is it?"

"A quarry."

"Why?"

"Just is."

I stood there for a while, feeling afraid and very small, like every choice I'd ever made had been wrong, if for no other reason than it had brought me here.

Mom was dead.

Dad was dead.

Andy was dead.

Had I ever done anything right?

"Look!"

I scanned the horizon and saw it. A heron, tall and thin, was gliding across the glassy water as silent as a water skimmer. She rose up, tipping her blue-gray wings before landing on the top of the wall across from us.

"Birdy!"

She alighted on a patch of green, and I noticed how much everything had changed over the years. The burned yellow of that summer had turned now. Trees poked up through the sides of the quarry. Wildflowers painted the field on both sides pink and yellow.

This whole place was alive. It didn't remember the horrible things that had happened here. Those were all so far in the past, and the only thing left for nature to do was get on with living. I was alive too, and so was the boy at my side. We all had Andy to thank for that. Somehow, I managed a smile, and Andrew and I walked back, holding hands.

★　　★　　★

That's almost all there is to tell. I did end up keeping the bear. After it was all said and done, I found it sitting there on the floor, right where the Thief had dropped it. I wanted to burn it the second I saw it, to pretend like that moment, and all the moments after, were just a bad dream, something I could forget seconds after it ended. But I couldn't do it then, and I still can't do it now. I threw the bear into a plastic bag and tossed it in the closet. I thought about it every night when I lay down, obsessing over it, changing it into something warped and obscene, something forever tainted. Then, when I finally worked up the nerve to pull the bag out and peer in, all I saw were cotton, buttons, the same metal clasp.

I took it out, washed it by hand once, twice, three times, and once all the dirt and grime were washed away, I saw it for what it was: a simple gesture, a gift given by a woman and man who loved me very much. I still have it. It's threadbare and worn, but I keep it in a box in my closet. Every once in a while I take it out, just to make sure it's still there, that it hasn't vanished in the night. Every time, I consider giving it to Andrew, but I never have. This toy means a lot to me, the good and the horribly bad, and there's no reason to put my own messed-up shit on him. He's still so young. His own little dysfunctions are still waiting out there for him to go find.

I will tell you one more thing. About a week ago, a moment happened that made me consider writing all this down. Something that threw the whole thing into a new perspective. I've learned that most everything in life comes down to perspective in the end. I was cooking breakfast. It was a Saturday morning, and most weekends I get up and make French toast. It's Andrew's favorite. He was sitting at the kitchen counter, half watching me, half drawing with his crayons. That was when he said it.

"Momma?"

I stopped, spatula in my hand, feeling my eyes well a bit as I processed exactly what had just happened. I could tell by his voice that he didn't need anything, not really. He said my name three dozen times a day in that same bored, sweet tone. He might have needed some more milk, or a different set of crayons, or maybe a new sheet of paper to draw on. It didn't matter. The word, though. That meant everything.

Let's get one damn thing straight. I'm not his mom. I don't deserve that name, not yet at least. But I have to say that in that moment, I felt as if I could be, that maybe everything that happened, from Mom and Dad to Andy and me, had all been for something. That maybe, just maybe, something good had made it out of that cave intact.

I took a deep breath, and I answered.

"Yes, baby?"

FLAME TREE PRESS
FICTION WITHOUT FRONTIERS
Award-Winning Authors & Original Voices

Flame Tree Press is the trade fiction imprint of Flame Tree Publishing, focusing on excellent writing in horror and the supernatural, crime and mystery, science fiction and fantasy. Our aim is to explore beyond the boundaries of the everyday, with tales from both award-winning authors and original voices.

•

Other titles available include:

Thirteen Days by Sunset Beach by Ramsey Campbell
Think Yourself Lucky by Ramsey Campbell
The House by the Cemetery by John Everson
The Siren and the Specter by Jonathan Janz
The Sorrows by Jonathan Janz
Kosmos by Adrian Laing
The Sky Woman by J.D. Moyer
Creature by Hunter Shea
The Bad Neighbor by David Tallerman
Ten Thousand Thunders by Brian Trent
Night Shift by Robin Triggs
The Mouth of the Dark by Tim Waggoner

•

Join our mailing list for free short stories, new release details, news about our authors and special promotions:

flametreepress.com